MW00624004

Sarah walked t ... d
her earphones snugly ... ...
ful, blissful ignorance. Sarah, her eyes glued to the book, walked between two opposing cars as she crossed the street.

Neither man saw Sarah walk into the street. The businessman looked up and saw her, but in his panic, slammed his foot against the accelerator. Both cars drove toward a head on collision with Sarah caught in the middle.

*I love it when my appointments are on time.*

Sarah realized what was about to happen and froze. The proverbial "deer in the headlights", Lorelai had heard once. The perfect storm of fate and irony.

Others would gather for the drivers caught up in the catastrophe Lorelai would find pleasure in leaving behind. But, she was there for Sarah. She would need Lorelai to guide her way.
Lorelai was focused so hard on the drama unfolding before her that she took little notice of "Mister I'm not a junkie but I am a junkie". He ran as fast as he could, right for Sarah. A split second before the collision, he grabbed her and jumped free.

It was at that very moment something happened. The appointment reminder for Sarah disappeared.

In the eons of existence Lorelai had seen come and go, she never had an appointment go dark. The moment was pivotal. To what extent, Lorelai wasn't sure. She was certain it was a moment that would alter cosmos. She had to investigate everything. The man, the moment, whatever it was that just happened.

Bystanders raced in to pull both men from the wreckage, just as Lorelai anticipated. To fill their tank of good deeds.
Instead, Lorelai chose to find the junkie, who was seated next to Sarah. Lorelai invoked the persona of a concerned passerby and offered him help up from the ground.

"Are you ok?" Lorelai asked.

She felt excited. Possibly the most excited she had felt in

eons. As soon as her hand touched his, it all came to her. Everything she needed to know.

His name was Gabe, and his story started the same as any other. He was born, grew up, and had dreams as most humans did. He chased those dreams by running away from his small hometown to become a big time country singer.

Unfortunately, those dreams led him to drugs. The drugs led him to a life of living for survival. He worked odd jobs, but the poison he pushed through his veins corrupted his mind. Purse snatching was the least of it. He had done much more than that.

Of all the Christian and mortal sins he had done, the one he couldn't seem to bring himself to fulfill was to kill another. It wasn't some sort of code he had. He was just too much of a coward.

The monkey on Gabe's back was enough to cause him to reconsider. He was too scared of going to Hell. Little did he know, that was exactly where he was headed, whether he had committed murder or not. Until that moment. The one where he derailed Sarah's fate.

Gabe balanced the book. In the seconds it took him to make the choice to save Sarah, he created a soul. One trapped on the mortal plane for eternity with an impossibility for any end of existence to occur.

A coin had been flipped, and against all probability, it landed on the edge.

Gabe looked at Lorelai with blank eyes and stammered, "Yeah, I'm good. Is the kid ok?"

"She's fine."

Lorelai looked from Gabe's perplexed expression toward Sarah, "Go home kid. We'll need to reschedule."

Sarah looked at Lorelai, a healthy dose of cynicism rudied her prepubescent features, and replied, "Whatever, crazy lady."

With her book tucked snuggly under her arm and nothing more than a few scrapes, Sarah ran off without another word.

"Are you hungry?" Lorelai asked Gabe.

The thought of food snapped him back to reality. Gabe couldn't recall the last time he had a decent meal.

"Let me at least reward you for your good deed. It's obvious the girl didn't acknowledge what you did, but she's young. She will learn to appreciate the gift you have given her in due time," Lorelai added with a pleasant, yet upbeat note in her voice. It bothered Lorelai. She needed to know what made him so special.

If there is one thing Lorelai had learned in all her eons of existence, it was the universe hated anything that created an imbalance. The ripples had not yet started, but they soon would. Chaos would erupt in every facet of existence.

Lorelai took Gabe back to the restaurant where they were greeted by Edward, punctual and eager to serve. No doubt from the tip Lorelai left only but an hour before.

Edward led them to a table on the patio and asked, "What can I get for you this afternoon?"

"I would love another round of what I had earlier and whatever my friend here wants," Lorelai said, a slight flick of the wrist toward Gabe.

Edward went from eager to disgusted within an instant. He had seen Gabe around and knew what he was because Edward used to be a junkie. All of them were thieves, criminals or homeless. Edward felt superior to Gabe because he had gotten away from that life. He pulled himself from the gutter and would never go back.

He scratched his arm out of habit. His uniform-issued shirt hid the healed track marks, but he still scratched them when nervous. He stammered his next few words, trying to hide his obvious lack of character.

"Wha…What w..would you like….." He looked at his pad, waiting for Gabe's order.

Before Gabe could say anything, Lorelai grabbed Edwards wrist and hissed, "What would you like, sir?"

With terror in his eyes, Edward asked, "I'm sorry?"

"A little courtesy is not a hard thing to give. You may wind up worse off than my friend here if you're not mindful of your actions in the future."

Lorelai graced Edward with the glimpse of a possible fate. It was an instantaneous flash. Edward lived out decades of homelessness and hunger within that moment. It was not his true future, but it was enough to get her point across. The life Gabe had lived was not easy. Another dose of his experiences would do Edward some good to remember just how fortunate he was.

"You're right. I am so very, very sorry," Edward said in a voice laced with humility. He looked to Gabe, "What would you like, sir?"

Gabe could have ordered anything he wanted, but he chose a cheeseburger, fries and a beer.

*A simple meal for a simple man. I can respect that.*

Lorelai feigned interest in Gabe's life. Like most men, he ate up the attention. He went on and on about stories of his childhood and present struggles. Lorelai learned that his addiction started shortly after his parents were killed in a fire, at home while they slept in the bed they shared. Rather than kill himself, he used drugs to deal with the pain. He became a shadow of the man he once was. Far from the man his father had been.

Gabe confided to Lorelai the many things he had done to "score". He told her of how he nearly beat a man to death because the man tried to steal his "H", as he called it. Gabe babbled on for more than two hours. It was then, he shook himself and said, "Why am I telling you all of this?"

Clearly confused by the amount of himself he gave freely to a complete stranger.

"I just have that effect on people." Lorelai licked the cappuccino foam from her lips and smiled knowingly.

"No, it's more than that," Gabe paused, a look of embarrassment marred his face. "This is going to sound like a line, but I swear it's not. I just feel comfortable with you. I feel safe. Like I have known you my whole life."

Gabe's eyes filled with a near innocence that could not be explained. Lorelai wasn't ready for such a statement to come from him, nor anyone else for that matter.

"You're right, it does sound like a lie, but I believe you." Lorelai said softly. She took a moment to collect her thoughts before continuing on with her real purpose. "I have to explain why I really brought you here."

"You said it was for my good deed."

"Which is true, but there is an ulterior motive as well. If I am to tell you what that motive is, I will have to explain a few things."

Lorelai attempted to calm Gabe's nervous nature. His hands wrung in his lap, giving off an air of unease.

"What do you have to explain?" He asked quizzically.

"Gabe, I am not good with subtlety. So, I am going to say this right out. I am Death."

With that small statement, Lorelai tried to sum up the infinite. *How can a human fathom the complexity of what I am and how entwined I am within the fabric of the universe,* Loralai thought.

Gabe didn't quite seem to comprehend the statement. He laughed and asked, "You mean, like you will be the death of me?"

Lorelai shook her head.

"Yeah, right. You're Death? Where are the robes and sickle?" He laughed even harder.

"Do you want proof?" Lorelai asked, the offense heavy in her otherwise flowery tone.

Her arms crossed in annoyance. She couldn't believe he had the audacity to laugh in the face of the infinite. His laughter mocking her very existence.

"Sure. Prove it," He said, the smile never leaving his scungy face.

"Think of somewhere you have always wanted to go. Don't tell me, think it," she said.

Lorelai tried to keep her voice calm and steady. Without hesitation, Gabe thought of the Great Wall of China. A point high in the mountains he once saw in a magazine.

Lorelai leaned forward across the candlelit table where they sat, laid her smooth hand atop his, and they were transported. The exact spot of Gabe's thoughts greeted them. The wind of the great mountains howled in welcome.

"What the hell? How....but you-" Gabe stammered.

"Just wait," Lorelai yelled over the fury of wind. "There is more."

In another instant they were in a bedroom. The appointment Lorelai delegated to a subordinate earlier in the day. A man in obvious emotional pain sat on the edge of his well-made bed with a ring in one hand and a gun in the other. On the desk to his left was a long, drawn-out note. A simplified explanation of his choices.

Lorelai and Gabe stood stoic in the shadows as she explained, the man had put on a facade to impress the love of his life, Lilith. He spent more money than he had, trying to give everything to make her happy. Lilith rejected his proposal of marriage.

"Wait, you mean he's gonna—," Gabe started.

He tried to move toward the man. Lorelai saw the man's in her mind.

*Christopher.*

"You can't help Christopher. He has chosen his fate. Besides, he doesn't sense you are here. It is not your place to intervene."

She explained in a flat, even tone. Even though this was not the appointment as it happened, she began to feel the numbness steal its way into her mind. Lorelai and her subordinates had to devoid themselves of emotions until the task was done.

Gabe watched in horror.

"You can choose to stop him. If you don't, it's murder. I will be an accomplice to murder. I have to help him."

Gabe pulled away from Lorelai with every fiber of his mortal being. To Gabe's dismay, Lorelai's otherworldly strength was no match for him.

Even though she overpowered him, Lorelai thought, *I wouldn't have thought a mere human could have such strength. It's taking every ounce of concentration to hold him here.*

Christopher put the never-worn solitaire between his chin and the barrel of the gun. As the moment drew closer, time slowed, but it was only a heightened sense taking control.

When a life chose to self-terminate, time slowed for Lorelai and her kind. Life had a choice. Until the bullet flew, the rope snapped taught, the last drop of blood flowed from the vein, the drug stopped the heart, or whatever horrific way they chose to die, there in it lay a choice.

As the firing pin hit the primer, Gabe pulled free of Lorelai's hold. They were transported back to the restaurant, sitting as if they never moved.

The bags accentuated under his eyes and the scarring of his once smooth cheeks were made worse by the horror the moment had brought. An expression of understanding covered his face as the light of day waned.

His jaw dropped wide, a look of near madness overtook the blue in his eyes, "You.You." His voice dripping with hatred. "You killed my parents. You're the reason for everything that has happened to me. You're evil. You let that guy kill himself. You just stood by and let it happen and… and-"

He lost his words in the bafflement.

"It is what I was created for. It is why I exist. My only purpose. I take life energy to its next existence or recycle it. Without me, life would overwhelm the universe," Lorelai said in a near whisper..

"Yeah, right. You're evil. You're the reason so many are afraid to really live. You're the reason so many people in the world, like me, get hooked on drugs. We can't face the thought of you. We can't stand the thought of leaving this world," Gabe ranted.

Lorelai felt her anger rise. Her thoughts had become overwhelming.

*Why? I have heard this kind of rant millions of times in my infinite eons of existence. This insignificant mortal being, who I believed was a coward, is standing up to me with the fury of a god. Somehow, this human found a spine I never thought any human could possess. So why anger? Why this emotional response? Yes, I can feel emotion until the moment I need to be detached. No mortal being has ever provoked such a response.*

"Another thing, most humans would see it as a blessing to live without the fear of death."

Gabe continued on, but Lorelai hardly heard him. At the same time, his words pierced the very fiber of what she was. Her control slipped and there was nothing she could do. She wasn't going to stand for these insults. Her brow furrowed, she clenched her fists, and slammed them onto the table. Her coffee cup wobbled, almost falling to the ground.

"Listen here, you pathetic excuse for a man. Hear my words." Lorelai's voice took on a vibrato outside of this world.

"I am neither good nor evil. I simply am. I have been since the beginning and will be until all is gone to nothing. I will still be, when what you think of as an existence is reborn in another form," she hissed and began a rant herself. "You mortals are the real evil. When a microbe dies on some termite mound, I don't see you shedding a tear, but yet, I am there.

You mortals are the problem. Even when you create something, you destroy something in return. Your kind is the most self-destructive force in this universe. You find more and more horrifically ingenious ways to destroy others.

I was there, in Hiroshima and Nagasaki. I had to take those souls, which had nothing to do with the war. I had to erase their fear and their pain. That's what happens to those who die horrific deaths. Such a horrific species and I have seen the worst of it. Through all that I have stood alone."

Gabe moved as if to add something to Lorelai's monologue.

"Shut it! I am necessary. Just as the light needs the dark. So, life needs death. Is it my fault? No. It's your creators' fault. Their flawed design of the universe. If I did not exist, no creature would have to evolve or procreate. Which means you wouldn't exist."

"How do you figure that?" Gabe asked with increased defiance. He had sat quite long enough, allowing Lorelai her moment. "We would still grow and evolve without you. That's what every being's purpose is. We exist to pass on our knowledge, our DNA, our very essence to the next generation."

With all the sarcasm Lorelai could muster, she mocked him, "Really? What purpose would there have been for evolution if I didn't exist? The most basic of single celled organisms would have flourished with no need to make more of themselves. Let's put it this way, where would you mortals be if the dinosaurs were never extinguished. This world would be a very different place.

This paradise of steel, concrete, and glass would probably never have been built!"

A spark of understanding appeared in Gabe's eyes, "I didn't think of that."

"Exactly. You mortals don't think about anything outside your own existence," Lorelai said as she returned to her normal state of calm. Her hand relaxed and she leaned back in the Adirondack chair.

"So, now I am going to give you something else to think about, but it may be too big for your mind. I don't say that to be insulting. I say that as a matter of fact. When faced with the intricacies of the universe and the infinite, your minds have a tendency to snap."

"Try me," Gabe said, poured from a confidence few mortals show.

Lorelai could see the poison in his veins bake off of him. It was as if his sheer will had made him well and stronger.

"Understand this, everything dies in a precise order. That order can be altered by choices you make and choices that others make," Lorelai began.

"You mean, fate, destiny, and all that stuff?"

"Precisely," she continued. "That is the most apt description mortals have for it. It is more complex than that of course,"

"Don't dumb it down for me," he said. "Just say what you have to."

"So, what happens if something comes along and disrupts that plan? What if something so small to normally be insignificant became something pivotal in the universe. There are only two constants in the universe, the plan and the balance. Everything must have a counter to it."

"Dark and light. Good and evil. Life and death. Am I on the right track?" Gabe asked as he smiled. His face seemed to have lost the look of a junkie. Lorelai saw the man Gabe had wanted to be. His eyes glowing with a newfound fire. "If something were to come along and throw a monkey wrench into the machine, the universe might implode. Something like that would upset the balance, right?"

"Exactly. So, this is where things will get difficult for you. You are that monkey wrench."

Lorelai didn't know how else to put it. Abrupt was her only way.

"How?" He questioned. "I'm nobody. I'm a guy who is barely surviving."

"Yes. You're also a thief, a cheater, a liar, and much, much worse," Lorelai said as coldly as she could. She said it to make him realize she knew everything about him. "You lived a life that had corrupted your energy. You lived a life where there was only one place for you to go."

"You mean, I'm going to Hell? That's what you said you do. You take life energy to the next existence and mine is Hell. You can't recycle me like you said? You can't reincarnate me?" The panic rose in Gabe's voice at the realization. "I didn't kill anyone. So what made me– "

Lorelai cut him off, "I said you were headed in that direction."

"Wait. What?" Relief and confusion came to his expression. "What do you mean?"

"The little girl. I was there for her. That one selfless act balanced your energy so perfectly that you become that pivotal point. You are that monkey wrench in the universe. Good and evil will come to destroy you. If that were to happen, it would upset the balance and the universe would tear itself apart," she explained further. "You created a blank space. Never once in my existence, or in all of existence for that matter, has that happened. You should have died in her place."

"First, I save a little girl, and now I am responsible for destroying everything? Give me a minute to wrap my head around this." Gabe's hands ran through his greasy hair. He wasn't sure how to process all of this. He's had some crazy trips before, but nothing like this. "I need to go to the restroom and splash some water on my face."

He stood and moved from the outdoor dining and into the restaurant. Lorelai saw fear in his mind but knew he would return.

She ordered another cup of coffee and waited for him to return. In the meantime, a couple sat down at the table across the patio. The woman wore a maroon business dress that seemed a bit too heavy for such mild weather. She appeared comfortable enough. Long black hair, with a streak of silver, hung down over her shoulders accentuating her beauty.

Her companion was also dressed in a business suit, but his was made of very plain, gray linen. His bald head only served to make his simple features less impressive. Where she was attention-grabbing, he was common and unremarkable.

"Lorelai," the woman said.

The name seemed to pour from her lips like an oil slick on the ocean.

Lorelai replied, "Lucy, you look show-stealing as always, but I never thought you'd appear as a woman."

As the man began to speak, time froze.

"You know why we are here," he said.

"Funny you didn't send one of your children," Lorelai said, mocking him. "Since when does The All Mighty, The All-Father, or whatever name you choose to use, come down from his throne?"

"This is too important for either of us not to be here–," Lucy hissed.

"What Lucifer means is, you know what is at stake," the man said, cutting off the woman. "You need to decide that mortal's fate. If not, we will not hesitate to do so. Destroy him eternally, so he cannot reincarnate."

"You and your son don't have that power. I choose. I decide, for I am Death," Lorelai said in defiance.

She straightened, now finding herself across the terrace and leaning toward where the couple sat.

"And you can be replaced!" Lucifer roared "You are not all-powerful. You are nothing."

"Such a petulant child. You should have taught him some manners," Lorelai said looking at the man. She looked back at Lucifer, "The only reason you have a kingdom to rule is that he couldn't defeat you. You are the ones that are replaceable. Remember, I have been here from the beginning. I saw you come into being just as I will see you both fall."

"We are infinite," The man said, looking unsure of himself. "We know all, we see all."

Lorelai laughed. It was a sound that rocked both Lucifer and his father. Her laughter shook heaven, Hell and all other realms. With her next seven words, she challenged everything. She placed a seed of doubt in their very existence.

"Then why didn't you know about him?" Lorelai asked, still on the cusp of laughter. "Because you are not omnipotent. Maybe there is something greater at work here."

"There is nothing greater than us!" Lucifer shot up, palm raised, and pulled the bowstring tight to strike Lorelai.

As if Lorelai was protected by some form of a shield, Lucifer was knocked to the ground in a poor attempt at retaliation.

Lorelai, now enraged, her calm demeanor replaced with something no human could imagine. She had no real form, appearing as if to turn to smoke, but yet remained corporeal. Terror had come to life, and it had a purpose.

Lorelai grabbed both of them, holding them completely immobile. Her voice slithered into the recesses of their minds, as one older than existence itself could do.

"I will take care of this. His fate is mine to decide. Now sit down and shut up. I've had enough of both of you." Lorelai slammed them into their vacated patio chairs, rattling the scones left cold on the table. They sat like rag dolls, quiet in their astonishment.

Lorelai situated herself, now back at her own table, and straightened the hem of her red dress when an idea of what to do came. Lorelai raised her cup of lukewarm coffee to them and nodded. They were on edge. That was good.

Gabe returned with a newfound calmness. "Ok, so where do we go from here?"

"I have been thinking about that very thing and I have a proposition for you."

"Oh, God. You sound like a used car salesman," Gabe chuckled.

Lorelai found the phrase humorous in light of recent events.

She smiled and replied, "Well, as I see it, you have two options. You can go back to that moment and change your choice," Lorelai said.

"Yeah, and go to Hell? What's option B?"

"You can take your chances with them."

Lorelai pointed to the couple on their left. They smiled and raised their cups in greeting. The smiles never reaching their eyes. They were cold, devoid of any compassion.

Gabe might not have noticed the slight shift in their demeanor, but Lorelai did. The once shaken pair had nearly returned to their prior sense of calm. Not good. She didn't have a lot of time.

"Is that–?" Gabe stammered. "Are they who I think they are?"

"I believe so," she said, faking an unknowing tone. "I am

not sure why they are here but it can't be good. Especially if they are sitting there as calmly as they appear."

"You said you have a proposal. Which I am guessing is option C," his eagerness apparent.

"Well, I like you. You have attributes I rarely see in mortals nowadays. You stand with courage in the face of Death." Lorelai smirked, finding herself rather quirky. "You also have knowledge of mortals which I do not possess. So, I ask you to be my companion. My link to understand mortals better and be forever removed from their game," she said, pointing over to the inhumane couple.

Lucifer and his father looked stunned. They had not anticipated the outcome. Keeping them off balance and in the dark was the best thing Lorelai could do.

"I have a few questions," Gabe said. "If I were to do this, what would I be? Would I be expected to take souls? Would I be alive or dead?"

"You would still be human, but you would be immortal. And no, I would not ask you to take appointments. I would ask that you teach me and show me existence through your mortal eyes."

His face became still, deep in thought. Thousands of thoughts could be seen racing through his eyes. His past and his family, dreams, and aspirations. Something occurred to Gabe Lorelai had not anticipated.

The steel resolve returned to his eyes, "Ok. Let's do this."

The couple vanished as if they had never been there. "I'm not going to do this because of the fate of the universe or because of them." Gabe gestured to the now empty table.

"Why are you going to do it then?"

"I'm doing it because of something you said and a silly human belief."

"What did I say?" Lorelai was confused.

She didn't recall having ever said anything other than the truth.

"That you have been alone through it all." Gabe smiled.

"And what is your belief?" Lorelai asked with genuine curiosity.

"Maybe it was something beyond them and beyond you that brought us together. Maybe someone, or something, is giving you what you desperately need. Maybe the universe is giving you a challenge."

Lorelai mused at her own thoughts and considered maybe it was possible.

"That's not a silly belief. That is beautiful. Poetic even." Lorelai felt emotions stir she couldn't seem to put into words.

"So, what do you really look like?" Gabe asked.

Lorelai was caught by surprise at the ask. She took great pleasure in donning a look mortals found worthy to gaze at.

"This is what you will always see when you look at me. So, this is what I look like.

"What do I call you?" He asked softly.

"I am called many names," she responded. "However, I have always liked the name Lorelai."

Gabe held out his hand. It was warm and strong. A lifetime of difference from the man she met earlier in the day. They shook hands gently. "It's nice to meet you, Gabe."

"It's nice to meet you, Lorelai. So, what now?"

"I have no idea, Gabe. I have no idea. And you know what?" Lorelai asked as she took a long bite of her cheesecake.

"What?"

"I like it."

# Hope's Bargain
By Tom Elmquist

The metal door opened, and a pleasant voice from the other side said, "Time for meds, Hope."

Hope got up and quickly took her meds. She opened her mouth wide and stuck out her tongue to show proof she swallowed it.

The nurse on the other side of the door said, "Good girl. Lights out in an hour."

Hope nodded and laid down on her bed. She knew she had to take the meds. If she didn't they would stick her, and Hope hated that. She lay waiting for the meds to take hold.

It was a day like any other. Hope and Danny walked hand in hand down Main Street to the garage where Danny worked. Danny was the love of Hope's life. They talked about school, plans, and dreams.

"Hey! Why don't I take the day off, and the two of us go to a movie?" Danny asked suddenly.

"No, babe, you work tonight. We can go to a movie this weekend. Besides, your Dad will kill you if you don't show up," she said.

Besides, she had something to do today. Had she known how the day would have ended, she might have changed those plans.

"Baby," he started.

"Ssssshh," she said and pushed a finger to his lips. "I promise this weekend I am all yours. We'll go to any movie you want, and a picnic on Saturday."

"Okay. I'm gonna hold you to it," Danny said with a grin.

They walked the half-mile to the garage. When they got there, Danny's dad waved. "Hi, Hope! Would you tell my son to get a move on? He has a tune-up to do."

Danny's dad loved Hope like his own. So, this was a playful question.

"Yes, sir!" Hope said and snapped a little salute. "You heard the man. Get a move on."

Danny kissed her, smiled, and said, "I'm gonna marry you. One day."

"One day," she repeated and hugged him.

He hugged her a little too tight, and she winced in pain. It was a reminder of her errand today.

"You, ok?" Danny asked, instantly knowing something was wrong.

"Just a little sore. I flattened when I should have tucked in the gym," Hope lied. "I'll be fine. Now, go on before he gets mad."

Hope threw a little look over her shoulder at Danny's dad.

"Alright, babe, love you," Danny said and hustled into the shop.

"Have a good day," Hope yelled and waved.

Both Danny and his dad waved back.

Hope turned, walking toward Maple Street. Everyone knew about the woman who lived on Maple Street. The rumors were, she was a witch. All Hope knew for a fact was she helped people with problems, and Hope had a huge problem.

Her ribs throbbed as if she needed a reminder of that problem. Her father had gone on one of his drunk tirades, and Hope was pushed into the kitchen counter. Her mother received much worse.

Hope's mother looked like she had been in a boxing match. Hope's dad had blacked her eye and split her lip. It wasn't the first time, but it wasn't the worst either. The last time her mother wound up in the hospital with four fractured ribs, a bruised liver, and a broken jaw. Hope's father got away with it because her mother refused to press charges. Hope's mother either loved the man very much or was too afraid of him to do anything. She once said she would kill him if he ever hurt Hope.

Hope knew her mother would never hurt a fly, but she was scared her mother would finally snap. Hope's mother was a sweet woman. She worked with her church to help and feed the homeless. In Hope's eyes, her mother was a saint, and Hope would give anything to keep her that way.

For the next fifteen minutes, she walked and thought.

No. She didn't think.

She daydreamed.

She dreamed of the wedding she and Danny would have. She dreamed of the two kids they would have together. She dreamed of the house where they would live. It would be a ranch-style house with three bedrooms, two baths, and a two-car garage.

That image was quickly replaced with a far more ominous one. Hope found herself standing in front of the house on Maple Street. There was nothing particularly creepy about it. It was a well-maintained house built in the 1800s. It had a big front porch that wrapped around to the left. To the right of the porch was a big bay window. It had lots of windows with faux shutters and, at the top, an attic that reminded her of a belfry.

On the porch sat a beautiful woman in her mid-thirties. She sipped iced tea and read a book. As Hope approached the front steps, the woman looked up from her book.

"Well, don't just stand there gawking," The woman said in a hefty Irish accent.

Without thought, Hope stepped up onto the porch. The woman stood and held her hand to Hope. Hope took the woman's hand and shook it..

"I am Mary Flynn. Named after my grandmother, who was the original owner of this house. And you are?" Mary asked with a bit of sparkle in her eye and a wide, inviting smile. She had fiery red hair and deep green eyes. Her skin as smooth as porcelain. She had very little make-up on, if any, and wore a black t-shirt with denim shorts.

Shaking the dumbfounded look off her face, Hope introduced herself. "I am Hope Elderidge. I have—"

"Come to see if I was a witch or some nonsense. No doubt," Mary said, cutting Hope off.

"Not exactly."

"Confidence girl, always have confidence when ye speak. Women have not been fighting for decades and longer to be timid little mice," Mary said as she moved back to her chair. "Please. Come sit and tell me why you have come to me home t'day."

Hope moved to the chair and noticed two glasses were waiting. Hope thought to herself, *There was only one glass. Wasn't there?*

Hope sat down and smiled at Mary. Mary smiled back with perfect teeth and asked, "Would you like some iced tea? It's a perfect refreshment for Spring days such as this." Mary noticed Hope staring at the glass. "I always have a second glass ready. Just in case someone like you happens to stop by. My mother was big on manners and being prepared."

This set Hope's mind at ease. "Please and Thank you."

"Thank you for the company," Mary said. "Most people are scared of this place. So, I don't get many visitors. What can I do for such a beautiful, young lady?"

"I have heard you do favors for people. Favors that can't be taken care of by normal means," Hope began.

"I see. What troubles you? A rival for some boy's heart? A way to get away from this sleepy little town guilt-free, perhaps?" Mary asked, a slight tone of sarcasm in her voice. All the while, her smile never faltered.

"No, nothing like that. I have a boyfriend and I love him with all my heart. We have already talked about getting married. You might have seen him. His dad runs the garage in town," Hope babbled.

"Oh, yes. A wonderful family. I know his father, and his father knew my mother," Mary said with genuine delight. "Well, it sounds like you have a good life. What brings you to me?"

Hope noticed a slight irritation in Mary's voice, but her smile stayed perfectly in place.

As if to remind her of purpose, or someone telling her to get on with it, Hope sneezed hard enough to make her wince and grab her bruised ribs.

Hope thought Mary's accent got thicker for a second "I'll fix you right up."

"It's-" Hope began.

"It's nothing? Yes, yes, I know. I have heard that many times. Inside," Mary commanded and led Hope inside.

The house was much cooler than outside. It was beautiful, and Hope stared in awe. "Have you maintained this all by yourself?"

"Oh no. I wouldn't know a nail from a thumb tack." It sounded like tum tac. "I have a handyman for all the house needs," Mary said.

They finally reached the kitchen, which was bright, warm, and inviting. Mary sat Hope in an old oak chair. "Now, let me see, Missy." Hope lifted her shirt, exposing a very purple bruise. "Who did this to you?" Mary asked.

Hope couldn't help the lie. It came out as an involuntary reflex. "I fell."

"Hmmm," Mary poked and prodded for a few seconds. "A little aloe and witch hazel will help that. Perhaps some chamomile tea to soothe your soul."

"I don't want to be any trouble," Hope began.

"Nonsense, ye came to Mary Flynn for help, and help you I will." Mary put water on for tea. She strolled across the small kitchen to a huge cabinet and rummaged inside.

She mumbled something Hope couldn't quite hear before closing the cupboard and setting a bottle and bowl next to Hope. She moved to the window and snipped a big piece from an aloe plant, dropping it into the bowl. Mary sat down and began to mix the ingredients.

"So, you are a witch," Hope said and immediately regretted it.

"I've been called that and much worse," Mary said smiling. This smile was different to Hope. It seemed warmer and more genuine than the smile she gave Hope on the porch.

"I mean, I'm not scared. Everyone has belief systems," Hope prayed. She was terrified out of her mind.

As if reading Hope's mind, Mary said, "Yes, you are. I can smell it coming off you like a bad perfume. It's alright to be afraid. Fear keeps us alert, but know I have no ill will or intent."

"Ok, I'm scared. I'm scared of you. I'm scared of what you can do," Hope said. A weight coming off her soul.

She had never admitted when she was afraid, not to anyone, even Danny.

"But ye came to me for help. Shirt up, girl," Hope raised her shirt obediently. "Now this is going to be cold and probably sting some."

It was cold, but it brought a feeling of bliss. It didn't sting at all. As Mary finished applying the salve, the teapot whistled. When Mary finished making the tea, she picked up the tray and asked, "Shall we have our tea in the living room?"

To Hope, it sounded more like a demand rather than a question. Hope followed. They sat on the couch. Mary poured the tea and handed a cup to Hope.

"Thank you. I wanted to tell you that you have a beautiful home," Hope said. The compliment sounded forced, and she immediately wished she hadn't said it.

"Enough of that. Sip your tea, and then we will speak of business. You came to ask a favor, and I will grant it if it is in my power. However, the favor may come at a small price," Mary said the last part as if practiced a thousand times before.

Hope did, and instantly she felt more at ease. "Before I begin, may I ask you a question?" Mary nodded. "How old are you?"

Hope dropped her shoulders and her gaze from Mary.

"Timid as a mouse ye are," Mary said and chuckled. "I'm older than you think but younger than you fear."

Hope began to feel uneasy again but started her story anyway.

She told Mary about her drunk and abusive father. She told Mary about her mother and how saintly Hope thought she was. She described the beatings and the nights she lost sleep because of the screaming. She went on and on for what felt like hours.

"Is he the one who did that?" Mary asked and gestured to Hope's ribs.

Hope nodded, dropping her gaze again. "Yes, ma'am. He

pushed me into a counter to get at my mom."

"So, what is it ye want?" Mary asked, a knowing look in her eyes.

She raised her eyebrows as if to accentuate the fact she already knew.

"Don't get me wrong. I don't want my mother to hurt him, but I want him to stop hurting her. I want him to stop hurting her and leave me—I mean, leave us. The sooner, the better," Hope said. She felt like she was begging,

Mary thought. She sat still for a long time, just staring off into space. Hope made a move to say something, but Mary waved a hand.

"I can help you, but it's going to cost you. I also need to do something before I fully agree."

Hope felt hope for the first time in a long time. "Yes. Anything."

"Are you pure?"

Hope knew what Mary wanted to know and answered with hesitation. "Yes. Danny and I,"

"I don't need all that," Mary snapped. "A simple yes will do. Are you willing to do anything I ask to have this favor granted"

"Yes. Anything. Do you want my firstborn or something like that?"

"In that case, hold out your hand,"

Hope obeyed. In an instant, three things happened. Hope felt the cold, steely pain of her palm being sliced. A white handkerchief appeared in her palm, soaking up the blood.

Finally, a roll of gauze appeared in Mary's hand. It happened so fast. Hope wasn't sure it had happened until Mary took the handkerchief and began wrapping Hope's hand.

"What the—" Hope screamed.

"Quiet. Our bargain is done, but there is one rule you

must follow. First, speak about this to no one, even if your young man asks about your hand. Lie. If someone you know asks about it. Lie. This bargain never happened. You were never here. Understood?" Mary asked, still bandaging Hope's hand.

"Yes," Hope nodded.

"You wait one hour to leave for home. Talk to your young man or something. Again, do not go home for one hour," Mary commanded

"I won't. I swear." Hope had no intention of crossing this woman.

"Now go, I have work," Mary ordered.

Hope didn't hesitate and ran out the front door, down the steps, and passed the mailbox. She didn't stop running for several blocks. When Hope slowed, she was close to the garage. Hope did as Mary told her, but the garage was closed when she got there. She thought it was odd but decided to walk to Danny's house.

She walked for the twenty minutes it took to get to Danny's house. Again, she thought it was odd but walked away. She looked at her watch. She still had twenty minutes before she could go home, and it was a thirty-minute walk. So, she turned north toward home.

She thought, *What could Mary do to make things better at home?"*

As if to answer, there was a searing pain in her hand. It felt like the worst steam burn she'd ever had. By instinct, she pulled the bandage off and saw her hand was healed. There was barely a scar, but it was there. She knew it would serve as a reminder of whatever bargain was struck between them.

At that point, she smelled it. There was smoke in the air. It wasn't the pleasant smell of a barbecue or a bonfire. It was the smoke of a burning building. Hope looked toward her house; a massive plume of smoke came from that direction.

"Oh God, no," Hope screamed, and she ran to her home. She got there to see her home engulfed in flames. A crowd had gathered. Hope's eyes were pulled directly to Danny and his family.

"Hope!" Danny yelled, catching Hope in his arms. "Thank God you weren't in there." Danny's Mom and Dad hugged Hope as well.

"Where are my parents?" Hope asked. A look of dawning horror in her eyes.

"They're still," Danny's dad started.

"Nooooooo," Hope screamed and pulled away from them. She ran past the fire trucks, intent on saving her mother. A firefighter grabbed her.

"Miss, you can't go in there. *We* can't even go in yet." As if to add emphasis to his statement, two windows exploded.

"No no no no no," Hope sobbed.

Danny and his parents pulled Hope back to safety. They sat in the grass of the house across the street. Mrs. Santini came down from her porch. She was in a housecoat and slippers, which were typical for her. Mrs. Santini had taken Hope's mother to the hospital a few times.

"Hope?" Mrs. Santini questioned. "Your father said I should give this to you."

"What is it?" Hope asked.

"He just said if anything happened today to give you this envelope.

Hope took it, tore it open, and read it aloud.

*Hope, I'm sorry I hurt you. I can't hurt you or your mother anymore. Be free. Dad*

Hope screamed as she threw the paper aside, howling in agony.

Danny's mom picked up the letter and handed it to a police officer nearby.

Hope calmed to sobs. Then a look of understanding came over her face. Her eyes widened, and her jaw dropped wide. "What did she do? Oh my God, what did she do?"

"What did who do?" Danny asked.

"No one. I mean, I'll explain later. Just wait here or meet me back at your house. I have to go do something," Hope said.

Danny went to say something, but Hope ran toward the house on Maple Street. She could feel the hatred grow with each step. She had no idea what she would do when she got there, but she was out for blood.

The biggest shock was yet to come. All the houses on Maple Street were there, all the streetlights were on. Yet, there was something different. As she got to Mary Flynn's place, she saw the house appeared abandoned. More than abandoned, it looked like it was about to fall down. There was a condemned sign on the front door.

"What the hell?" Hope asked out loud.

As if to answer her question, the flag popped up on the now rusted mailbox. Hope moved to it and opened it. Inside was a single envelope. When she touched it, she realized it was made of old paper. It had a sweet smell to it. The scent immediately made her think of some of the old books in her grandmother's house.

She sat on the steps and read the letter enclosed in the envelope.

*Dearest Hope,*

*I trust this finds you well. I know you must hate me, but you mustn't. All I did today was free myself of the curse placed on me by a prominent citizen of this town—a citizen who condemned me to live because she was sentenced to die.*

*Yes, I was a witch, but so was your great great grandmother. She was the witch that cursed me with her dying breath. I remember those words all too well.*

*She said, "As I die, may you never know peace. As I die, may you live for eternity and watch all you love die. Only the pure blood of your enemy can set you free."*

*She thought I turned her in as a witch to save my skin, but I didn't. It was your man's great great grandmother. His family prospered from that deed.*

*So, through all these years, all I wanted was to rest. I searched for a way to get the blood I needed to free myself.*

*Now, here is the last sane thought that will be in your head. Did I do anything to your parents, or did I just know it would happen the way things did? Would things have been different if you and your man went to the movies? Would any of this have taken place had you changed anything at all? What would things have changed had you not heeded my warning not to go home?*

*I must ask your forgiveness. I meant no harm to you. I wanted to be free, and now I am. There will be no evidence if you tell anyone of what happened today. Please, take solace in the fact you righted a wrong.*

Mary

The letter and the envelope disintegrated in her hands. Hope sobbed and turned into a peal of insane laughter. She sat on that stoop and laughed for hours. She was found later by Danny and his parents. When she caught sight of Danny, she began punching him and laughing the entire time.

It took everything Danny's father had to hold her down. She still laughed through it all. The Paramedics arrived and took Hope to the hospital. She was sedated and put into an isolation ward. She has been there ever since.

She laughed at the pain, the precision of fate, or the art of chaos that caused the events to happen. She laughed because maybe she could have stopped it.

She eventually told the doctors the story of the day's

events. They labeled her and stuffed her away in that tiny cell. Her last thought as she fell to sleep was.
What if......

## The Lonely Fox
By S.E. Reed

The secret wasn't in the way Ríona made the potion. The secret was in *who* she made the potion for. Love was a complicated matter. Sure, she could pluck a few hairs and throw them into a cauldron of boiling rose water to create a little spark. The drinker might garner a quick kiss at the end of a dinner date. But real love? That took time, concentration, and supplies she didn't keep stocked in her Apothecary Shop. But, Ríona was a woman of many talents, and never shied away from a challenge.

She preferred not to describe herself as a witch. She was more of a businesswoman. An entrepreneur. She knew how to discreetly find the right patron for her magic— one with deep pockets and a burning desire.

The key to her powerful love potion was the *actual* burning desire. The sickening feeling of lust for human contact. The tiresome longing for affection you'd do almost anything for. She'd met many men and women who wanted to purchase love. They believed they were ready for a marriage union and sought the easy way out. Why go through the hassle of a courtship when you could drink a love potion? What they failed to understand was, that without the burning, passionate, rip-your-heart-out desire for true love, Ríona's potion was useless.

That's why Ríona had become so particular for whom she brewed the love potion. If her potions did not work, it meant angry customers. And angry customers often lent to pitchforks, bricks through her shop windows, and even the occasional burning at the stake. Which by the way, was terrible for Ríona's complexion. It was hard enough to stay moisturized in the harsh New England weather.

Ríona had spent the last several weeks brewing a love potion for one particular patron, a very nice-looking gentleman in his early thirties named Donovan Butler...

Donovan Butler was born into poverty in East London. But, with his intelligence and eye for detail, he had elevated his stature. They called him a self-made man. However, without a prominent family name, Donovan never found an appropriate female match—so, he decided to sail to America.

In America, it was all about hard work and ingenuity, not family lineage. He'd also heard women in America desired men with rugged good looks and a large coin purse. Donovan wasn't sure how rugged his looks were, but he'd often been told he was an attractive man and his coin purse extremely full. However, after years of working in Boston and attending countless dinner parties and galas, Donovan still had not found true love.

Ríona found him weeping softly with a whiskey in his hand, standing alone at the back of a bar. They had both been attending an opera performance at Concert Hall across the street.

"I followed you here," Ríona said casually to Donovan. He looked up from his drink, unsure if he was observing a woman or a ghost. She had a dove white complexion, complimented by her midnight hair.

"For sport, perhaps?"

"I suppose you could call it that, if I may be the hound and you the fox," she said in jest.

"Ah, to be the fox, running from thy vicious bark. You, my lady, seem neither vicious nor loud—so, what do I owe your affections to?" Donovan responded with mild angst.

He wasn't sure if it was the whiskey or the woman. Something about both American varieties made him anxious.

"I do love you Brits. The wit. The clever banter. But I'm not surprised you haven't found a woman to wed." Ríona leaned in and sniffed him. "Or to bed. When was the last time you felt the bare breasts of a woman upon your nakedness?"

Donovan choked out the whiskey he'd just sipped. Spraying it on Ríona's chest. His face flushed a deep shade of pink as he looked around to see if anyone in the bar noticed what had happened. He'd never been propositioned by a prostitute before. Was this what it was like? Because the woman in front of him looked too fine a creature, smelled too clean, dressed in finery—there was no way she was an elicit creature of the night.

"Why sir, you have spit your drink on me," Ríona said. Then she let out a delightful laugh. One he was not expecting at all. Something inside of him stirred. Desire.

"I'm very sorry, you just—your question startled me." Donovan tried to apologize but Ríona waved it off.

"My name is Ríona. I own an Apothecary Shop outside of Boston. I make special tinctures and potions for those in need. And you sir, are in need of love. I watched you tonight, alone at the Opera. A man of your means should never be out alone," Ríona said.

Donovan was speechless.

"I am staying the night at the Parker Hotel in room 202. If you are interested in a love potion, you may slip the required funds under my door before sunrise. I will return here with your potion in exactly one month."

Ríona leaned into Donovan, who was still shocked into silence by the transpiring events. She whispered a ridiculous sum into his ear. The closeness of her lips aroused him.

The next morning when Ríona awoke, there was an envelope with money slid under her hotel room door. Inside of it, Donovan had written her a letter. No man had ever written her a letter before. In it, he thanked her for her offer of the love potion. But said it was no use—he described his youth, living on the streets of East London, and his rise to stature and wealth through sheer determination. But, without a proper surname, he'd never truly been accepted. Donovan went on to describe his woes with love and his move to America, where his woes continued. Finally, proclaimed he was broken, unable to find or give love.

He finished the letter by saying the money was a gift, nothing more. He expected no love potion in return. There was no hope for a lonely fox. Especially from such a beautiful and mysterious hound.

"Oh sir, you have underestimated my abilities," Ríona said to herself after reading the letter several times. If ever a love potion was to be brewed, it was for Donovan Butler.

***

One month to the day, Ríona returned to the bar. She arrived early, to hide in the shadows and watch for Donovan. He'd come back, she knew he would. The magic blue love potion was in a vial in her handbag. It was aching to be drunk. It had been the most difficult potion to brew— Ríona found herself reading the letter from Donovan so many times she became distracted by her own obsession for the man. It was hard to picture him with any woman other than herself. Which, if she was not careful, could be detrimental to the potion's effectiveness for Donovan.

It was then the door opened and handsome Donovan Butler waltzed in. He had a beautiful young woman on his arm.

She was exquisite. Everything Ríona might have hoped her potion could bring him. Her own heart ached at the sight. Ríona sighed and set the vial down on the bar— upholding her end of the bargain, regardless of Donovan gifting her the money.

Love was a complicated matter.

# I'm Not a Witch (Just a Bitch)
By S.E. Reed

"I wouldn't go so far as to say I'm an evil villain. Bitchy? Yes. Selfish? A little. But let's not get ahead of ourselves here people," I announce to the crowd forming around my cage.

"Gut her!"

"Cut out her eyes!"

"Burn her alive!"

Chants and ranting by a bunch of half-wits. Every piss poor town is the same. A beautiful young woman moves in and opens a small apothecary shop, trying to mind her own business—then BAM! Here I am, locked in a cage, and put on display while they decide how to kill me. Seriously, if it wasn't so predictable, my feelings might be hurt.

Who are we kidding? It would be a cold day in hell if my feelings were ever hurt by these morons. Truthfully, I'm not sure I even have any feelings…

"Witch! You poisoned my Isabelle!" A woman comes forward wailing. Lamenting. I roll my eyes.

"Uh, lady? Yeah, you. Isabelle's mom." I point at the

crying woman. "I'll have you know I am not a witch. I do not belong to a coven. Your precious Isabelle got herself knocked up and came to me for help. It's not my fault she was so stupid and mixed the tea wrong. I told her, one part wormwood to one part—"

"LIAR! You poisoned her! You're a witch!"

I didn't.

And I'm not.

Yeah, okay, maybe Mom is the High Priestess in her coven and you don't have to remind me that my father may-or-may-not be Lucifer (What? It was the 1680s. Shit was wild back then! You can't blame Mom for getting around). But I did not join Mom's crew, no matter how hard she tried to force me.

I am not a witch.

If growing up in Salem taught me one thing, it was to stay the hell out of the affairs of witches. Because, when I mix in, shit gets dark. So, I have spent the last 200 years making my own way, running a legitimate business selling delicate herb teas and masterful love potions. Which isn't easy when you're absolutely not a witch. Thank you very much.

"Kill the witch! Destroy her!"

"Burn her shop, she kills children!" Cheers rain from the crowd while pitchforks and torches wave along, fueled by rage, fear, and old-fashioned ignorance.

"Yes, yes, go burn down my shop. How clever of you." I smile to the crowd as they turn and run across the town square.

"Now, time for a little magic."

I fumble a small vial out from the folds of my skirt and sprinkle black powder into the lock on my temporary prison. I pull out a striking match.

CRASH!

I look up briefly to see the windows of my quaint apothecary shop being smashed by bricks. There's at least twenty grown men inside ripping everything to shreds. How annoying– I just finished building those shelves!

"Here goes nothing," I say and strike the match.

I quickly stick its wooden end into the lock and back as far to the side of the cage as I can. I put my hands over my head to protect it from the– BLAST! Bits of twisted metal burst from the lock, just enough to loosen it where I can kick the metal door wide open. I step forward and brush myself off.

"SHE'S ESCAPING!"

"Awe, shit." I run.

At least they didn't shackle my feet. I hate running with my feet bound together, it's hard to get any real momentum. I've always been a good runner, but it's not my favorite pastime or anything.

Mostly for escaping.

"That fucking horse better be where I left her," I mutter. You'd think someone could invent better shoes. These brown leather boots with pointy toes and wedge heels are murdering my feet. Not to mention the clip-clop-bullshit on the cobblestones. I might as well scream and yell, "I'm here! Look at me!"

I turn left to head down an alley between the tavern and livery, diving into the back of the stables.

"Hey Jon, heads up– angry mob on their way," I say, kicking the man asleep on a pile of straw.

I get inside the last stall, slamming the deadbolt to trap me and Penelope behind the thick door. She snorts.

"I'm sorry, okay! Don't look at me like that, Penelope. This place is full of losers. It's time to hit the road." I apologize to my horse as I load a pack on her back.

I always keep the essentials ready in her stable for a hasty getaway; you know, clean pantaloons, rose water, a jar of dried magots (don't ask). I hear the front of the livery open up.

"She's got to be in here. I saw her turn this way!"

"No torches 'round the horses! Are you feckers mad? Get the fuck out of my stables!" Jon yells at the crowd.

He might be an old drunk, but he does care about the safety of the horses.

"You hiding that witch in here?" The mob shouts.

The smell of rage and manure is thick. Penelope's nostrils flare. The other horses are stomping and neighing. This is getting ugly. We've gotta get out of here, now.

I boot open the secret backdoor I built in Penelope's stall. No one will think of going around back. There's never been a door this way and by the time Jon lets one of them in to search for me, Penelope and I will be long gone. Good riddance. Assholes.

\*\*\*

"Ríona, again?" Mairenn says as she sits down next to me at the fire.

I'm exhausted and pissed off to be at her outdoor camp in the woods instead of a swanky hotel downtown.

"It took me three days to get here– I really don't want to get into the particulars of my latest misadventures right now," I croak.

My half-sister frowns. She looks a lot like me– except shorter. We both have big, round dark eyes, long black hair, and curves that make grown men cry like infants when we disrobe. I nudge her with my shoulder. She takes a blanket, throws it over me and snaps her fingers. A dirty former tavern wench, by the smell of her, appears with a tray of food and mugs of elderberry wine. The meat looks pretty suspicious. I pass and only take the wine. My face contorts at the sweetness.

"You should eat," Mairenn urges me.

"I'd rather not spend the next week shitting in the woods." I point to the witch who delivered the tray. "That one's definitely got some sort of venereal disease."

"You are so weird, Ríona," Mairenn complains.

"Hey, when you've been alive as long as I have, you'll understand. You're what? Sixty? Seventy?" I ask.

"Seventy-nine next week actually. Mother said me and the girls can go into Boston and meet up with the Princes of Darkness for my birthday. They've got a club downtown. I've always wanted to let one suck my blood, and maybe a few other places too." Mairenn's eyes glow brightly with lust.
She finishes her wine in one gulp and reaches for the meat.

"Seriously, don't eat that," I say and smack her hand as the witch who served us cackles.

"Ohhh, I have a wicked idea! You should come with us for my birthday! Please Ríona."

"Mairenn, you know I don't party with witches," I remind her.

"But it's not fair! You are always out there trying to live with the humans and hide who you really are. Look where it's gotten you, kicked out of every town from here to New York. Just stay with us for a while. Pleeeeease," she begs.

I let out a long sigh.

Mairenn has no idea what she's asking me! The darkness in my soul is real. There is a reason I don't hang out with witches; I may have a bit of a self-control problem when it comes to magic. I'm liable to do anything when it takes me over. But, as I look at the faces of the women sitting around the fire, all young, eager, (and to be honest, super gross) something about them pulls at my dark heart strings.

I know one thing for sure—

If I'm staying, my first mission is to brew up rose hips and lavender. There's nothing worse than a smelly witch! Every single one needs a hot bath. Especially my sister. Mairenn's never going to get sucked by one of those stupid Princes if she rolls into the club like some forest skank.

"Fine. I'll stay and go to your birthday, but after that I'm leaving. A few years ago, I met a retired pirate— he said if I was ever down South to look him up, maybe I'll head that way for a while. He was actually pretty hot for an old guy," I tell Mairenn.

She looks at me sideways.

"What? Don't judge me."

"No! I'm just so happy you'll stay for my birthday!" Mairenn squeals with delight before bursting into tears as she leans in to hug me. I back away.

"Relax. Don't get all sappy and romantic. I have one stipulation. Tomorrow you are going to help me find some herbs and oils. This place stinks," I say loudly. "Yeah, I'm looking at all of you. You smell like a bunch of dirty vaginas. How can Mom stand it?"

"Oh, she's not around much. She's got a new boyfriend— some Professor Longfellow at Harvard. He's all like, Elspeth, you're sooooo beautiful. More beautiful than all the stars in the sky. Here, let me build you an observatory on campus so we can gaze at the stars together. Bunch of corny shit. I don't know how she fell for it." Mairenn looks distressed.

It's no wonder everyone here is crusty. Mom's not been here to manage her own coven. She's left Mairenn in charge and she's a child in the witch world.

I've known Mom long enough to know— she's up to *something*. A Professor? She's a smart woman, but a Professor? No, that's not her speed at all. There's some ulterior motive at play, but it's none of my business. I don't care what she does. I never have.

I'm not a witch.

\*\*\*

The next few days at camp are hectic.

Who knew getting ten witches cleaned up and presentable would be this difficult. I mean, I make lotions and potions and creams and hair tonics for a living! But, out here in the woods, I'm forced to scrounge up what I need without any of my tools or workshop to blend and chop. Plus, it seems this particular batch of young witches have grown accustomed to living like filthy twats.

"Hold still." I pull on Gretchen's blonde hair.

"Ow, Ríona, you're hurting me. Don't tug so hard," she whimpers.

"I'm hurting you? Well, it hurts me to see all these fucking lice in your hair. I can literally see them crawling when I sit across the fire from you. Have some pride in your appearance. If you want to get anywhere in life, you have to use your feminine wiles," I scold. "That goes for all of you. Being a witch means using your womanhood to your advantage," I shout before going back to picking and killing the nits in her hair. "God, you're so gross."

"I'm sorry, Ríona. I don't know what's happened." Mairenn comes closer to inspect my work.

"I know damn well what's happened here. You've all gotten lazy. Soft. You think because the High Priestess is off banging some Harvard professor you can forget your training? Well, you've got another thing coming to you. I may not be a witch, but I am still a woman. Once Elspeth has finished her little game with the professor, she will return to you, her coven. You'll all be burned alive at the stake if she spends more than ten minutes with you," I tell them and spit into the fire. The flames burst green and blue. I hear whispering and see shivers crawl up their spines.

Seriously. Mom's really been slacking. But she won't take responsibility for this when she comes home. She'll blame this mess on Mairenn. Just like she used to do with me, until I left to make my own way in the world. Not that I care. I'm not a fucking witch and this isn't my coven! My heart races and my face burns with agitation. A gust of wind blows the sweet river air through my hair, temporarily cooling me off. I let out a long sigh. I don't know why I let this get to me—

"Thanks for staying, sis. I guess I really needed you. You're completely right. We've been lazy with Mom gone so much. I mean, out here in the woods, there's not a lot to do." Marienne leans and tries to hug me when I finally finish picking Gretchen's disgusting hair.

"What's with this hugging shit? Stop trying to touch me. You're a witch, go draw a pentagram or cut off a dog's tail or something spooky." I march off to the river to wash my hands and face.

"Wait, Ríona, don't be like that, all angry and bitter. It's been so long since you've been around and I've missed you. Can't I be happy to see you? Can't I hug you?" Mairenn chases after me.

The river is rushing wild and bloated from the spring thaw. If I was smart, I'd jump in and swim away. But instead I spin around and stare at her. I want to be angry, not at her, not really, so when she looks at me with those doe eyes… I sigh… She really is a beauty.

"Yes, you can be happy."

She smiles slyly. I know that look. It would do her some good to have a night on the town. To let loose, to feel free, and to suck face with a Prince of Darkness.

"Do you have any other clothes? Because you are not wearing that to your birthday party, it's dreadful."

"Um, actually, I was hoping we could go into town early and go shopping. Me and the girls have some money saved from a seance we performed for some rich assholes a few months ago. Enough to buy all of us a new gown. I'll get you one too." She smiles and bats her eyes.

\*\*\*

"I'm not sure why I agreed to this," I inhale sharply as

the woman behind me pulls the laces on the whale bone bustier as tight as she can.

"Because you looooove me," Mairenn teases as she comes into the dressing room.

The little shit attendant cinches me tighter and tighter, trying to torture me.

"Stop it." I smack her.

"Here sis, try this one." Mairenn holds up a red-wine velvet gown.

It's exquisite. Sumptuous. Like it was made for me. My chest is in my throat, but it's my reflection in the mirror that takes my breath away.

"God, Ríona. You look like a fallen angel!" My sister gasps.

My blood tingles and pulses through my body. I know this feeling. Okay, okay, so maybe *I do* have feelings. I just choose to bury them most of the time, because once I let them out, they are really hard to control, and they make me do some really fucked up shit.

But Mairenn wanted this, right?

She's the one who asked me to stay and party with her and Mom's coven, knowing full well what might happen if the real me was unleashed. I look at myself in the mirror again. My reflection blows me a kiss, clapping with delight when it sees my eyes flare with lust and desire.

"Uh oh," I whisper.

Reflection me, the witch in me, laughs as she watches my human form shed the chains of self-control that normally bind me.

*Ah fuck, here we go.*

There's no stopping what's happening, and I don't want to. I want to lose all control. I want to be a witch again, at least for tonight. I grab a parasol that's meant to show how demure and dainty we are as women and that we must protect our precious skin from the harsh sunlight. I thrust it into the air like a wand and roar.

"Ladies, we are going to take Boston by storm! Whatever we want is ours! Men, women, freaks, geeks, the Princes of fucking Darkness! Tonight we drink, we dance, we shed blood! It's all ours for the taking."

"Agh! You're a monster!" The idiot who laced me up screams and faints, hitting the floor with a thud.

I put my foot on her chest and look around the room.

"Boo."

The witches start laughing.

I'm such a bitch sometimes.

I love it.

I flick a coin over my shoulder and push open the doors of the dress shop. We hit the streets— a gang of beautiful savages. Boston doesn't have any idea what kind of hell has been unleashed. A boom of thunder and a bolt of lightning strike the horizon as me and Mairenn march in front of the coven to the beat of our own drum. Hmmm, maybe it was Zeus. That whole daddy thing is still debatable.

"Ladies. I think a drink is in order. Let's get this party started!" I lift the heavy skirts of my new gown and step onto the muddy street.

You'd think a city like Boston could cobblestone the main roads. I shake my head. Pathetic. Horses and buggies come to a halt as men scream and shout at us to get out of their way. We take our time crossing the road.

"Move it!" One driver shouts.

"Outta the way! Women don't belong out here alone!"

I suck in a deep breath and look at the driver. "Say it again— I dare you," I hiss, showing my teeth.

"Freak!" He yells back.

"Oh, no you didn't."

I take a running charge at him. His horse realizes she's in danger and rears up, twisting to the side, and snapping the wooden and leather straps connecting her to the carriage. I wink as she runs away and nods. I may be a fucking psycho, but I'm not into killing animals.

*I'm not a real witch.*

It all happens so fast; the driver's whip is mid-air like his horse is still connected to the buggy. And what if she was? Would he have just rammed through me, my sister, and Mom's coven? As I rush him, the witches' instincts take over. They lift their new dresses and run at the carriage in perfect unison (like that ever happens). They take a flying leap into the air and land on the man.

Their blood lust takes over. I don't even have to lift a finger. They tear him to bits.

\*\*\*

"Did you see the look in his eye?" I lift my glass at dinner. The girls all shriek and clap for me.

"Cheers to Ríona!" Gretchen shouts.

"No, cheers to Mairenn. Happy birthday, Sister!"

We spend the next three hours drinking and feasting. Fresh oysters with herbs. Roasted duck simmered in blood oranges. Thick black truffle souffle. French champagne in crystal goblets. It's decadent, over the top. I haven't indulged like this in decades. It's to die for!

"Ríona, I can't thank you enough for—" Mairenn looks at me with her big doe eyes. My eyes. Our Mom's eyes.

"Bitch, shut up and drink," I take the bottle closest to me and pour it straight into her mouth.

"You women need to pay your bill and leave." The squatty owner of the restaurant comes over to our table. "You've scared away every other paying patron in my fine establishment."

He sweats profusely.

"I'd be scared too, if I was you." I stand, ready to rumble with this pathetic man. But the clock on the wall chimes. "Lucky you, saved by the bell." I push him aside.

"Midnight!" The witches start clapping and laughing.

I snap my fingers as we leave and every oil lamp in the restaurant explodes.

What?

Obviously, I like dramatic exits.

***

"It's supposed to be right here," Mairenn looks side to side.

We stand in an alley between two rundown buildings. Everything is dark. My blood lust and booze begin to wear off. If we don't find this club soon, we'll have to find some shitty street tavern to keep the party alive. Cringe.

"Mairenn, I thought you said this place would be packed. There's not a living soul around," one of the witches complains.

She's right. There should be some kind of sign, like stumbling drunks, the smell of blood and liquor, or notes of music marking this as the entrance. Anything. I sniff the air, straining my ears to listen for anything– that's when I hear her laugh. Coming from the shadows.

Elspeth.

She's gorgeous. Glowing and evil. Of course, she'd show up just in time for the party.

"Ladies, ladies! Don't you look ravishing. Good enough to eat! Although, I'm sure that was the point. The club is this way, follow me. The Princes are waiting for you. My consort, Professor Longfellow, and I have been speaking highly of you all night," her deep voice is like a summoning spell.

Her coven lines up to follow her. Including Mairenn. I'd forgotten what it was like to be around Mom when she acted like a real High Priestess.

"Ríona, nice to see you. I heard you were with the girls. Will you be joining us this evening?" Mom's tone is cool. Calculating. But I'm not really listening– I'm focused on the scene unfolding in front of me as we walk into the club that's appeared out of thin air.

Ah. I'm so stupid. It was here the entire time.

I blink a few times. "Yeah, yeah, Mom. Here for Mairenn's birthday," I say as I walk into the center of the club. Musicians in tuxedos are playing on a stage, hundreds of Boston's finest are dancing, singing, drinking under a heavy layer of magic hanging in the air. There are pentagrams drawn on the wall. Black flamed candles in the chandeliers.

The Princes are easy to spot. Beautiful male specimens wearing clothes from Paris and London. Some of them aren't wearing shirts at all. The witches are drawn to them – moth-to-flame bullshit. I smile, watching Mairenn descend upon the male with the biggest crowd around him. *You know what they say about men with big crowds.*

His teeth are fully exposed, blood drips from them.

She doesn't even wait her turn.

"Atta girl, take what you want!" I scream.

The music starts to play louder and the lust in my veins peaks again. Time to party!

"Now just hold on a minute, young lady." Mom grabs my arm. "Before you go all crazy, I'd like you to meet my consort, Professor Longfellow. He's a Harvard man, you know, talented, brilliant, great in the sack."

Mom pulls a paunchy little man with a goatee over and gives him a big sloppy kiss before turning him to face me.

"Charming," I yawn.

I don't give a shit what game she's up to.

"Don't be rude, Ríona," she slights. "Longfellow and I

are getting ready to go on a trip to Europe. That whole French Revolution thing– the climate is perfect for me to recruit and train a new coven before heading to Romania. Longfellow is going to help me secure a castle there, aren't you, my dear."

"Yes, yes, I have a large financial grant from Harvard. I will be placing an observatory on several castles in middle Europe, we are going to triangulate the–"

"Alright, that's enough. Go get me a drink," Mom says and shoves him toward the bar.

"I don't care what it is you're up to." I turn to walk away.

"Stop right there." She uses her voice, the deep one, like with her coven. She's trying to force me to obey.

"Ha, idiot. I'm not in your coven. You can't bend me to your will," I laugh in her face.

"You are a part of me. You don't have to be in my coven to be a witch. You are MY witch. I own you, child," she sneers.

"What crawled up your ass and died? Relax! I'm just not interested in whatever you're doing. I'm only here for my sister. She wanted me to come to her birthday party. I cleaned up your sleazy witches, so they might have a chance to hook up tonight," I tell her. "Now if you don't mind, I'm going to get a drink, and enjoy myself!"

I walk away from Mom. Who the fuck does she think she is? Grabbing me like that. Trying to bend me to her will! She's infuriating!

I grab a drink off a tray and chug it. Then another. And another.

This is so typical of Mom.

I know exactly what that bitch is up to. She thinks she can force me into her coven. To take over for her while she goes gallivanting around Europe with that putz Longfellow. Yeah, well, it's not going to work.

"I'm not a fucking witch!" I scream as loud as I can.

Everyone in the room stops.

The music screeches to a halt.

"Yeah, I like that– I'M NOT A FUCKING WITCH!" One of the Princes of Darkness bellows into the air. The crowd erupts into a frenzy and everyone in the club starts jumping and dancing and cheering.

"Real nice, Ríona." Mom stares at me with her glowing round eyes.

"Are you two alright?" Mairenn approaches, holding on to a super hot shirtless male with bloody fangs. Her neck is punctured in multiple spots. "I'm having sooooo much fun! I hope you aren't over here fighting."

"No, we're fine," Mom and I both say at the same time. Mairenn smiles.

"Come on, Franco. Let's find a dark corner. I have a few other places I want you to stick those fangs." Mairenn pulls on her new friend, and they disappear into the chaos of the club.

"What happened to you out there with the humans? You've turned into such a mean-spirited bitch. This is worse than that time in Salem." Mom spits at me.

"First of all, I was a child when that shit in Salem happened and how am I the pathetic one? I've been an independent businesswoman for over a century. Do you even know what you're sorry, good-for-nothing coven looked like when I found them?" I spit right back at her. "Those women are YOUR responsibility. Not mine!"

"I didn't ask you to take over my coven. You're out of your mind, Ríona– you're the last person I'd put in charge!" She laughs. Outright cackles.

"I don't need this shit, I'm out of here," I rage and push past all of the dancing assholes. I flick my fingers before walking out the doors and the lights explode. The club screams and cheers. Opposite of what I wanted to happen.

Mom thinks she's so perfect. So clever. Bringing up Salem. Like I did all that on purpose. I mean come on, how was I supposed to know that whole trial would happen? How would I know half of Mom's coven would be burned at the stake? I didn't mean to show my magic to that little priss from town, but that's a time and place I'm tired of reliving. This is exactly why I'm not in her coven.

Why I'm not a witch.

***

I spend the next few hours wandering the streets of Boston looking for a fight. I've got to get the rest of these vile feelings out of my system before I regret it. Plus, it's about time I head south, and Penelope really hates it when I go on weird magic-blood lusty benders. (This isn't the first time). She can smell it on me for days and makes the riding as difficult as possible. Fucking horses.

"Hey pretty lady, you lost?"

"Come here sweetie, we ain't gonna hurt you."

*Bingo.*

Two burly men lean up against a building waiting for prey. The sun just starts to peak, making the early morning fog give a false sense of anonymity for them to attack. I keep walking, but slower, tempting them to come closer. I cave in my shoulders and look back nervously. A tease. I stop and shiver, making sure they still see me. Slowly, now— slowly, one foot in front of the other. But the blood inside me pulses furiously, and I can feel my eyes turn red. All I want to do is turn around and—

"Slow down, slut. I asked if you were lost. You gonna answer me or what?" The bigger of the two men trots over and puts his hand on my back.

*There it is.*

I spin around and claw him in the face, my nails pull his skin loose, and blood spurts across the front of my dress. I punch him in the nose with my other hand.

"What the fuck!" He screams, flying backward and slamming into a building.

"AGHHHH!" His friend rushes toward me with his hands out, like he's going to choke me.

I laugh and put my hands up. They are literally red, flaming from anger. I grab him seconds before he reaches my throat.

He doesn't know what to do.

His eyes blaze with pain.

"F-f-f-FIRE! The bitch is burning me, man!" He screams and tries to get out of my grip. But I'm strong. Stronger than he is.

The piece of shit I punched finally comes to his senses and clambers up off the ground, lunging toward me. But I'm fast. Faster than he is. I side-kick him, except this goddamn dress is in my way and my boot gets caught up in all the fabric. My foot comes down, so does the dress. Fighting in my bloomers has never stopped me before.

"You think women are weak?" I ask my boot to his gut.

"You think I'm scared of you?" My elbow to his jaw.

"Fuck you." I spit in his face.

"Ríona! Ríona! Are you okay?" Mairenn comes rushing toward me. Mom's coven is right behind her, running with wild eyes. The two assholes moan on the ground behind me. I don't even have to watch. I can hear the witches ripping the men apart. Tearing them limb from limb. I let out a sigh. My blood lust is nearly gone…

Now, all I feel is regret.

Not for the two assholes, they deserved what they got.

"Where's Mom?" I ask Mairenn.

"She's really upset, you know. She and Professor Longfellow went back to their hotel. They are leaving on the first ship to France. What did you say to her?" Mairenn puts her arm around me.

I let out a sigh. "I don't know, she just pisses me off so bad! Whenever I'm around her, I know she's judging me– she hates my life and she's furious I'm not one of you. It's really hard being the oldest, you know? It's like everything I do is never good enough. And here you are, her little princess, and she's leaving you in charge of the coven while she goes to France." My voice is shaky.

I'm not supposed to have feelings! I just want to get back to Penelope and get the hell out of here. Put some space between me and the coven.

"Mom didn't leave me in charge, dummy. She's taking the coven with her. She'd never abandon us! She loves us, in her own sort of way. We just came to find you– Mom wants you to come! She's really excited for you to set up an apothecary shop in the village outside of the castle. Come on, we've got to get down to their hotel– they've got all the tickets for the ship." Mairenn squeezes me in a half hug.

I don't even push her away.

So, Mom wants me to open an apothecary outside of her castle? She's totally up to something. I bet she thinks she can trick me into joining her coven. Yeah, well she's got another thing coming. But, look at my little sister, those eyes glimmering with magic. She's going to need someone like me to guide her and teach her how to live in the real world.

I have always wanted to go to Europe. I can almost smell the French Lavender and sweet Sorel. And– we all know how nasty her coven gets when she's too busy to keep an eye on them. Setting up an entire castle with Longfellow means she's going to be very busy, utterly distracted even! Who else will be there to keep all those foul witches clean? Oh, who are we kidding– I love my sister and I would do anything for her. I would kill for her. I would die for her.

Shut up about the feelings already!

Speaking of someone, or something, I have feelings for…

"What about Penelope? I can't just leave her. We've been together a long time. She's kind of my go-to," I say and blink a few times, the final layer of blood lust and rage clearing from my head. I feel all soft and mushy.

"Bring her! It's not like the ship captain will say anything about a horse. I mean, come on, our Mom is a High Priestess."

"True. Okay little sis, what the hell? Let's go to Europe!" I throw my arms up.

Mairenn laughs with delight. "Oh, Ríona, this will be amazing! Can you imagine? All of us in Europe? This is what you and Mom need to reconnect. I promise you aren't going to regret this! Plus, I heard the clubs there are insane and the men are to die for."

"You're such a child. Boy crazy!" I elbow her.

She throws her arm around me, and we start following the coven down the street toward the hotel. I can't believe I'm doing this. What am I thinking? But it's not like I have a home to go back to, or anything really. Shit– I don't even have proper clothing on.

"Stop!" I shout. "One of you witches give me your shawl. I'm literally walking in my fucking pantaloons here. Boy, I have so much to teach you wicked ladies. None of you have any manners, grace, or style."

Gretchen quickly hands me her shawl and I tie it around my waste.

"You don't have to be so rude about everything, sis," Mairenn chides.

"Um, yes I do. I mean, *I am a bitch, not a witch.*"

"Ríona!"

I laugh. "What? It's true!"

# antecedent

By Johnny Francis Wolf

Hovering, a face in whist —
suspended by a wire, frame.
Less like black than starless mist
enfolded round the face aflame

in gilded chroma, canvas swabbed
with auric brush and crimson comb.
Whiskers grew from oils daubed,
rouge and russet. Metronome

was counting quivers, rhythms pulsed
on harpsichord as playing Bach.
His ghostly mirrored eyes avulsed
an augury, when heard a knock.

***

"Sir," the servant's mien contrived,
"Your wife, it seems, has taken ill.
Doctor sent for has arrived."
His bearing matched by master's chill.

"See to it and leave me pen
a dirge to honor final flight."
The poser for the painting, then,
composed a keen with lyrics light.

"There was a lass, a maiden fair —"
Parchment balled and brashly thrown.
"Beguiling beauty, flaxen hair ——"
He spit disdain, as often prone.

\*\*\*

"CURS-ED WITCH and BANEFUL SHREW
who left me little choice but cull
my bed of her. WHERE ONCE WAS TWO
is now a bless-ed one and skull."

Contented with his odic air
quilled to honor strangled wife,
upon his portrait long didst stare.
"A handsome man, afresh my life."

Little left of neck he kissed,
rarely rendered sonnet sweet.
Hovering, a face in whist —
suspended noose and flailing feet.

# Daylight
By C.L. Galan

She stared at the street in front of her, hidden within a canopy of trees that shrouded her in essential darkness.

She watched him. Gabriel. As he spoke with a girl she could only call an obstacle.

For a man, she'd met centuries ago, had told her upon his death bed of a prophecy he'd seen. A prophecy that would give her the true love she'd craved so desperately.

A prophecy that required sacrifice.

She was told a man named Gabriel would be born and raised in the same place as she. This prophecy foretold that Gabriel would first feel love for another. For he had two soulmates. She would have to end this other girl's life to be with him.

She thought, *though that girl has to die, so does Gabriel. He needs to die to become like me. And once he's like me, he'll take her life himself!*

In her mind, it was the perfect plan. The prophecy told that she would be waiting a long, long time to be with him.

*Three centuries must be enough time*, she thought.

She loved him deeply. She knew he was her future, and she was desperate to make him her's as quickly as she could.

Once the other girl left, the sky darkened, and she was able to leave her shroud.

"Gabriel," she said softly to draw his attention. She knew her beauty and their connection would draw him in. Her raven hair and dark purple eyes.

All he had to do was look.

He turned toward her, "Who are you?"

"Your soulmate. Your future. Your eternal love."

He didn't react to her words, entranced by her beauty, just as she expected.

"Come closer, Gabriel. So, we can see each other clearer within the darkness."

He walked toward her, each step sounded louder and louder to her. Soon, her three-century wait would be over.

She had no clue.

It was just beginning.

"I'm not ready to go," he said slowly. "Please, don't make me leave her."

"Hush. You enjoy it. Don't you?" She glided her fangs back to his pale neck.

He couldn't answer, instead, a gasp fell from his dry lips.

She was taking too much. He felt weak and oh so tired. He just wanted to sleep. But the thought of Ally's beautiful, burgundy hair had him holding onto his life.

He knew it was his own fault any of this was happening. He should never have followed that sweet voice into the dark of the tree canopy. She had his head spinning the moment they touched, and her first bite was the end for him.

Now, he would die, and the girl he loved would be alone. He, just as the woman stealing his life away, would never walk in the daylight again.

As he faded and his eyes struggled to stay open, he heard her voice. It was his mind playing tricks.

Ally couldn't be here.

She shouted out, "Gabe!"

She really was here. His eyes opened long enough to see her hair. She ran toward him. He could see her tears.

"Hold on! Please, don't go." Her sobs drowned him. It was the worst sound he'd ever heard.

He couldn't speak.

She held his hand.

Where had his killer gone?

His eyes closed. He was sure it would be for good.

There was silence, his senses must be shutting down. Then he heard a loud crack. Ally must've stopped crying.

"You can be mine now, Gabriel. She's gone and you'll be with me for eternity."

A tear left his eye as he felt the cold begin to set in around him. She was dead and he was about to be.

He took his last breath as he felt his life abandon him.

***

Her cold body was the first thing he felt. Then his own frozen skin.

There was a sorrow there he was sure would never leave, then a boiling rage filled him. He bolted up, landing on his feet, and ready to attack.

Except, the sun was setting, and it gleamed right where he stood. The shock of pain shot through him as the dwindling rays caressed his skin. He ran as far as he could from the light of day.

He never thought the sunlight could be so dangerous, but here he was, his skin on fire. He tripped into a lake, hitting rocks but putting out the fire.

He stood again; his skin healed. He walked back through the overcast of dusk, finding Ally on the ground where they'd died. His heart sunk as he saw no bite marks on her neck. What that wench had said was true. Ally was dead for good, and he'd have to live an eternity without her.

The woman with the silk black hair walked up behind him, "Come with me now, Gabriel."

He turned toward her, baring his fangs out in an endless rage. "You killed the love of my life."

"I killed her so we could be together."

"I don't even know your name, you evil-"

"My name's Sabrina and we are destined, Gabriel. You will be mine. I'll leave you time to grieve, but the day I return, you will love me."

Sabrina kissed him, grabbing his face so he couldn't pull away, and disappeared into the night.

All he could do was stare at the space she'd left.

He turned to Ally and walked to her side, feeling the dry evening air. He turned her onto her back and stroked her face.

"I'm sorry, my love. I'm so sorry I couldn't fight her. Now, I'll spend the rest of my life running from the daylight without you." He placed a gentle kiss on her forehead, a tear dripping onto her pale, frozen skin.

"Goodbye."

He moved her body out to the sidewalk, placing her carefully down.

He ran into the woods, tears glimmering behind in the moonlight. The only things on his mind were his lost love, and his hate for the evil vampire that stole her away.

If only he'd stayed through the night.

\*\*\*

She awoke with a gasp.

Her neck hurt. Her hair was a mess.

*Why was she on the sidewalk?*

She thought back, what happened?

Her memories returned like a fog lifting and tears fell from her eyes.

She ran back into the woods, following the trail he'd left. He wasn't there.

*Where is he? Where's his body? He was dying. Did I save him?*

She had come to save him. She knew something was wrong. She could sense it earlier that day by the look in his eyes. By how pale his skin had become.

She'd done a spell before leaving. An amulet that would bring life. It was usually used to ensure a safe birth, but her spell shifted the use to something more powerful.

She must've put it on him.

She reached in her pocket, but it was still there.

She must not have had time to place it then.

So what happened? How did he survive?

She understood now, why she'd survived.

Her amulet had protected her. Saved her life. Or it had restored it. Either way, she was alive.

And he was out there somewhere.

She felt it in her heart. She had to find him.

Her love.

Her light.

Her life.

She looked up at the sky and silently begged for the daylight to guide her to him. Guide her home.

# Just a Comment
By C.L. Galan

I know it wasn't his fault. Not directly. But he lined up the dominos and knocked the first one down. With a few throw-away words in a comment on the internet, he ruined my life.

I commented that if he had placed a block here rather than where he did, the design would look better. Just a comment. Some constructive criticism that wasn't even real criticism.

My phone started buzzing and it wouldn't stop. At first, people were liking my comment, bringing it up the comment wall. But, as it traveled up, more people saw it, and finally, he replied to me.

I was so excited to see that he'd replied to me, but I was also anxious about what he may have said. I hesitated to click for a moment before allowing my finger to hit the screen.

"I went back to look at the block placement you were talking about... I'll move it."

I didn't know what to think. Was he saying my suggestion was good or was he doing it because my comment was now on top? Being at the top meant most of his viewers agreed with what I said.

There'd been a lot of replies to my comments as well, to the point I had to turn off the notifications. Most of them agreed with me or suggested other places to put it. All in all, aside from the bots, my comment reply section was free of the toxic side of his fandom.

That was before he replied.

After he replied, people in the toxic part of his fandom started looking at it. And when they saw his reply, they must've thought similarly to how I did. But like I said, they were on the toxic side.

They started yelling at me in their replies, saying I was forcing him to do something he didn't have to. Saying I was being toxic. I understood they were toxic fans, so I ignored them. I still had my notifications turned off.

But then they started commenting under posts on my other socials. Calling me names, saying awful things, making accusations out of left field. I saw this was getting more serious. Especially when the death threat DMs started showing up. I started searching my social media accounts for anything that could lead them to me.

I sighed in relief when I found there was nothing leading to me directly. I'd been careful. I knew though, within the toxic fan groups are those that know how to hack. I refused to let my social media accounts be their opening, so I privated my socials and deleted the account that started it all. The account hadn't mattered all that much to me because I'd never posted anything on it, so deleting it didn't mean much. I started using it with a guest account instead.

I even started a VPN subscription to be safe. They were always advertising those things, so I hoped it would be enough. I should've just deleted all of those accounts.

It was only quiet for a day. Then, I started getting calls and texts from people I didn't know. My accounts were hacked. When I scrolled through my socials, I saw screenshots of my emails. Billing and shipping information. My credit card number was leaked, so I immediately froze all my accounts.

Soon, I saw pictures of my house. My address was being shared. The names of people in my family.

I was being doxed. I was being doxed for giving my favorite content creator a suggestion for his build.

What is wrong with this world? How can people be this cruel?

I didn't know how much worse it would get. I packed my valuables, whatever else I could grab, and quickly went to my friend's apartment for safety.

Those death threats would have become reality if I'd stayed home. I got a call later that day telling me my apartment had burned down. The entire building was set aflame and burnt to the ground. I was in shock. I didn't think they would go this far. That they could.

My friend kept a close eye on what they were doing on social media and was careful not to interact with any of it. The guy who set this all in motion hadn't addressed it at all. His latest post was about how adorable his dog was with a photo of it playing with a chew toy. As if none of this was happening.

It was late that night when an officer knocked on my door. My friend opened it and the officer declared I was under arrest for arson and murder. I didn't understand who they were saying I murdered, so I asked.

No one told me three people died in that fire.

I was horrified, as you could imagine. My situation was worse than I'd initially thought. I didn't have the money for a lawyer, so I was given a state-appointed lawyer. The stereotype, a state-appointed attorney who doesn't care and is hoping to make it quick.

He did.

I was given a temporary release, but there would be a hearing.

The days between my release and the start of the hearing were tense. I had two panic attacks, which my friend tried to help me through. I just couldn't process it all.

How did a comment lead to a hearing?

The hearing came and the judge decided my case wasn't worth pursuing. I wanted to bring up the doxing part, to see if I could get something for that situation. Some sort of protection maybe?

I'd need a proper lawyer for that, so I didn't try to do anything more about it.

Time went by and things quieted. Patrol cars made their rounds near my friend's apartment, probably trying to make sure I didn't burn down another one. I rolled my eyes at the thought. It had made the rounds online; I'd been arrested for murder. Finally, that guy addressed the issue.

Not the issue you'd hope for.

I guess all he saw was the headline. He posted that he was sorry a murderer had been allowed a part of his community and he didn't condone my actions.

I shouted, "What the hell!"

Because what the hell was wrong with this guy? It said nothing about a viewer getting doxed for saying something to him but talked about A HEADLINE without any sort of context.

I still couldn't understand, but moreover, I was pissed.

"I don't condone murder, my ass. He didn't do anything. And then he says this. Newsflash, I'm not the fucking murderer!"

My friend was close to very done watching all of this gets said on social media.

She replied to the guy's post when I wasn't looking. It was about a day later when she got her first death threat call.

Neither of us was safe.

We ran to the police station and told them what was going on. We even showed them screenshots of the posts about the fire. All they said was we could've edited the screenshots and we needed to get out so they could be ready for a real emergency.

I didn't know where to go or what to do. My friend decided we should just go back to her place and deal with whatever happened next.

What happened next broke my heart.

One of them broke in while we were asleep. I'm not a strong guy, so even though I woke in time to fight them off, I wasn't able to. I was knocked out. When I finally woke, I was in the hospital and my friend was dead.

After I failed at processing it, I tried using one of those adrenaline shots. I just couldn't take it anymore, and that should do it, shouldn't it? Well, my hand was pulled away before the needle went in

I spent the next week or so in the hospital's mental health ward. I was eventually told I'd been shipped off to a city nearby because I'd had severe brain bleeding from the attack.

I was also eventually told I couldn't stay there anymore. That was fine. I didn't want to. I wanted to find out who did this. Who killed all of these people? I wanted to make them pay.

And now? Well, now I just wonder what my life would've been like if I hadn't made that comment.

Maybe I wouldn't be holding a bloody knife over the corpses of those arsonist murderers. Maybe I wouldn't be laughing. Maybe I wouldn't be looking across the street hoping the neighbor's home and hoping they would let me in.

Who knows?

Now if you'll excuse me, my knife wants more blood. Maybe I should buy a sword?

# The Keeper of the Abyss
By James Hanna

Child molesters were rarely harassed at the Indiana Penal Farm, a medium-security prison where I once worked as a counselor. This revelation surprised me at first, but it now seems rather redundant. Molesters are masters of disguise, so their dark deeds are not on display, and many have the sort of job skills a prison is likely to value. Most of the inmate plumbers and carpenters were convicted child molesters as were a lot of the clerks in the prison law library. Passive and well-behaved, they blended seamlessly into the inmate population, respected for their abilities rather than damned for their crimes.

But abusing a child does not lend itself to internal solitude. For this reason, some of them spoke candidly to me in the privacy of my office. They would often admit their modus for courting and seducing minors, and they sometimes volunteered the fact that they were child-abuse victims themselves. I would listen to them politely, unwilling to pass any judgment. I felt as though I had fallen into the role of a confessional priest.

Accustomed to discretion on the part of molesters, I was not prepared for Dan Geegax—a serial pedophile from Muncie who ended up on my caseload. Shortly after he arrived at the penal farm, he sent me a request slip. His request was written in a childish script, so I was surprised by his artful language.

*To: Thomas Hemmings, Dorm 12 Counselor*
*Date: July 21, 1979*
*From: Daniel Geegax, DOC-982251*
*Location: Law Library*
*RE: Request to be transferred.*

*I look forward to meeting you, Mister Hemmings. Sadly, I need a friend. Excuse my penchant for puns, but I'm hoping you'll do me a solid. As an intellectual, I must admit that I am out of my element here. I'm not saying an honor camp would be much improvement, but in my current position, I am willing to settle for scraps. Please toss me a bone, Mister Hemmings, and I will forever be your amigo.*

I could have ignored his presumptuous request, but I decided to call him into my office instead. Since he had just been placed on my caseload, I needed to prepare his visiting list. Besides, as an aspiring wordsmith myself, I looked forward to having a chat with someone so able to turn a phrase. The penal farm was as bare as a moonscape where culture was concerned.

I sent a pass to the law library where he had been assigned to work as a clerk. Minutes later, he entered my office and sat down on the chair by my desk. He was a tall, boney man in his sixties with large uneven teeth, and his clear-blue eyes were enlarged several times by a pair of bottle-thick glasses.

He squinted as though he were looking at me from the bottom of a well, then he smiled solicitously and handed me a pamphlet from the American Man-Boy Society. "Son, don't look so shocked," he said in a cheerful, reedy voice. "When karma catches up with a fella, a mission will set him free."

I tossed the pamphlet into my wastebasket. "I wouldn't be circulating these," I warned. "Some of our inmates are touchy when it comes to sex with children. One of them might get pissed off and beat the shit out of you."

"Wouldn't be the first time," he laughed.

"Maybe not. But prison is not a good place to make enemies."

"Point taken," he said with a wink. "You seem a bit self-righteous, buddy, but I won't hold that against ya. I'm always happy to listen to what a young fella has to say."

"Then hear me out," I said. "I can't recommend you for honor camp."

"How come?"

"You don't qualify. They don't take pedophiles there."

He slapped his chest as though wounded. "Can'tcha pull some strings, Mister Hemmings?"

"No, I can't bend the rules quite that far."

He snorted. "You don't seem like the sort who gets off on enforcing rules."

As a child of the turbulent sixties, I had no fetish for rules. I had smoked my share of pot, I had protested the Vietnam War, I had even been arrested during the '68 Siege of Chicago. But rules were not unappealing to me when it came to Daniel Geegax.

"In your case, the rules have their place," I admitted.

He sat back in the chair and chuckled. "If you're supposed to be my guru, buddy, what can you do for me?"

I shrugged. "I can make out your visiting list."

"That ain't gonna cut it," he said. "Why would I want *anyone* to come see me in a place like this?"

"That's up to you."

He studied me as though he were taking notes. "Save yer paper, son," he laughed. "Go scribble a story on it."

"I've written a few short stories," I confessed since he seemed to know this already. I was not surprised by his astuteness—child molesters are excellent profilers. Still, it made me uncomfortable to make this admission to him.

"Short stories," he scoffed. "No money in them—they're like contemplating your navel. What are you, some kind of idealist?"

"I just like to write," I muttered.

"Well, write for money—that's what I do. Don't end up like Herman Melville. He hadda work in a custom house because no one bought his book about whales."

"So what do *you* write?"

"I write porn," he said proudly. "My pen name is Hardy Peters. You've probably read some of my books if you're into that sort of stuff."

"I hope you're not talking about kiddie porn."

He narrowed his eyes like a gunfighter and stared at me woodenly. Whatever his depth of depravity, he was not without limitations. "I would never write porn about children," he snapped. "Kids are sacred to me."

"What then?" I asked him, shaking my head.

"Just run-of-the-mill, standard-issue porn. I used to be a journalist, but smut pays a whole lot better. I make two thousand dollars a book, and I can write one in three or four weeks. Jesus, I've written dozens of 'em and my publisher keeps asking for more."

"You've written dozens of books?" I said. I could not help but be impressed.

"Naw," he said. "When it comes to porn, there's no room for variety. Basically, I wrote the same fucking book a coupla dozen times. Sometimes, I just changed the title and the book sold anyhow."

"Impressive," I said sarcastically.

He rolled his eyes and shrugged. "Those books are nothing to brag about. I've done better work writing screenplays. Didja ever see *Lesbian Lunch*? That won a Flint award."

That the movie was actually familiar to me made me blush to the roots of my hair. Sensing my embarrassment, he patted me on the wrist.

"It ain't as good as *Deep Throat*," he said, "but I'm proud of it anyhow. It was my first stab at a screenplay, and it won a Flint award."

"I haven't seen *Lesbian Lunch*," I lied.

"No, I'm sure you haven't," he laughed. "But I got hope for you, buddy. If you ever need an editor, I'll be happy to look at your stuff."

***

After Dan Geegax left my office, I felt a deep despair. Had I given up too much when I became a civil servant? A decade ago, I dropped out of college and spent seven years roaming Australia. I had herded cattle in the Northern Outback, I had traveled with a carnival, and I even worked on lobster boats off the rugged coast of Tasmania. Had these adventures so exhausted me that I now craved moderation? Was I content to sit in an office all day and make out visiting lists? It was clear that Daniel Geegax pitied me and that his pity had some foundation. My menial scribblings could hardly compete with his many publications, and my waning sense of adventure was dwarfed by his cavalier recklessness.

I was also perturbed that my warning had had no effect upon him. When I walked through the prison yard later that day, I spotted him handing out his pamphlets to inmates. *It won't be long*, I thought, *until someone beats the shit out of him*, and the anticipation of this gave me a hollow satisfaction.

But months went by and nobody held Daniel Geegax to account. This was probably due to the skill he displayed as a hearing advocate. I chaired a conduct adjustment board when I wasn't making out visiting lists, and most of the inmates facing disciplinary hearings asked that the law library assign them Dan Geegax to help them present their cases. He was remarkable at reviewing writeups and spotting the seams in them, and he was frequently successful in getting charges reduced or thrown out. "Yeah," he might argue, "Ol' Bubba here was caught jacking off in his bunk, but the officers who work the midnight shift let him get away with it all the time. If you're gonna run a prison, ya gotta have consistency."

Daniel also turned out to be a very reliable snitch—a role for which the prison recruited him after he had been there only a week. To avoid suspicion, he reported to me instead of the office of the investigation sergeant. After providing information about drug trafficking, which I relayed to the investigator, he would give me his car salesman grin and tell me about his day. Once, he said, "Ya know, Mister Hemmings, I think I've made a few converts."

"We have enough pedophiles here," I said, "without you recruiting more."

"I'm a man on a mission, son," he boasted. "Are you going to fault me for that?"

"Why do you need to have converts?" I said. "Can't you whitewash your crimes on your own?"

"Do you really think I believe that line about teaching boys how to make love?"

"Don't you?" I asked.

"Naw," he replied. "I'm just a fucking pervert, and I'm willing to live with that."

"So why do you pass out those pamphlets?"

"Ya ever read *The Scarlet Letter,* son—that eighteenth-century chestnut about an adulteress named Hester Prynne. You seem like a literary fella, so I shouldn't have to spell it out for you."

"What's Hester Prynne got to do with it?"

"Be true to yerself—that's the sage advice with which Hawthorne ends the book. If you wear your sins upon your chest, they're easier to bear."

"It seems you've thought this through," I said.

"Exactly," he replied. "Hester Prynne was a sinner—not that adultery is much of a sin—but she was also the type of person who helped out other people. Now the whole damn town poo-pooed on the bitch for stepping out on her husband, but even those Puritans loved the slut for all the good deeds she did. 'Be true, be true'—Hawthorne had it right. But be true to your total self. If you keep your sins secret, yer conscience will punish you a lot more than other people will."

"Incredible," I said. I was almost impressed. "You're a modern-day Hester Prynne."

"I wouldn't go quite that far," he laughed, "but I wanna be true to myself. If it's good enough for ol' Hester, it's good enough for me."

\*\*\*

As a prison informant, Daniel spent a great deal of time in my office. He was a constant source of knowledge regarding inmates smuggling in drugs, and, of course, he bartered this information for personal favors. I allowed him to use my office phone to call his publisher and his attorney, and soon he started to treat me as though I were at his beck and call. So great was his sense of entitlement that one day he asked me if I wouldn't mind storing his pamphlets inside my desk.

"Do me a solid and hide 'em," he said. "If a dorm officer shakes down my footlocker, he might think they're contraband."

I handed the pamphlets back to him. "No big loss," I

replied

"Like hell," he said with a chuckle. "I *need* my scarlet letter."

Having reread *The Scarlet Letter,* I decided to challenge him. "Your analogy is crap," I said.

"What are ya saying, buddy?"

"Hester Prynne was beautiful, but you're not much to look at. She also felt genuine guilt. I'm not so sure you do."

"That all you got?"

"There's more," I replied. "Hester Prynne wasn't a snitch. The Church wanted her to name her lover, but she protected him. She had too much integrity to throw anyone under the bus."

"Didja just read that book again, Hemmings? It sounds like she gave you a hard-on."

"They punished her way too much," I snapped. "That hardly applies to you."

Dan cracked his knuckles one by one. "*All* analogies are crap," he said. "How come you're picking on mine?"

"I'm your counselor," I said, "and it's obvious you don't know how to serve time."

He stuffed his pamphlets back into his shirt then looked at me curiously. "You're not much of a guru, Hemmings. Ya talk like you've lost your nerve."

"Maybe so, but don't look to Hawthorne to sanctify your hubris. After her bust, Hester lived out her life in a shack at the edge of town. She didn't run around preaching adultery and putting her life on the line."

"Are you suggesting I pick another book? Like maybe *Don Quixote.*"

"I'm suggesting you check into our segregation dorm before somebody bumps you off."

"Now who's exaggerating?" he laughed. "You're starting to sound like Tom Sawyer."

"You're serving four years," I reminded him, "and you're drawing the wrong kind of attention. If you keep living in a novel, you'll be deader than Mark Twain."

He looked at me as though I were a stranger then drew a labored breath. "Ya mean well, Hemmings," he said. "I'm grateful to you for that. But I ain't gonna take no advice from a fella who hides in his office all day."

\*\*\*

Almost a year went by, and Geegax kept serving his time recklessly. He cheerily dropped a dime on inmates possessing pot and cocaine—inmates he later defended in front of the conduct adjustment board. He argued that contraband found in footlockers was no evidence of possession—that the stuff could have easily been planted to set an inmate up. This argument was so persuasive that I threw out dozens of cases, which eventually earned me a letter of reprimand from the warden.

Geegax bragged to me that he charged his clients up to ten dollars a case. These fees were payable in cigarettes and homemade hooch, and he was not above accepting blowjobs from some of his younger clients. When I remarked that these sounded like petty returns for a man who made two grand a book, he laughed and said, "Hemmings, it's about the hustle. It ain't about the prize."

We were sitting in my office, having one of our chats, and our conversation once again drifted to the pitfalls of doing time. "If you want to serve easy time," I said, "why don't you just read Proust?"

He pinched his nose as though I had farted. "I'm sure you know all about easy time, Hemmings, but don't bother bending my ear. I don't believe in serving time. I think time oughta serve me."

"A great book will serve you as well as a hustle, and you won't have to watch your back."

"I've read all the great books, Hemmings," he said, "so don't bother suggesting one. Especially not Proust—that long-winded fag will put a fella to sleep."

"What about Hemingway?"

"Overrated. His writing's too damn thin."

"Steinbeck?"

"Too fucking preachy. He makes me feel like I'm in church."

"Have you read Nabokov?"

"I slogged through *Lolita*. I thought it had racy parts. But there wasn't a bit of sex in the book—it just dragged on and on about nothing."

I shrugged. I was out of suggestions.

He said, "Why don't we talk about you? Ya married, Hemmings?"

"No."

"Have ya ever been in a fight?"

"Not lately."

"Ya ever had a roll with a hooker or fucked yer neighbor's wife?"

When I told him I'd rather go fishing, he snorted then grinned like a ghoul. "So whaddya do when the fish ain't biting? Do ya sit in the boat reading Proust?"

He laughed when I didn't reply and said, "Ya don't gotta answer that question. Ya strike me as the sort of fella who's read a whole lot of Proust."

*** 

My next conversation with Geegax took place in the Special Housing Unit, a starfish-shaped building at the core of the prison where unruly inmates were kept. His dorm officers had shaken his bed area down and had found a shank under his mattress—a footlong piece of metal that had been ground to razor sharpness. I suspected one of the guards had been ordered to plant the shank, but there was nothing I could do about it. Geegax had appeared in front of the conduct adjustment board while I was attending a training session, and the board had found him guilty of possessing a deadly weapon. The board had recommended that he be confined to a cell pending a transfer to the Indiana State Prison. The hearing report described him as a dangerous predator.

After his hearing, Geegax had sent me a request slip asking me to pay him a visit. Although deemed a dangerous predator, his message was typically light.

*To: Thomas Hemmings, Counselor Dorm 12*
*Date: June 23, 1980*
*From: Daniel Geegax, DOC 982251*
*Location: SHU*
*RE: I told you so.*

> *Hemmings, I hope you're not the sort to say, "I told you so." Not when my saboteurs showed no originality at all. Why couldn't they have planted a penis stretcher instead of a fucking knife? I'm not well-hung for a predator and could use a couple more inches.*

> *Anyhow, I hope you drop by and see me. I'm in A Range, Cell 17. I'd like to summarize Proust with you before I head for the big house.*

As I waited for him in the conference room of the Special Housing Unit, I wished I had picked a better time to stop by for a visit. Some A-Range inmates had blocked up their toilets, which had flooded most of the range, so it was an hour before an officer fetched Geegax from his cell. His hands were linked to a waist chain, he was wearing ankle irons and he stumbled like a drunk as the officer herded him into the room.

He stood as still as a statue while the officer removed his restraints, then he sat on a chair by the conference table and sadly shook his head. "I guess my being a snitch ain't enough for this fucking place."

"Being a snitch may have bought you some time, but you were bound to get set up."

"Spare me the lecture, Hemmings," he said. "I knew it was gonna happen."

"If you saw it coming, why didn't you bail? Why did you keep winning cases?"

"Why did you let me keep winning them, Hemmings? If you had been a hardass conduct board chairman, I wouldn't have rocked the boat."

"I hope you appeal the decision."

He stretched like a feline and smiled. "Your guilt won't save ya, Hemmings, so let's just talk about books. I ain't gonna waste my time bucking a frame-up that the warden probably ordered."

"Shall I bring you something by Proust?" I joked.

"Naw, I'm rereading Ken Kesey's book. The chaplain slipped me a copy of *One Flew Over the Cuckoo's Nest.*"

"I'm sure it will keep your attention. It's got plenty of taboo sex."

"You're missing the point," he laughed. "The point is the hero had enough balls to shake up a looney bin. Get yer mind out of the gutter, Hemmings, if ya wanna discuss a great book."

"Listen," I said, "when you get to the State Prison, don't act like the guy in that book. They kill known child molesters there, so keep out of the main population."

"Why are you telling me this?" he said.

"You need some sage advice."

"Ya ain't acting like a counselor, ya know. You're acting like a pal. Just 'cause I have a good side don't mean I wantcha to be my pal."

"I'm just doing my job," I insisted. "There's something you may not know. Every week, we transfer troublemakers to the Indiana State Prison. Most of them know you're a pedophile and they're bound to spread the word. A reception will be awaiting you the moment you step into the yard."

"Hemmings, ya got noble intentions," he said, "but you're giving me pussy advice. If you wanna turn me into a wimp, I won't letcha be my pal."

"I'm trying to save your life," I said.

"By making my life not worth saving? What kind of friend are you?"

"You won't last a day if you don't check into segregation. There's going to be a bounty on you."

He arched his eyebrows in mock alarm then laughed as though watching a skit. "A bounty? My, my. That sounds so cloak-and-dagger, but don't let it getcha down. At least my life will have value if I end it in the yard."

\*\*\*

The following week, I stood by the watchtower inside the main sally port, and I watched Geegax trip toward a transport van bound for the Indiana State Prison. He was draped in so many chains that he looked like Marley's ghost, a compatible image since I had little doubt that he was a dead man walking.

He noticed me standing there and grinned. "Hemmings!" he called. "I'll write cha, and I'll come see ya after I get out!"

I nodded warily and watched him slip into the van. I wondered; *How will it happen if they don't get him in the yard? Will they corner him on a catwalk? Will they trap him in his cell? Will they gang-jump him in the showers after diverting the guards?* I only knew that the hit would be quick—he wouldn't see it coming—and the knife would be passed off several times before his heart stopped beating.

I relived our last conversation as I watched the van pull away. He had actually had the temerity to recite Nietzsche's most famous quote. "Hemmings," he'd said, wagging his head. "What am I gonna do with you? You know, if ya stare into the abyss, the abyss stares back at you."

How unsettling it felt to know that I had opened myself to the abyss and that, despite its villainry, the abyss was just toying with me. "So, what did you see?" I muttered.

His face was full of pity, and he dropped his probing gaze. "Son," he said, "don't take this wrong, but you're a hopeless case."

***

Three weeks later, my prison mail included a letter from Geegax. That he had lived long enough to write it suggested he might have listened to me. I did not particularly want to credit myself for salvaging his life, and when I read the letter, I was relieved to discover that this had not been the case.

*July 23, 1980,*
*Hemmings,*

*I have to say this about karma: it doesn't sting with precision. From everything you told me, I should be a specter by now. I don't want to upset your apple cart because I'll bet you're disappointed, so let's just say that the Birdman of Alcatraz hasn't got much on me. He was a pedophile too, you know, and he thrived like a fucking weed.*

*They've assigned me to the prison library, so I won't be arguing any more cases. But that's just as well because it gives me time to court my randy muse. Watch out D.H. Lawrence—that's all I've got to say. I know I can write much classier smut than* Lady Chatterley's Lover—*that book is so repetitious it almost put me to sleep.*

*Do you remember our talk about* The Brothers Karamazov? *I just read that monster again—the library here has a copy—and I've got to say that maybe you got it wrong again, bucko. You said those three brothers were existentially different, but my guess is they're all Dostoyevsky. Ivan he's Dostoyevsky's mind—his powerful, unflinching mind. Alyosha he's the D Man's heart because he keeps getting led astray. And Dimitri, that lecherous fucker, has got to be the loins. You're kind of like Alyosha, a well-meaning ideologue. Me, I'm more like Ivan, but I like Dimitri best.*

*Hemmings don't bother writing me back—I don't want the brass slapping your wrist. I'll drop you a line from time to time if my muse abandons me.*

Daniel

***

It was almost two months before he wrote me again, so his muse must not have strayed far. But how he had managed to stay alive remained a mystery to me. His letter did not show a hint of concern that someone might cut his throat. Like the canny protagonist in *The Shawshank Redemption*, he was making his time serve him.

*September 14, 1980,*
*Hemmings,*

*Today I'm down to ten months. If you factor in the good time I'm earning, that's all I've got left to serve. That means I'll disenthrall myself a whole lot sooner than you will—I'll bet you've got twenty years to go before you can fish all day.*

*I'm the head librarian now, so the guards don't watch me much. I wish they would because I'm buying and smoking too much goddamn weed. Pot blunts my creativity, you know, and my muse is getting lonely.*

*Yesterday, I took a break and reread* The Old Man and the Sea. *The book is way too sentimental, but I'll give ol' Papa a pass. With all the brain cells he zapped with his boozing, I'm surprised he could write it at all. The book's supposed to be a tragedy, but I say the old man was blessed. Hell, the marlin was way too big to be lashed to the side of a skiff, and that graybeard was too damned stubborn to cut that fucker loose. If the sharks hadn't been peckish that day, the skiff would have probably sunk, and the dumb piscator would have ended up in Davey Jones' chest.*

*I ain't quite sure what I'm saying, bucko, but I think there's a deep message here. And since you're so fond of fishing, I'm hoping you'll figure it out.*

Daniel

Although it had deemed me a charity case, the abyss was baiting me still, but I saw no enduring reason to keep on playing the game. Having never fished for anything bigger than crappies and bass, who was I to speculate on the agenda of the abyss?

Five weeks passed before I received another letter from Gee-gax. He keeps popping up like a jig bait, I thought as I tore open the envelope.

*October 20, 1980,*

*Hemmings,*

*On a pedestrian note, I'm going to clue you as to what's been happening here. Some con shanked a guard and the prison is on lockdown, so I've been stuck all week in my cell. The guard was a newbie who was stupid enough to try to be friends with the inmates, and a gang leader must have ordered one of his soldiers to take the asshole out. Most inmates don't want a guard for a pal—it makes them look like snitches—so take heed, bucko. Don't make a habit of overstepping your bounds. Still, I wish the gang had just warned the guard instead of knocking him off. Having to sit in my cell all day long is giving me cabin fever.*

*I'm still the head librarian here, and I've managed to hang onto my good time. I've even adopted a cat—can you believe that Hemmings? The cellblocks here are crawling with cats, so it's not too hard to adopt one. She's a marmalade-colored tabby and I call her Molly Bloom. I won her over by feeding her guppies from my aquarium. Most cells here have aquar-*

*iums, but the brass is now hauling them off. It's too easy to hide a shank in one—you just stick it under the sand. We get to keep our televisions though, and the World Series starts today. I've bet an ounce of weed on the Phillies—they oughta win it in six games.*

*Hemmings, I wish you hadn't told me your favorite book is* Paradise Lost. *I dug a copy out of the library just to see what the fuss was about, and I had to blow off three layers of dust before I could open it up. Be honest, is this really your favorite book, or are you just trying to show off? My god, the dead language and Hebraism could drive a reader nuts. I will say this about Milton, though: He knew the Church was corrupt, and that it's better to be a law unto yourself than to let some priest fuck you up. I just don't see how that pertains to you—it's not like you're bucking the system. If you want to have a favorite book, Hemmings, stick to* The Scarlet Letter. *Don't start quoting from* Paradise Lost *because I think you'll be out of your depth.*

*I've got to go, for now, Hemmings. My fish-watching days are up. Some guards have stormed the catwalk, and they're taking the aquariums out. All the damn racket they're making has upset Molly Bloom, so I'm going to feed her the rest of the guppies and hope that improves her mood.*

Daniel

\*\*\*

Three months later, I received yet another letter from Daniel. He had sketched a harpooned marlin on the back of the envelope, and underneath the marlin, he had written, "The jig is up." The letter was short, the writing looked hurried, and his nonchalance seemed forced.

*January 20, 1981,*
*Hemmings,*

"*Ask for me tomorrow, and you shall find me a grave man.*"

*Mercutio couldn't have said it better after Tybalt ran him through. But don't bother asking for me, Hemmings—I have no more tomorrows. By the time this letter reaches you, I'll be pushing up daisies too.*

*I'm not going to tell you the details—that's something you don't need to know. Let's just say that the interest is due on all my borrowed time. Now I ain't a fellow to dodge his debts, so I'm not going to check into seg. Hell, what would old Milton think of me if I took the coward's way out?*

*Once the piper is paid, and I've been planted in the ground, I'm hoping a flock of fallen angels will give me a livelier home. I'm not saying a lake of eternal flame is a perfect place to dwell, but given how fucked-up heaven must be, I'll be happier in hell.*

Daniel

\*\*\*

Six months passed, and I did not receive another letter from Daniel. Given his compulsion to taunt me, I could only conclude he was dead. I did not have enough of Alyosha in me to regret his leaving this world, but I did hope the hit had come quickly and he had not lingered in death.

I found myself watching for Daniel's ghost when I fished the pond at the prison's north quarter, a forested preserve where prison staff was allowed to picnic and fish. I compulsively looked for ghosts when I fished there, having recently seen a couple. Staff suicides were not uncommon at the Indiana Penal Farm, and over the years, two guards drowned themselves in the pond. Their ghosts had approached me a month ago while I was casting from the shore and had gazed at me like gophers before wandering away. Since these shades were without an agenda, I chose to contain my fear. Although chilled by this glimpse of the netherworld, I went on with my fishing.

On a hazy afternoon, six months after Geegax had written me last, I was casting a jig from a dinghy, which I had rowed to the middle of the pond. Since the fish were not biting that afternoon, my eyes drifted toward the shore, and that's when I spotted a misty figure standing on the dock. The form was as stiff as a sentry and was watching me like a voyeur, so I dipped the blades into the water and pulled toward the dock. It unnerved me to think that this presence had unfinished business with me, but the fog was so thick and cottony that I rowed as though I were drugged.

"Hemmings," a reedy voice shouted as the prow of the boat touched the dock, "if you're catching lotsa fish, I hope you're tossin' the little ones back."

"For a spook, you sound rather cheery," I quipped. I chastised myself as I spoke, hoping the Great Beyond would not fault me for feigning a lack of respect.

The dinghy swayed like a pendulum as Geegax eased himself into it. "Hemmings don't be so smug," he said as he seated himself at the prow. "If I'd had the option to haunt you, I'd have done it before now."

His face lacked the insularity I associated with ghosts, and the potbelly he had developed suggested he still had a grip on this world. When I realized he was still alive, my pulse began to race. I would have been far less startled if he had come to me as a spook.

"You're real!" I exclaimed. I started to sweat.

He saluted me and laughed. "Didja have me dead and buried, Hemmings? Yeah, I'll bet ya did."

"You told me your time had run out. You put that in your last letter."

"A moment of weakness," he shrugged. "We all have 'em now and then. I finished serving my bit last month, and now I'm out on parole."

"When your letters stopped, I thought your time had run out long ago."

"Naw, I just got tired of writing you, bucko. You kind of

bore me, ya know?"

"So, what are you doing here? This is private property."

"I see ya still have a hard-on for boundaries," he laughed. "Well, I did drive up to the prison to see you, but the shift captain said you'd gone fishing. He said it was okay with him if I came to see you here."

"How?" I said.

"How do you think? I took the service road."

"I mean how did you last a whole year in state prison? There had to be a bounty on you?"

He shook his head and snorted. "There was one for a while. When I wrote ya last, it was after some dickhead lunged at me with a shank. But a coupla shot callers grabbed the fucker and pulled him away from me. They said the gangs would protect me as long as I shared my lewd writing with them."

"Did you share it?" I said.

"Of course, I did, and I wrote 'em a whole bunch more. Since ya can't buy cock books in prison, my work was in high demand."

"So, you gave them smut and they gave you your life."

"Hemmings, they gave me more than that. Pot, blow-jobs, commissary snacks—whatever I wanted was mine. Just as long as I used the library printer to launch a new book every month."

"It sounds as though you were inspired."

"How could I not be, Hemmings? I was writing for my life. Watch for new titles by Hardy Peters because I snuck those books out on disks."

"Amazing," I said.

He grinned like a jackal. "I guess you could call it that. Those books are the best damn writing that I have ever done. Fully-fleshed characters, powerful imagery, stunning metaphors. DH Lawrence and Nabokov are gonna be turning in their graves."

Given my weakness for boundaries, I struggled to catch my breath. It felt as though a steel cable had tightened around my chest. "It's amazing you're still alive," I muttered. "That's what I meant to say."

"Don't ever go into politics, son, if you think criminals can't be bought."

"But you bought them with books you call literature?"

"Well, the subtext went over their heads. But as long as I put lots of smut in those books, the dipshits ate 'em up."

"So why are you here?"

He looked at me sternly—as though I had stood him up. It was then I remembered his pledge to come see me after he got out.

We sat for a minute in silence then he climbed back onto the dock. Standing above me, he arched his eyebrows then chuckled like a clown. "Go back to yer fishing," he teased. "It seems I'm rocking yer boat. Anyhow, I won't get my books on the market if I stay here gabbing with you."

He pushed the boat away from the dock as though ridding himself of a load. I watched as the fog reclaimed him, and then I started to row.

# Room # 23
By Alice de Crowley

Interrogation room #23. Fluorescent lights cast hollow reflections against the linoleum floor and cheap metal table. The stale scent of spent cigarettes oozes from every surface. No cameras.

Not the sort of environment Dick Rawls was expecting. He despised every inch of it. The District Attorney called him personally to secure an interview with the subject. A rare moment, but not without precedent. On previous occasions, he was watched intently. This time, he was without any surveillance at all.

This was foremost on his mind as he sat at the table and began to arrange his files.

Across the table from him was the most beautiful woman he had ever seen. Her eyes followed his hands, watching closely as he shuffled the files, finally bringing her own to the top. He took a sharp inhale of breath and opened the file.

"What's your name, Detective?" She asked.

Her mellifluous voice took him by surprise.

"Richard Rawls."

"Nice to meet you." He noted her playful, flirtatious tone and thought he saw her bright blue eyes twinkle. "Are you here to break the case wide open and bring the black widow to justice?"

"Just the opposite." Dick tilted his head slightly to the side, arching his right brow and awaiting her response. She was completely placid, except for a slight expansion of her pupils that indicated, in this particular context, relief. At any rate, it was the hypothesis he was going with for the duration. "I'm here to make sure there are absolutely no discrepancies or irregularities in your version of events."

"Why?"

"Because the DA wants to be absolutely certain that dropping the charges against you won't result in political problems for him later on. At least, that's how he pitched it to me."

Now, it was she who tilted her head slightly to the side. Her brow furrowed. "Can I smoke in here?"

Dick motioned with his head around the room, running his gaze along the edge of the ceiling. She did the same. "No cameras in here. No problem. Wait a second."

With that, he stood, leaving the files on the table, and turned toward the door. He rapped his knuckles gently against the small glass window above the handle. Outside, a uniformed officer fumbled with his keys before opening the door wide enough to peer inside.

"We need a cup of water, no ice. And— two coffees. Black."

"Yes, sir. Right away." The officer closed the door and locked it behind him. Dick could hear his steps recede down the hallway.

Turning, he looked her in the eyes, letting a couple of seconds pass before speaking.

"So, you're the infamous Melody Montblanc."

"I am she, yes. Infamous? I like that. I'm certainly not going to escape the public eye now, am I?"

"You never were out of the public eye. People have been fascinated by you ever since the first murder."

"It was NOT a murder," Melody sighed. She broke eye contact with Dick to stare at the stack of files on the table. "The jury found me innocent."

"The jury acquitted you. It's not the same thing. You were hardly innocent then, and you're no more innocent now. I mean that in the general sense. I would have voted to acquit you. I was there the last day of the trial. I saw you testify."

"Oh? What did you think of my testimony?" Her eyes met his again and she smiled faintly.

Dick shifted on his heels to fully face her and nodded his head in a gesture of respect. "It was the most compelling testimony I've ever heard. I'll never forget the sounds coming from the jury box. Wasn't one of the jurors crying at one point?"

"I don't remember that. I do remember a couple of times, some of the jurors gasped while I detailed some of the things my father did to me. I was just focused on maintaining my composure, which… as you saw for yourself, I failed to do at the end."

"It was pitch perfect. Something I would expect to see in a movie. If I weren't convinced you were telling the truth, I'd have lobbied for you to get an Oscar for that performance."

Melody's face betrayed the sadness that overcame her. "I might have won an Oscar someday, if not for all of that. I used to love dancing and singing so much. That was my dream, you know, to become a famous actress. My friends were mostly obsessed with their wedding trousseaus. I was obsessed with the theater." She sighed. "It was not meant to be."

"You did alright for yourself. At least for a while. I remember reading in the papers you ended up with your father's fortune after all was said and done."

"That's right. After the acquittal, all the money was legally mine. I went from being a stupid teenage girl, desperately in love with her own father, to a notorious murderess, to a fantastically wealthy heiress. All in the space of a year. I saw him die, you remember?"

"Yes, that was the hinge that turned the trial around. I can almost see it myself, the way you described it. I guess that's my first question…"

It was then he heard the officer's footfall, turning back toward the door. The lock clicked as the officer proffered a small tray with three Styrofoam cups on it, some packs of sugar, and a small metal decanter of cream.

"Black was fine, but thanks all the same," Dick said. The officer didn't respond as he closed the door and locked it.

"You said you were going to let me go, right? Why do you keep locking the door?" Melody looked genuinely puzzled, and a bit nervous.

"First of all, I'm not responsible for any of this. I'm not a cop. I'm a private detective. The DA is currently planning to let you go unless I find something problematic in your version of events. Something problematic beyond the fact that two fully grown men have met their ends at the bottom of the same staircase. Your staircase. That's clearly problematic in and of itself. They lock the door as a matter of routine. We're in this room for a reason. No cameras. Which is weird, but there could be a number of reasons for that."

Dick placed the tray on the table, took a swig of the water, and placed the cup on the table. Reaching into his inner breast pocket, he removed a pack of Lucky Strikes and placed them on the table. From his pants pocket, he pulled a worn Zippo lighter and lay it next to the cigarettes. Finally, he sat and pulled his chair up to the table.

Melody reached for the cigarettes Turning the pack upside down, she gently tapped on the bottom before pulling out two. She placed one the table, the other between her lips. Dick found everything about her to be maddeningly distracting. At this moment, it was her perfect set of full, red lips. He noted that she wasn't wearing any makeup. The thought was enough to bring his mind back into focus, if for no other reason than to resist the incredible magnetism surrounding Melody, inexorably rousing his senses.

In one smooth motion, he took the lighter in his left hand and deftly flicked the lid out of the way while running his thumb across the flint, sparking a flame that he slowly brought forward for her. In turn, she leaned forward, eyes locking on his, and drew deeply on her cigarette. She let a small wisp of smoke escape her mouth before drawing it into her nostrils. A moment passed before she leaned her head back and exhaled a long column of smoke.

Dick took the other cigarette, placed it in his lips, and pulled on the flame of the lighter brusquely before snapping it shut. He placed it back on the table, next to the cup of water and the cigarette pack. He waited, watching her savor the smoke until enough ash accumulated at the tip for her to tap it on the rim of the cup. The motion produced a very quiet sound as the ash cooled in the water.

"Okay, so. I've got your file here. My first question is about your father's death. Your testimony at the trial. It's been five years since then. Have any of your memories changed?"

"No. I still wake up in the middle of the night, sometimes, remembering him tumble down the stairs."

"So, every detail…I want to be perfectly clear. You are 100% immune from any sort of legal liability if anything has changed. No  court can touch you. Double jeopardy. You get that, right?"

"Yes, I get that. I was absolutely honest to the best of my ability back then, and nothing has changed."

"Okay. Wait, what do you mean by 'the best of my ability', is that a dodge?"

"No, no. I made a couple of remarks during my testimony that weren't...we rehearsed that; you know? They said it was normal to do that before trial. I said a couple of things in rehearsal that my attorney told me not to say, because the prosecutor would object to them. I screwed up and said something I know I wasn't supposed to say. It was, ah, hearsay? Anyways, when I said it on the stand, there was no objection. That's all I meant."

Dick chuckled softly. "It was the bit about your father losing interest in you, wasn't it?"

She looked a bit surprised. "Yeah, that was the bit I was talking about."

"That surprised me. It's why I remember it so clearly. I think the prosecutor was completely stunned at that point. Probably overwhelmed by your testimony as everyone else was. Okay, so...moving forward to the husband. I know you've told this story over and over again already, but I'm going to need you to tell it one more time. I want you to go in the order of events as they happened, and I'm going to interrupt you from time to time with questions. Okay?"

"I'm ready, Dick." Melody's eyes twinkled again. Dick raised his brow to quietly acknowledge her flirtation without responding verbally. He opened the file and flipped through the first few pages which included Melody's arrest report, mug shots, and biographical details. He scanned the next tranche of pages, the transcript of her testimony during her murder trial. His curiosity aroused by a memory of the first trial, he raised his eyes to meet hers again.

"Oh, wait. I do have one more question about the first

trial. It was a brilliant move, but did your attorney ever explain to you why he moved for you to be tried as an adult? That took guts."

"He tried to explain it to me, but I still don't really understand why. Something about 'disparity and contrast' and…I think he wanted the prosecution to be rough on me, and then show the jury who I really was, a very sad teenage girl who had been to Hell and back. At least, that's what I think he was going for. It certainly did the trick, as far as winning the case. Right?"

"I was always a bit curious about that, and the question came back to me just now. On to your husband's death."

"Well, we were in the bedroom, and…"

"No, let's go back further. Tell me about your relationship with him. When did it begin?"

"Oh, I'd known him for years. He was a friend of my father, came by the house all the time for dinner and drinks and such."

"Was he involved in the sexual abuse at all?"

"God, no. He once told me he would have killed my father himself if he had known, and I believed him. He was certainly no angel, my Jack. Neither was my father. I didn't know until after we were married that he was more than just a friend to my father, but they were friends first and foremost, I think."

"That was three years ago, the wedding, is that right?"

"Almost three years. Our anniversary is…was…coming up in a few weeks. September 21st."

"Okay, tell me about your marriage. Was it happy? How deeply were you involved in his business interests, if at all? Tell me something you haven't told the police that will give me a better sense of how things were between the two of you."

"I wasn't involved in his business at all. We kept separate portfolios, at his insistence. I gave him half of my inheritance, that was my insistence. It wasn't until after the IRS I even knew anything about what my father was up to, and I'm still not 100% sure Jack was the gangster they're saying he was. I suppose the accountants will figure it all out…"

The silence between them became pregnant. It was a common device he used to get his subjects talking at length. He wanted them to feel slightly uncomfortable, to fill the empty air with the sound of their own voices.

"Were we happy? Oh, yes. I love my Jack." She cast her gaze at the table for a moment. "I loved my Jack. No. I love my Jack. I can't believe he's dead. I think it started for me when I was in jail waiting for the first trial. No bail for me, I was a flight risk. He was so gentle, and so kind, even more than he was when my father was alive. He came to see me every day, just to visit. He was taking care of the house at that point, looking after the horses. I felt safe when he visited, even though I was locked in a cage.

He was there for me every day during the trial, too. That's how I was able to keep my composure for so long, just looking him in the eyes as I regaled everyone on planet Earth with my sordid tale of incestual woe. I only started crying when I saw tears gathering in his eyes. That's when I lost it, right at the end. He didn't lose it, though. He pulled himself together. I could feel his strength surrounding me, and it somehow felt like we were the only people in the room in that moment. Everyone else just disappeared, and I cried. I cried for myself, but I also cried for him. I think I was already in love with him by then, and I was starting to really feel it when I was on the stand, after I had borne my soul before so many strangers. Does that answer all of your questions?"

"You're doing great. Tell me about a typical day in the life of Mr. and Mrs. Montblanc."

"It was a life of leisure for me. My father's money made me fantastically wealthy. Have you ever seen our house?"

"I wouldn't describe it as a house, but yes. It's one of the biggest estates in Beverly Hills. Nice stables, pretty horses. The informal gardens are a very nice touch."

"That was Jack's idea. I love to spend my mornings taking tea under the arcade at the back of the house. It's only been three days, right? I hope nobody's left. We...I...have a very fine team of people who work very hard to make my life pleasant and comfortable.

So, a typical day, right? Tea in the morning for me. Jack's at work in the office, making calls, and taking meetings. That goes on throughout the day. I'm usually at the stables, working the horses, or if the weather is nice, out on the trail. Then, lunch. I don't usually eat breakfast. Jack and I almost always eat together. After, we plan the evening, then he goes back to work. I might go shopping for clothes, or take a nap, or read a book. In the evening, dinner, sometimes with guests. Then, drinks and cigars for the men. I'm usually upstairs, tending to myself before bed. That's more or less a typical day."

"Sounds nice."

"It IS nice. Well, it WAS nice." A flash of anguish passed over Melody's beautiful face, and Dick felt a lump in his throat. He was beginning to understand, to feel, the power of her story. Damn, it's no wonder DA Roberts doesn't want to touch this case with a ten-foot pole. Pulling himself together, he went on with the interview.

"Okay. Tell me about the day your husband died. Was it a typical day?"

"It was pretty typical at first, yes. He seemed a bit distracted during lunch, but I didn't think anything of it at the time. Men and their business, as they say. I think they say that? Whatever, it's been said. I went riding that afternoon. My favorite gelding, Rooster. He's an Arab, and a very fine ride. Chocolate brown. Do you ride?"

"I do, yes. Been riding since I was a kid. Never could afford a pony of my own, so I traded work at Bar S for the chance to ride the horses, and a bit of spare change."

"Oh, I know Bar S, that's in Glendale, by the equestrian center. I sometimes go there to watch the dressage ponies go through their paces. I don't suppose you ride English?"

"I like the saddles, but I prefer cowboy boots. I'm told it's a funny sight, but it works for me." Dick gently tapped his boot on the linoleum floor and watched Melody's face light up with a broad smile.

"I have a lovely Crosby close-contact saddle you might like."

"Certainly, that's something I'd like to see. So, Jack seemed a bit distracted at lunch, and later, you went for a ride. This was up in the hills, I presume. Then, what?"

"Yes, the house…the estate if you must…borders the scrub at the back edge of the property. There's a trail head there that leads up and around the hills. After my ride, I must've spent some time with Rooster in the stable, cooling him down, and grooming him. I let the hands muck the stalls and that sort of thing, but I do enjoy spending time with my horses after a good ride. Let's see…

I don't remember much else before dinner. We had guests that night…"

"Oh, who was present for dinner? I don't see any mention of that."

"No one asked before you, just now. I didn't know any of them actually. There were three men. Mr. Vuille, his first name was Jacque, which is easy to remember. Mr. Gutierrez. I'm not sure if his first name was Don, or if that was a title. He was very well-dressed, in a double-breasted suit. And…There was another man, but I don't remember his name. He seemed a bit out of place."

"Why out of place?"

"His suit wasn't the sort of bespoke, tailored array that Jack's business partners usually wore to dinner. I think maybe he worked for Mr. Vuille or Mr. Gutierrez, or maybe both. He didn't say much, and always nodded his head in agreement when any one of the other men spoke."

"Okay. Do you remember what you ate?"

"I do. The main course was filet mignon. We had roasted asparagus and rice, as well. Hmmm. Oh. The hors d'oeuvre, was escargot, which was a bit unusual, but it paired perfectly with steak as the main course. Red wine, I don't remember the vintage. No soup, but we had a second appetizer of avocado bruschetta. Dessert was ice cream. French vanilla with cinnamon flakes, one of my favorites. Then, a plate of cheeses."

"That sounds…delightful. How was Jack during the meal?"

"He was drinking a bit much. There were five of us, and I think we went through three bottles of wine. I always try to match him when we drink around other people."

"Don't take this wrong way, but you're…well, you're very voluptuous, but also pretty short. I have a picture of you and Jack together and he must have been twice your size."

"Well, it was my father who taught me how to drink, and I'd like to think I can hold my liquor pretty well. But you're right. It's always a ready excuse for Jack to relieve our guests when he's done for the evening. That wasn't the end of the night's drinking, though. After our guests left, Jack's demeanor changed. Something was clearly bothering him, but I know better than to ask about such things."

"Why, does he become hostile when you do that?"

"No, no. He starts cooing and reassuring me like a little girl asking questions that she wouldn't understand the answers to. It was actually quite adorable the first year, but I eventually gave up the exercise, a pointless adventure.

No, he seemed bothered, and I think he was drinking to shake off whatever he was feeling. We went upstairs and made love. That was the last time…" Melody's voice lost its music as it trailed off, Dick caught the moisture in her eyes.

"Melody. Look at me." Melody did as she was told. The two of them looked into each other's eyes for a few moments as she pulled herself together. Dick was in trouble, and he knew it. Dick's voice broke their reverie. "What happened next?"

"More drinks. He was drinking gin and tonics. I was drinking club soda at that point, as I was pretty hammered already. The wine. His mood was lighter after, and he began to smile and laugh. He pulled me off the bed and lead me through a waltz that he was humming. One of Strauss's, I think. We were both stark naked.

I don't know what got into him. I remember he said something along the lines of 'your father was a complete bastard and deserved everything he got'. He opened the bedroom door. Have you seen it, the double door that leads to the balcony above…the stairs?"

"I've seen pictures of it from time to time. Usually in one of the gossip magazines that seem to survive by retelling the story of the first trial."

"First trial? Aren't you…isn't the DA going to release me?" Again, puzzle, and concern flashed briefly across her face.

"No, I didn't mean it like that. Besides, there's still plenty of time for you to commit nefarious crimes. You're young, after all."

"Not too young, I hope." This time, it was Melody who tilted her head slightly to the side and gently arched her brow. Dick chuckled again softly and didn't bother to resist the sly smile on his face.

"Touché. I think part of the reason Roberts wanted me

to talk to you is because he thinks I have the self-control to resist your feminine wiles."

"Roberts? That's the DA's name, right?"

"Yes, we've been friends since high school. Went to the police academy together."

"So, you ARE a cop!"

"No, I was a beat cop for a couple of years before getting my gold badge. Lasted about a year after that, then jumped ship."

"Do you like what you do?"

"Mostly. I'm good at interviewing people. I notice details that others miss. I like the money."

"The pay is good?"

"It's a helluva lot better than a police detective's salary, but nothing compared to your kind of money."

"You know, I don't think Jack had much money when I married him. I don't think like that. I don't think he did, either."

"I suspect you're right about him, if that's worth anything. So, what happened next?"

Melody's expression became somber. "He threw open the doors and spun around on the balcony. I was a bit worried. He was pretty drunk. I went to the door and scolded him. He laughed, and blurted out, "Look, I'm your stupid father. Come push me down the stairs, my love!" Those words are burned into my memory forever.

When I ran to him, yelling "No, no, no!", he went to the edge of the top stair, dancing drunkenly and spun around again. That's when he lost his footing. I was only a couple of feet away. Almost in time. I suppose I would have ended up going down with him, I don't know. I wish I had.

He tumbled head over heels down the entire staircase. I heard a sickening thud as his head hit the marble floor at the foot of the stairs. I watched in horror as a thick pool of bright red blood grew around his motionless body. I screamed. No, I howled, like a wild animal. I remember the maid coming in from the dining room. She screamed. That's the last thing I remember. When I came to, I was in the ambulance, cuffed to the gurney."

"Okay. Here, have a bit of coffee and just give yourself a minute."

Dick took a cup for himself. It was still warm, but only just so. He continued to observe Melody, but her eyes closed as she drained her cup. He could feel her trauma in his core. This was a credible witness with a credible story. A powerful story made even more powerful by her testimony on the witness stand during the trial following her father's death.

They sat in silence for several minutes. Finally, Melody looked up and locked eyes with Dick. She took a deep, halting breath before motioning towards the cigarettes. Dick pulled two from the pack, placed them on his lips, and lit them both before offering one to her. Melody looked genuinely grateful for that small kindness, and for his gentle, reassuring smile. They sat and smoked. Dick waited patiently for her to continue.

Taking another deep breath, she asked, "What happens next, detective?"

"I'm going to confer with the DA and make a couple of recommendations regarding this case."

"What recommendations, if I may ask?"

"You may, of course. First, I'm going to recommend you be released immediately. Second, I'm going to recommend I be retained for a follow-up investigation."

"A follow-up investigation? Investigation into what?"

"Not what, whom. Jack."

"Why?"

"It'll be a few hours before your paperwork gets processed, but that will start as soon as I'm done talking with the DA. I'll be seeing you, Melody."

"Do you have a card? Two cards. You are a private detective for hire, yes?" Her eyes took on a mischievous glint. Dick reached into his outer breast pocket and carefully peeled off two of his business cards. Flipping them like a set of playing cards, he presented them to her, and she quickly snatched them from his hand.

"How about a pen?" She moved her eyes from his, to the pen he held in his hand to make notes in her file. Dick tilted his head again. He held the pen out to her, and she scribbled something on the back of a card before handing the card and pen back to him. She smiled sweetly. Dick looked at the card. It read: "See You Soon."

See you soon, he thought to himself as he stood up, walked to the door, and gently rapped his knuckles on the small window above the knob. As the officer opened the door wide for him to step through, he glanced back at Melody. She was looking at him with an intense and earnest expression on her face that could only mean one thing.

"See you soon, Melody Montblanc." With that, Dick stepped out of room #23 into the cool hallway beyond. He imagined that she was listening carefully to his footsteps as he walked slowly and deliberately away. See you soon, he said again to himself.

## Sage-Green Eyes
By Victoria Holland

On December 21, 2035, there was a pulse of silver energy released from the center of the country of Haiti. A pillar of light rose into the sky. The northern phenomenon, known as the Aurora Borealis, stretched across the entire world. These lights could be seen in every night sky, on every continent, from every mountain, desert, ocean, and field. Governments from all over worked day and night to understand why this happened, to track the source of the event, and ultimately get the lights to recede back to the arctic circle.

The first two objectives were accomplished.

They were never able to get the lights to recede.

Over the next two years, several representatives from around the world started to stand and speak for the lights. However, their explanation for such a huge change was met with skepticism, shock, derision, and mocking.

You see, these representatives—*several million of them*—were throwing around words like "magic." Words like "voodoo." Words like *spirits, gods, alchemy,* and *astrology*. These people read cards, threw runes, worked herbalism, and worked with gods and spirits that hadn't been publicly acknowledged as legitimate for thousands of years. What shocked people was that most of them were not living in swamps or doing ritual sacrifices, though some certainly did.

No, these people lived in shitty apartments in New England, worked at the Pentagon, had children, and fought in the military. These people were nurses, lawyers, shopworkers, and taxi drivers. One was even in the cabinet for the Prime Minister of England.

First, it was the priests and priestesses in Haiti where the pulse initially came from.

Then it was several citizens of Greece who still privately worshiped the old pantheon.

Then it was neo-druids from England, swamp witches from Louisiana, diviners from France, medicine women in both rural and urban China.

Then it was neo-pagans and witches scattered around America, quickly followed by the complex network of psychics, mediums, and intuitive spanning across the entire world. It was mainstream representatives at first but then it was more modest practitioners, then it was private practitioners, then it was closeted practitioners. And then soon it was people who had magical potential but never talked about it.

That last category was the biggest demographic of all.

Within the next three years, three big events happened.

First, the governments of the world scrambled to handle the situation, silence it, and bring things back to normal, but they couldn't complete their mission with the growing population of voices. Many representatives tried to work with the governments to bring order, but it became quite clear that their goals severely diverged.

Second, as a direct result of the deception from the governments, an organization was started by a Haitian Voodoo High Priestess and a Magician trained in the Way of the Tree. The intention of this organization was "to bring people together, to unite the heavens with the earth, old traditions with new, and to help people remember their innate magic."

The third event was the biggest one of all because of the hurt, fear, and anger it caused. The UN did an extensive investigation of the pulse in Haiti, only to come to "inconclusive results" —which was immediately known as bullshit by the global magical community.

Soon after, the newly developed organization took root and grew rapidly. It was less of an institution and more of an energetic network, comprised of several million practitioners. It allowed for the exchange of information, provided services for those in need, and was completely undetectable. The governments knew something was going on, but they had no real proof.

The only "proof" they had was a convention held once a year at a castle in Scotland. One spy for the Russian military described it as "a cross between a Renaissance fair and a sci-fi convention."

Little did they know, this network worked day and night to maintain pulses of magic that appeared around the globe. They utilized cloaking techniques from the Veil, an energetic barrier of light that once stood to separate the magical from the mundane.

This organization was able to contain the situations and neutralize them. The meeting was a yearly exchange of developments among every practitioner from who wished to come. Among them was a married couple named Vienna and Remus Laurier.

Vienna Laurier was one of the founders of this organization, a magician trained in the Way of the Tree. Her husband, Remus, was a powerful healer and magic-user in his own right. Among many other agents, they were deployed when available to contain and neutralize potential magical threats. There was a lot to be said about this couple among their allies, their enemies, and their files in several top-secret facilities. If this couple was *ever* called on a mission, they would *neutralize. Never* kill. No matter what their orders were.

Some people respected this. Some people found it infuriating.

Either way, this was their goal with their present mission. Vienna and Remus were briefed beforehand that a cult leader by the name of John had utilized the conjoined energy of his followers to summon an unidentified energetic signature.

Vienna elected to fly there, having manifested white swan wings to carry her through the air, while her husband took the typical portal through the astral plane. He hated flying, but she loved it more than anything.

When Vienna landed about a block outside of the site, Remus appeared beside her through a portal, stepping through a window into reality framed by silver light. He was an attractive, Scottish guy with ginger hair, a ginger beard, white skin, and chocolate brown eyes. He looked to Vienna, a Mediterranean beauty with thick, black curly hair, olive skin, and sage-green eyes.

He asked her, "What did you see from the air?"

"Nothing. He's using the Veil."

Remus sighed, "They're getting smarter. Hopefully, we can talk him down."

"The others already tried that, hon. You read the report."

"Allow me to be optimistic. It's worked in the past."

"And yet, they still just want to shoot them in the head," Vienna replied. They hiked up a hill and made their way to a place on a cliff that looked like a patch of dirt with dry grass surrounding it. But Vienna only had to bang her fist against the invisible shield once for it to ripple with truth; toward the end of the cliff stood a hut made of earth and rotting wood. The moment their presence was detected, bodies rose from the ground—rotting corpses with the glowing blue eyes of the underworld.

"Oh, yay. Necromancy!" Vi said with a sarcastic smile. "Hades and Persephone will love that!"

"It's very high fantasy. This is kind of cool actually," Remus replied with a giddy smile.

"It is, yeah." They laughed before Vienna started to scan the area.

"I don't sense any soul energy in them. So, we won't have to worry about helping them cross over again," she said.

Remus scanned the area too, taking in the network of energy. "We can burn them, but I don't think it will weaken John. Sorry—he prefers 'Ares.'"

"I've met Ares and he's not Ares," Vienna replied, igniting a flame in her hand. However, the glow of the flame reached beneath her skin, showing an imbalance with her emotions.

Remus reached for her arm, "You good?"

"You know I don't like cult leaders. And you know those bodies are his followers."

Remus sucked his teeth, "Do you think burning them is disrespectful?"

With one kick, Vienna shattered the barrier just enough so a hole appeared for her to walk through. She ducked, stepped through, and in one fluid motion burned the corpses with a swirl of her fire. They collapsed into ash.

As she turned back to Remus, the fire in her hands faded

and the air around her swirled. She gathered the heaps of ash with the wind and mixed them with the earth, returning their remains from where they once came.

"I know it's not ceremonial, but we don't have time," Vienna said.

"That might come back to bite us in the ass, Vi," Remus replied, ducking past the shield. "Their families probably would have wanted their bodies back."

Vienna sighed, "Yeah, you're right. I'm sorry about that."

"You had good—" but he stopped. Remus felt a ripple cut through the air, like a rip in the wall of reality.

Vienna felt it half-a-second after him and whispered, "Chaos."

"You gotta be fucking kidding me."

"He invoked a chaos god," Vienna replied. She placed her hands together, "Do you think it's Loki? He's powerful but he's not primordial. We could probably disconnect John from—"

"You know it's primordial."

Vienna sighed, "Never mind. This isn't fun."

"Yeah, but a god is a god no matter which way it swings. The same rules apply whether he is primordial or demi. You know that. You *told me that.*"

"I've never dealt with primordial gods. But you're probably right."

"So, the same plan?"

"The same plan."

Again, their goal was always to neutralize. Killing was more effective certainly but, because of their rule, they had the chance to get creative. Sometimes they even went theatrical.

But with this situation, a direct approach was best.

The first thing they saw as they entered the hut was the head cultist, John, standing behind a stone altar dressed in a white robe. There were heaps of dead bodies he had sacrificed. The chaos god John had invoked was channeled through John's body and the sheer power of it could not be held within.

John's face had warped and twisted with purple chaos energy, spiraling off into infinity, into the background, into the god he had found. Vienna felt the power of this god the second she and John made eye contact.

She forced herself to ignore the bodies. She could still feel John, despite the god possessing him, and he was in *so much pain.*

"Set up the anchor," she said to Remus.

Her husband stepped to the side, writing out sigils in the earth to begin their ritual. Vienna stepped forward to deal with John and his god directly.

"What is your preferred name, Chaos?" she asked the god.

"I have no name."

"So, is no-name good?"

The god stopped for a moment as if to consider her question. Then, he said, "I think so."

"Is this what you wanted from this guy?" Vienna asked.

"I have been whispering in his ear since childhood."

"So, the mass ritual sacrifice and possession of a body that can't hold you is what you wanted, no-name?"

"I am Chaos, and I am desperate."

Vienna respected his candor. "Fair enough. So, there is no way to sway you from this vessel?"

"This vessel will not be for long, mage."

Vienna knew his goal. It was supervillain-y and not very creative, but he wanted to be re-released into the world. He had not been worshiped in a very long time, and John had given everything just to feel him for a few minutes. All these people died for nothing. If they could at the very least spare John's life then that would mean this wasn't a *completely awful* situation.

Vienna said no more. She sensed the shift in the air as her husband's sigils activated. She could also sense the power of this god and a little voice inside her said she may have to bend on her ethics to neutralize this threat. But she looked that voice in the face and said—*Not if I can help it.*

And so, it began.

She projected an energetic core into the center of John's mind, right behind his eyes where the god was looking. She stretched her fingers out and projected the core outward so that it took the shape of a sphere of mirrors. John and the god looked around confused, staring back at their warped face reflected back to them a thousand times. Remus and Vienna summoned shields to be ready.

But this method always worked.

They waited patiently until they heard John shout "GET IT OUT OF ME!"

The power of his rejection created a temporary wedge between his soul and no-name's energy. Vienna waited until she could sense it and then grabbed for it instantly. She inflamed it, making it grow bigger and bigger and bigger. John's fear and need for survival grew larger and larger until she heard the struggling cry of the god. Vienna made the wedge expand so much it shattered through the mirrors. The god pulled back from John's face—not completely, but enough for John's face to reshape.

Remus drew a sigil in the air, brought his palm behind it, and shoved it straight into John's chest. The power of it was enough to push no-name out of him. He was a swirling, formless shape of energy.

Vienna instantly gathered up the residual, nervous energy of John's fear and used it to generate a tube that no-name was sucked through. She bent it through the air, using the first two fingers of her hands to aim with precision. Her husband caught it with the same technique and siphoned it into the sigil drawn into the dirt.

"The planet is more powerful than him. She should accept it," Remus replied, though he only ever used 'should' when he doubted the tactic.

Vienna was about to respond when she saw John collapse to the ground. He had aged twenty years, his eyes wide with knowledge and pain that no human should ever know. He looked around, at his sacrificed followers, and tears poured down his face.

"*I'm sorry,*" he croaked. Vienna knew he meant it.

But she had a horrible feeling. A rushing feeling. The plan was going fine but she could still sense no-name and he was *happy.* Her eyes went wide and she watched John's face twist in terror before his possessor took him once more, causing his mouth to twist in a sickening smile.

"Remus—" but no-name spoke once and Vienna was thrown back. She hit the wall and fell to the ground, dizzy from the impact.

She heard a faint shout from her husband. John's corpse walked toward him, fully possessed by no-name. She couldn't sense John in that body anymore.

The siphoned energy faded; Remus's sigils burned up. He stumbled backward.

Vienna could sense what he was about to do.

She stood and found her balance again. She could sense the dense energy gathering in her husband's hands, but she was quicker with battle magic. She gathered red energy, a gift from Ares she never wanted to use, and drew a bloody red line through the air, breaking John's neck.

He collapsed to the ground. With no vessel, no-name's energy dissipated into dust through the corpse's mouth. Remus was breathing hard, looking at his wife in shock.

With the sight of the dead body, it took Vienna a few moments to fully process what she had just done. Her eyes widened and she stumbled. Fire gathered in her chest. She barred her teeth like a wolf and turned, letting out a roar, a fury of fire that blew out the side of the hut they stood in.

Remus was about to speak when Vienna turned to him with tears pouring down her face.

"I couldn't let you do that!" she shouted at him before storming out of the hut.

Remus got to his feet, shaken from the event. He looked down at the dead body at his feet. For a few moments, he couldn't look away.

But he willed himself to.

He followed his wife out of the hut.

She reached the edge of the cliff and let out another scream, this time without any magic. It echoed into the valley beyond. She collapsed to the ground, holding her head in her hands.

Remus could feel her pain. He could feel her shame.

He walked up to her.

Vienna said from beneath her hands, "Doing that would have killed you."

"I would have been fine."

Vienna lowered her hands, her face puffy with tears. She shook her head, "No, you wouldn't have been."

"And you are?"

"I can handle it better than you."

"Vi—"

"It's not a good thing, trust me." She looked up at him, "How are you? Are you okay?"

"I'm fine. Stop side-stepping the question."

"Are you okay?" she repeated firmly.

Remus sighed and fell to the ground beside her. "No, of course not. Someone's..." his voice cracked as he said, *"someone's dead."*

Vienna said nothing. Her shame grew more intense. There was something she was hiding.

"Talk to me. You know I could never hate you," Remus reassured her.

Vienna sighed. She took his hand, and he squeezed it back, "There's a reason I can handle it. There's something I haven't told you."

Remus gestured to her, showing that he was listening.

"It was a long time ago… in another life."

*1480 A.D.—Spain*

*It was pain that reminded them who they were.*

*Flesh. Bone.*

*Sinners.*

*The symbol at the center of their village was familiar to Santiago. It was an ancient, Celtic symbol he worked very hard not to look at directly, for not only was it forbidden but it was also from his childhood. His mother, an Irish-Spaniard woman, had worked with that symbol. If he looked at it, he would remember too much, including her return to the Lord.*

*If his men realized he knew what it stood for, it would raise suspicion in a way that was unnecessary. It would break the mission. It would empower the people they were trying so desperately to save.*

*They were saving them.*

*Carving, paining, and branding them were one thing, but his method worked better. It was better if they did it to each other, because it would build a sense of community. They would be returned to the heart of the Lord if they did it to each other. It worked; Santiago knew.*

*He had been through it himself.*

*His back was covered with proof of his salvation.*

*"Inquisitor, are you sure this is—"*

*"Do not question your Inquisitor, knight," his second-in-command ordered.*

*Santiago turned to his second with his sage-green eyes, nodding at him. He was a younger man with ginger hair and beard and was just as dedicated to the cause as Santiago.*

*Santiago stood off to the side, his head turned away from the sinner population but hearing their screams all the same. He found himself looking over a cliff as he watched the sinners walk over to the ground below. He watched them fall one-by-one; their sacrifice covered with symbols of the Lord. They were returning to the Lord's arms, but he still heard wails of fear, of grief, of pain, of them demanding what they did to deserve this.*

*And that very question suddenly had him standing in a land far away, among thousands of people, as they heard their queen howling from her castle over the death of her beloved son. They could all hear her, and they raised their chins or bowed their heads. But they were all grieving with her, ready to receive her when she emerged from her castle.*

Santiago burst awake, gasping.

The sun was barely over the horizon.

He felt a hand on his shoulder and turned to see his second looking back at him with concern.

"I'm alright," Santiago replied. He brushed off his knight's hand.

He and his party all rose. They ate rabbit, as they had done for the past month. As Santiago washed his hands in the river, he saw his reflection. Burn scars from a previous mission along with the untreated eye injury from this last one left very little of his face from his youth.

One of Santiago's lower knights came to him with a letter. He took it from him, dismissed him, and opened it. It was from his adoptive father, Torquemada.

The tone was curt and expectant, as always.

But it was also... congratulatory.

It was a strange feeling for Santiago. He had relinquished the idea of ever pleasing his father because his father didn't deal in right or wrong. He only dealt in perdition or salvation. If you did things right, then you didn't receive congratulations. You should've been doing it that way in the first place. If your sake is perdition, you shall be educated under the love of the Lord until you are back in the place you should be—dead or alive. His job was to make sure others stayed where they were supposed to stay.

And yet, here Santiago was. He was holding a letter in his hand with the words:

*Your efforts are outstanding.*

Santiago hadn't realized he wanted to hear that until now.

And yet, somehow at the same time, he felt nothing at all.

He felt nothing at all because the letter confused him. Torquemada didn't give congratulations for anything, because none of them were in it for the glory. His mission had been successful, but the fact was this was his purpose. He shouldn't receive a reward for it.

He needed to ask his father what was special about this time.

This question remained at the back of his mind as he and his men rode their horses a half-day back to their town with the Inquisitor's fortress in the center of it. It was a black, looming castle that rose above the rest of the town. They had been away a month. When they entered their town, they were met with the usual fanfare for their duties. The townspeople thanked them, and one woman even took the hand of his second-in-command and thanked him for saving her daughter.

His second-in-command humbly nodded and gently

brushed her hand away. His eyes darted around sheepishly and, Santiago found it slightly endearing.

They made their way up to the fortress, their horses retrieved for the stables. His men went to the barracks, and Santiago was brought to his private quarters where his injuries could be tended to.

He had a dirty cloth over his eye and their resident physician pulled it away to reveal his injury. The physician, practiced in his craft, kept his voice and face calm. But by this point Santiago had been treated by him so many times, he could tell when the physician was concerned.

"You should have brought more resources with you, Santiago," the physician said, opening his purse of remedies. "It's severely infected. We may have to remove the eye."

"It's all for the mission," Santiago replied. "A loss of an eye means nothing."

"The Lord would want you to take care of yourself."

It was a peculiar thing for the physician to say. Perhaps he was right. But the Lord was a father and fathers kept their children in line. The Lord had done that to Santiago all his life, as did his own father, as would he to his own children if the time ever came. So, he replied with, "Any sacrifice for this mission is the right one. You know that as well as I."

"That is the reason I am a healer. If you are going to survive, Santiago, we need to do the procedure now. Would you like something to put you to sleep?"

"Enough to numb the pain. Not enough to knock me out."

"This particular procedure is deeply uncomfortable, even without the pain."

"To know pain is to know salvation."

The physician said nothing. He laid Santiago out over the table, gave him the numbing agent, and then got to work.

The feeling of the metal tools in his eye was deeply upsetting and invasive, as the physician warned, but Santiago could hold himself—

The door opened.

"We are busy—" the physician stopped when he saw who it was. He dropped the tools on a cloth and wiped his hands as he answered fearfully, "I-Inquisitor Torquemada. I meant no disrespect—"

"Please continue your procedure. I will not be here long."

"It would be best if we—"

"*I insist.*"

The physician blinked quickly before returning to his work. Santiago felt the tools within his eye socket, but he was unnerved at having his father beside him. He couldn't say anything at all, he was so overwhelmed. There was no pain, but it was deeply unpleasant and upsetting and his father knew this. So why—

"Your report was delivered to me yesterday by pigeon."

Santiago shook. His teeth pressed together as tightly as prison bars.

"I think it may have been your greatest work, Santiago."

He felt the physician remove what was left of his eye and watched him quickly place it on the table. Santiago was frozen to the spot.

"The precision, communication, and demonstration of our message was clear. I taught you well, my son. You have come far from the boy I saved from that village all those years ago. You have proven yourself to be a fine Inquisitor."

It was all Santiago ever wanted to hear and it was happening as an important organ was being removed from his face.

He felt nothing.

He felt everything.

They probably thought his body trembled from the procedure, but he felt a deep, dark, angry, hot something curdling in his gut and he didn't know why. All he knew was that the sound of his father's voice made him want to vomit.

"I leave tonight, but I wish to speak with you when I return. There are changes coming and your consultation on them will be valuable. Prepare while I am away." Torquemada left without another word.

The physician watched him leave and waited until the door was closed before asking, "Are you alright?"

Santiago swallowed. He could cry and the very thing he needed to cry from was gone.

"Just finish the procedure."

The physician did as he said.

Torquemada being gone meant Santiago was in charge. His second-in-command always got quietly ambitious, telling him to make changes. But he was only in charge once a month and his father had strict rules that one day wouldn't…

Santiago could barely think.

He was more bothered by what his father had done than the loss of his own eye.

He was so confused. His father had made it clear that, in their line of work, there were no rewards, but had rewarded him with praise twice. He had done it the second time in such a way that was… typical, and yet…

Why did it bother Santiago? Why did the reward bother him? Why was the way it was done bothering him?

He… He couldn't think about that now. He had a duty to fulfill.

His father's duties overcame his own; without him, the city would collapse. Governor Moreno was a kind, stupid, and easily corruptible man who did the same thing every month— when Santiago was in charge, Moreno would approach him with an offer to move the exchange of goods from the church to the market. It was such a simple request and would strengthen the merchant class in town, but it would weaken the hold the Church had over the people. And there was the tiny part that the money-grubbing merchants, and by extension the governor, would have more control to spread their corruption.

If Torquemada and the Church relented on that, then all the good they had accomplished would fall apart and their people would forget the call of their Lord. Spiritual salvation was more important than the calls of the flesh.

To be honest, such a demand had Santiago thinking. If Moreno was making this request, then it probably went all the way down. He was a stupid man who allowed the people to run his office, even though he would never admit that.

As a boy, any requests Santiago made for anyone not educated in the words of the Lord were quickly hushed by Torquemada's blatant, painful, and clear brand of education. That counted for any sinners, including a lost dog. The first marks of salvation on his back were from those educational sessions when he had defended said pup. And now, for the first time in his life, Santiago was praised for his work. He was watching Moreno make these demands and the answer came quite easily to Santiago.

He knew who was making these demands. So, he brought them to the center of town. As usual, a crowd gathered. He'd seen Torquemada do it so many times and was well within his rights to do it, too. It wasn't creative or original. He lined up the dissenting voices, chained them up in a line, made them face forward, and then simply repeated what he did with those pagans only a week ago.

He had their own kin step up and mark them with the symbols of the Lord. Their screams echoed into the air and Santiago almost rolled his eyes at their weakness.

He wasn't going to kill them. The knives had been

cleansed with fire. They would be fine.

This was his greatest work. It was what he had been trained for.

He was barely watching, though. He was barely hearing any of it. The screams echoed up and once again, he couldn't understand why his father congratulating him bothered him so much.

Santiago looked up and across the crowd. His second-in-command watched him, knowing something was bothering him.

Santiago looked down, showing nothing.

Those who resisted were brought to the interrogation chambers under the fortress. They wouldn't die. All they had to do was confess.

That's all they had to do.

Do that, and their souls would be spared.

That's what people didn't seem to understand.

He stepped away to continue the rest of his duties.

Everyone envied Santiago's position and the sway he had over the head Inquisitor was impressive. If he said it, odds are it would be put in effect.

However, there wasn't much freedom in what he could say. The reason his suggestions were taken was because they were tailored to exactly what Torquemada wanted to hear. There was no room for flexibility in this position. Mercy was only given to perpetrators if they confessed their sins, and the only mercy granted to them was banishment. Any other suggestion was considered heretical...

God, this was all so exhausting.

Santiago understood his role and how important this all was. But his role was taxing after a while and... and that vision never left his dreams.

Clans of ancient pagans coming together to hear the

wailing grief of their queen and Santiago could feel the magic of her grief, the magic of the land, their love and their compassion, and... it all led to perdition. These poor people had no idea.

And Santiago, truthfully, could say nothing about it because it would be misinterpreted.

As he said; he's tired.

The end of the day finally came. Santiago stood in a nondescript tower, almost as small as a storage closet. There was one bed, one chair, and one candle burning on the bedside table. No one knew about this room. It was buried so deep in the fortress you could only find it if you knew what to look for. There was a sizable window, though, and Santiago looked out into the night, past the firelight of the village, into the hills beyond. There, in the wilds, was pagan land. To go there alone would almost surely mean damnation. And yet, he wanted to disappear into its shadows.

He shoved down the impulse. He knew who he was and what he stood for.

The doorknob jangled and Santiago turned as he heard it unlock. A slight breeze entered the room, making the candlelight flicker as his second-in-command whispered, "Good evening."

Santiago, for the first time in a while, smiled. His knight stood before him, dressed in a brown cloak, white shirt, black slacks, and boots. His knight closed the door, double-checking that it was locked. Then, he revealed from beneath his cloak a bouquet of flowers. African daisies, red carnations, and— "Lilies?" Santiago asked as he took the bouquet, "Where did you get these?"

"They were brought in on one of the ships today," his knight replied with a smile.

Santiago inhaled the scent of the bouquet, like spicy

perfume. He placed the flowers on the table beside the candle and pulled his knight into an embrace he had been craving for a whole month. His knight returned it. He buried his face in Santiago's neck and Santiago pressed a tender kiss to his cheek. They pulled apart for a moment, their lips lingering inches from the other.

It would just be one kiss. No one would ever know.

Santiago almost gave in.

But, it was his knight who harbored self-control. He looked down for a moment before caressing Santiago's face with his thumb. He looked upon him, concerned. His thumb drifted just beneath the eyepatch covering his left eye, "How… How are you? Really?"

"We have the best healers, Ramón," Santiago replied, side-stepping the question.

"I know. I just hate to see you go through this," Ramón replied, taking off his cloak to place it on the chair in the corner. "You already carry so much and I don't want to give the people any other reason to misunderstand you."

Santiago sighed, "You noticed that?"

"We are only trying to help," Ramón replied, taking Santiago's hand in his. He gently guided him to the bed. The two men, free of armor and expectations, laid down together. "Though, you know how I feel about this."

"I can't think too much about it."

"But I can see that you are."

Santiago sighed, "What do you want me to say? The governor is a moron and the Inquisitor is extremely strict. It's a careful balance. If I suggest anything that could disrupt it, the power I already have could vanish."

"I hate to ask this, but do you feel you have any power at all?"

If anyone else asked Santiago that question, he would

demote, banish, or execute them. But Ramón had a… way with him. He trusted Santiago's mind and held Santiago's heart as tenderly as a baby bird. So, Santiago knew implicitly if Ramón was asking such a hard question…

"I ask myself that every day." He thought for a moment before adding, "There is heavy misinformation. We are sending waves and waves of knights to wipe out people who could lead us to perdition, but sometimes the things they bring back are not magic, paganism, or devil's work. It's—"

"—science?" Ramón smiled. He reached beneath his hanging cloak and pulled out a red, leather-bound journal for Santiago to see. "This is the private journal of an inventor and scientist we tried to arrest. By the time we got to his tower, he had gone."

Santiago smirked, "You kept the journal!" He took it and sat up.

Ramón jumped up in excitement. "You should have seen it, Santiago! He had gone but he left behind a plethora of instruments and tools made of brass and glass. Telescopes, sailor's tools, maps, books, and he even built a miniature mechanism copying the planets—"

"—with the sun in the middle?" Santiago asked, holding up the journal. There was a sketch of the planets circling around the sun. "We should burn this," he said, plopping it on the side table.

"But Santiago, I think he may be right."

Santiago raised a brow, "Be very careful what you say next, Ramón ."

He pulled Santiago up from the bed and pointed to the stars. He demonstrated how this scientist's theory was possible just by using the angles of the stars, of Mars and Venus, and by the end of it, all Santiago could say was "This is what I mean. I can understand our mission, but how could this knowledge be evil? We are simply learning more about who we are."

"And yet your father considers *La Divina Comedia* fact."

Santiago tried to hide his smile, "It's a good read, though. It is a reframing of the pagan world through the eyes of Christianity. It is helpful."

"As a story, certainly, but—"

"—hard fact? Oh, of course not. But it does worry me, again."

"This is why you should be running things."

"Even if I could, none of what I say here would be used to affect my decisions."

"Of course not. The moment I stepped into this room, it was heretical."

Santiago's stomach dropped. "How so? We are just friends."

Ramón stopped for a moment, a long pause at Santiago's words. The air became thick with tension because Santiago knew Ramón had always wanted more than that. Ramón was braver than him and Ramón had more freedom than him. If Santiago said the word, the two of them would pack up and leave forever. Ramón was always wounded, always disappointed, and always secretly angry because he would always choose Santiago over all of this, but Santiago probably wouldn't choose him. It wasn't because Santiago didn't love Ramón, it was because Santiago had grown up in this power, he *needed* it, and if he left it behind then he wouldn't know who he was anymore.

If he gave into Ramón's hold over him, this person Santiago built himself up as would crumble and the person who was hidden beneath the surface would rise and—

"This is our cocoon, Santiago," Ramón said, looking back at him, hurt in his eyes.

"You already have so much of me."

Ramón sighed, "I know." He turned to Santiago and despite his sadness, he smiled. "I know I do and I am honored you have shown me as much as you have."

Santiago sighed, and as always, the air calmed. The tension cleared. And, once more, he felt free and at home in the presence of his knight.

He held out his hand and Ramón took it, joining him on the bed. They pulled close next to each other and as they did every time they met they discussed what they would do if they left to never return. They would vanish into the hills of the pagans, to some remote village where they still used the stars to tell about the magics, the wilds for healing, and song and prayers to ancient spirits to give them their harvest. Where medicine men, midwives, and illiterate scholars could feel the changes in the weather, the cycle of the seasons, and the turning of the world.

"It would have to be a slow transition."

"There are some merits to their ways. It would just be more effective with God at the helm instead of the devil masking as fickle spirits," Santiago replied, shaking his head. "The Lord's punishment does seem to keep them in-line."

"Only for so long, though."

"Elaborate?"

"Pain can also breed rebellion and disobedience. And as you said, they have some helpful techniques... I could run a rehabilitation center. Teach them our healing modalities. We could help them transition to our more consistent methods." Ramón smiled, "Imagine if astrology really worked, though. It is a wonderful idea. For the stars to tell us what we need to know?"

Ramón could see beauty even in the worst situations.

He was the most open-minded person Santiago would ever know.

And at that moment, with all the pretenses dropped, Santiago wanted to tell him. He wanted to tell him about the visions he had every single night. He knew Ramón suspected something because Santiago always woke with a start. Ramón never asked and Santiago loved him for that, but he wanted to tell him.

About the pagan queen howling her grief into the night, so that all her clans could hear.

About the sheer magic pouring from the land and the queen and her people.

About how Santiago felt more at home in that vision than he ever had here.

About how sometimes when Santiago woke from his vision, he could see magic glittering in the air or faces in the darkness watching him or hear the call of that queen howling for him to meet her in the wilds.

About how sometimes Santiago felt so crushed under the weight of this life that he felt he couldn't breathe.

But he didn't. Instead, all he did was press a kiss to Ramón's cheek.

Ramón smiled at him, the gratitude between them so deep that it almost brought them both to tears. And as they always did, at these monthly meetings, they didn't sleep at all. They talked and talked and talked until the sun came up.

\*\*\*

Santiago was tired, one-eyed, and happy.

Everything else was a great sacrifice for his mission, but his exhaustion was a good exhaustion. His heart felt warm, and he could still feel the comfort of his knight's arms around him. It was always the morning after these meetings when Santiago felt most like himself—the leader his father had bred him to be, but with enough certainty he could almost confidently make his own decisions.

His own courage surprised him.

He looked over the village now with a renewed sense of

what needed to be done. He wondered if his knight had a point; threading a little kindness into the Inquisition's interaction with the people of the town could strengthen their relationship with the Church. It was an obvious change, really, and he wondered why his father had not come up with it already.

The kindness of his knight alone made Santiago better, stronger, and more loyal.

He was thinking all this over as he sat in his office, waiting on his father's assistant to bring him the paperwork that would usually go to his father. He had a cup of tila tea in front of him and the flowers Ramón brought him sitting in a metal vase on a table off to the side, in just the right spot to catch the sunlight.

The assistant knocked on the door and Santiago bid him enter.

He bowed his head to Santiago respectfully, and then handed each set of papers to him, briefly explaining what each one was. The last page was just a list: "These are the spies that have been found, investigated, and proven to be working against us."

Santiago scoffed, "They are idiots." He read through the list and every single one he had previously suspected. "They always think they are so slick and..." he trailed off. He read the last name on the list, ears ringing:

*Ramón Rosales*

His stomach dropped—
"Inquisitor?"
Santiago looked up at the assistant.
"Are you alright?"
Santiago's face hardened. Bluntly, he said, "Go about your duties."

The assistant nodded and disappeared from the room.

He waited until the door was well and properly closed, his heart racing in his chest. Santiago locked the door to his office and stumbled up to the window with the sun shining through.

He felt like a child.

All the times Torquemada had condemned someone he cared about right in front of him. Men, women, a skittish puppy... his own mother.

And now Ramón.

The image of the pagan queen howling in pain echoed through him. He felt her scream. He wanted to scream with her. He wanted to scream so loud it would break the glass of his office window. He glanced to his left and saw those flowers sitting on the table. African daisies, red carnations, and... lilies....

That flower meant condolences for grief.

Did... Did Ramón know he would be taken?

Santiago reached for the flowers and ripped them in half with his hands. He threw them ragefully into his wastebasket and as he looked out the window again, he eyed welled up. It was the dog all over again. It was his mother all over again. Every single time he had fought for something he cared about; he had been punished without fail.

*I need to talk to Ramón. I need to—*

His door opened. "The spies are ready for you."

"Put Ramón Rosales in a separate chamber."

"Why?"

Santiago thought out his words carefully. "Because he knew better than any of them," he replied, keeping his voice cold. He meant his words and he didn't.

He went about his duties like normal, but swiftly. Torquemada would be back by dusk and Santiago had to get all his ducks in a row before he made a decision on what to do with Ramón. He knew Torquemada was ruthless, but if he could find just one reason—*a solid one*—to grant Ramón mercy, it could save him.

He went by spy after spy. He knew most of them were working against them months in advance, so he gave them the typical spiel with his voice cold and his chin held high. He was aware his eyepatch only made him uglier and more menacing. He read them their last rights, their prayer for forgiveness and salvation for the Lord, and then left them to the interrogators. If need be, the executioners.

The interrogators then opened the door to Ramón's private chamber. Santiago commanded they leave, as the law did not prohibit him to have one final word with his own men before their condemnation.

They did as commanded, closing the door behind them, including the metal slat over the barred window. Santiago averted his gaze from his knight, waiting until the door was firmly locked behind him.

When he was sure no one would hear, he dropped all pretenses. He ran up to his knight, who was sweaty and dizzy, held down in one of the interrogation chairs. Without really realizing what he was doing, he gently took Ramón's face in his hands, "My love."

"S-Santiago," Ramón groaned.

"Say nothing. Do nothing. Admit to nothing. You have enough credibility from your service that we may be able to appeal for mercy for you. You would no longer be a knight—"

"I did do it, Santiago."

*"Say nothing,"* Santiago whispered sharply.

"That mission was horrible, Santiago. They did nothing," Ramón murmured, leaning into Santiago's touch. He was broken and saddened and defeated. "Those pagans only had healing skills we could use. They weren't harming anyone."

"The devil was their representative, Ramón."

"You don't..." Ramón trailed off. His tears fell and a small sob spilled from his lips. He was tired from the interrogation, but he was even more tired from everything else. "I am a *healer*, Santiago."

Santiago's bottom lip trembled.

"What we did was horrible."

His words were confusing Santiago, they truly were. Certainly, the two of them would discuss the hypocrisies of their mission in private but, just last night, Ramón was saying how they were only trying to help.

But he had also been a spy by then.

This whole thing was a tangled mess that he would have to talk to Ramón about after everything. Once again, he pleaded, "Say nothing more."

"I tried to save a single family. They hid in our cart."

*They were hiding in the city.* Santiago remembered the mother thanking Ramón when they entered the village, and the sheepish look on his face.

"I can't do this, Santiago. I did it. I did all of it."

Santiago was silent, but internally, he was screaming. The plan could still work, but Ramón would botch all of it because he knew who he was and what he wanted, and when he made up his mind, there was no changing it. Ramón was brave and Ramón was "Stupid," Santiago spat. He turned away, "So *stupid*."

"Don't leave me this way!"

Ramón's words shook Santiago. He stopped in his tracks, but it took all his self-control not to look back. "You made your choice. This is the path you walked."

Yet, he did not walk out right away. He was hoping Ramón would just say—

"Santiago," Ramón murmured so only he could hear. "The dream you have is not a vision. It's a memory. I-It's a story."

Santiago's eyes went wide. He turned—

The metal door opened and Torquemada was looking back at him with his beady, brown eyes. Santiago's face fell to stone and the door was pushed open for the interrogator and his assistants to enter the chamber. Torquemada called for him and Santiago hesitated for just a moment.

He thought he might throw up.

His mother. The dog.

And now Ramón.

Torquemada looked at him impatiently and expectantly. There were so many thoughts going through Santiago's mind, but all he could do was step toward his father. The world was a blur as the door closed behind him.

"You have truly impressed me," his father said.

Santiago remembered the eye procedure.

"Your dedication is unparalleled. To smell out your own man and bring him back to the love of the Lord," Torquemada said, placing a hand on Santiago's shoulder.

Santiago looked down. The hand was gloved in brown leather and he had only ever felt its touch when he was a problem. And now it was on his shoulder in congratulations.

While his best friend, his lover, his *knight* was—

He heard Ramón's scream and Santiago trembled.

"Betrayal is hard, my son," Torquemada said in a rare moment of compassion. There was even a hint of sadness in his eyes. And yet, he said, "But that is the sacrifice we must make for our mission."

Pain, when he was wrong. Pain, when he was right.

Santiago shook with rage.

*I'm going to kill you.*

*2040 A.D. - Present day*

"Santiago was a coward," Remus said.

"A coward who ended countless lives," Vienna replied with venom in her voice.

Remus hesitated before adding, "He was brainwashed, though. His entire life."

Vienna shook her head, "Please don't defend him. It's because of him that I can even *think* of doing... what I did."

Remus was about to reply when he was cut off by a sudden patch of black growing in the air in front of them. "What is that?" He asked.

Vienna had no chance to answer. The black cycled around her, pulling her into a void with barely any color coming through. She breathed hard, confused, and startled, the air around her stale. She couldn't see her breath, but she felt the cold deep in her bones all the same. Remus was nowhere to be found.

Vienna demanded bluntly, "Where am I?"

As she asked, she heard somebody else ask the same thing simultaneously. It echoed out of the darkness. As she squinted, she could make out a figure draped in black. She didn't logically know who he was, but everything inside of her screamed at her to run.

She tried to get away, but the void turned her around so that she found herself right in front of the figure she was trying to escape. He looked up at her, just as confused as she was.

He was an ugly motherfucker.

The right half of his face was burned away, covered by scars that never healed properly, and an eyepatch over his right eye. He wore a black mustache with a goatee. But, when his good eye met Vienna's, it was sage-green, just like her own.

"State your name," he commanded.

She did not answer, and for half-a-second, she didn't move either. Three things entered her mind at the exact same time: one, this was an opportunity given to her from some force above that she couldn't pass up. Two, she had the upper hand; he knew nothing, which meant she could do anything here. And three—a man was dead because of her and the fact that she could do such an abominable act started with the *bastard* standing in front of her.

She raised her chin defiantly, "I am Vienna Laurier. *You* are Santiago Rivera, second-in-command to Inquisitor Tomás de Torquemada. The only person who can come close to Torquemada's record of death and oppression is *you*."

Unfazed, Santiago asked, "So I have attempted to redeem you, then?"

"You consider torture, oppression, and genocide redemption?"

"I consider my work far too important for a pagan like you to understand. I work for God. The creator does not think in terms of life and death. He only wants us to be safe and whole."

"And you consider torture, oppression, and genocide the path to that wholeness?" Vienna demanded again; her face reddening with anger.

"Love is not always kind," Santiago replied without hesitation. Without a beat.

Vienna's rage went cold, "Santiago Rivera."

Her tone was powerful enough to catch his full attention.

"I am from the year 2040 AD, nearly 600 years from your lifetime." She started to walk and as she did, the energy in the void changed. It hummed to her presence, echoed to her footsteps, and shifted with her movements. She raised her hand to reveal the image of the curtain of light dancing across the horizon, reaching up into the sky.

"About five years ago, a pulse was released that reshaped the magical patterns around the planet. What do those lights look like, Santiago?"

Santiago paused for a moment before he said, "The northern lights."

"As the magical patterns reshaped, the northern lights stretched across the globe. You can see them in almost every area now," Vienna replied.

She raised her hands, creating images echoing in the void around them.

"To balance out the energies, many cultures had to work together with ancient rituals in order to anchor the lights."

In the images, they could see indigenous shamans vocalizing songs and prayers to connect with their spirits, pandits and pujari in India singing with other Hindu worshippers to generate the energy of their gods, neo-pagans burning candles on their altars to invoke their own energy and the energy of their deities, and northern indigenous people raising their hands to the northern spirits of sky, wind, and ice to properly tame the overflowing energy of the aurora borealis as it reached into the glaciers. Voodoo practitioners channeling their spirits, Norse medicine men and women reaching into their frozen lands, Santeria practitioners in Brazil, Uruguay, Mexico lighting their candles and praying to their saints. Muslims on their knees, Jews in their temples, and Christians in their churches, praying to Santiago's Lord, for the health of every other person he had seen in the visions around him.

As if clinging to the last remnants of his faith, he said to himself "I am being tempted."

Vienna crossed her arms as her sage-green eyes glowed. "Who am I, Santiago?"

"A witch or a demonic spirit in human form. I haven't decided yet."

Vienna shook her head slowly and she asked again, "Who am I, Santiago?"

"I just answered your question, *Witch*."

Vienna raised her chin defiantly. "*Santiago*," she hissed. "Who. Am. I?"

Santiago didn't know why, but she would not cease, and that made *him* want to run. He bolted into the darkness only to circle around and come right back face-to-face with Vienna.

He drew his sword and ran at her, shoving her up against the black walls around them.

*She* was doing this.

*She* was manipulating *all of this*. She must be!

The walls shook under their weight as Santiago held his blade to Vienna's throat. He was not calm and calculated like he always tried to be. He was rageful and hateful and— "You have damned the world!"

Vienna laughed despite the pressure against her throat and chest.

He still didn't *fucking get it!*

Vienna brought her free hand to the blade. Her fingertip glowed like the tip of a fire iron. She touched the blade and within seconds, the weapon was hot enough that Santiago had to drop it. Vienna landed on her feet and raised her leg, kicking Santiago square in the chest. He stumbled backwards as she demanded again, "WHO AM I!?"

Her sage-green eyes were glowing. She clenched her fists and her power gathered in her veins as glowing, fiery energy. She was ready to burn him alive.

He was afraid. He had nowhere to go... and his attention was drawn away from her. He was scared, but what he saw had him confused. Vienna turned to where he was looking... in the walls of shadow was a vision of crowds and crowds of pagans gathered in support as they listened to the howling grief of their queen.

From the vision, the darkness, they both heard... "*The dream you have is not a vision. It's a memory. It's a story.*"

The voice was that of Remus. But it was Ramón speaking.

Santiago trembled.

"That was my favorite story growing up," Vienna said.

The horrible, wailing grief of the queen and the hymns of her people… that was all they could give her…

What was Vienna doing?

Her fists loosened. The energy of her rage faded and the glow of her eyes dimmed back to its normal color. She remembered what her husband had said… He was brainwashed his entire life…

Santiago was… he was shaking. He was confused.

She spoke to him… she *willed herself* to speak calmly. Kindly. "Your thought that you had before you came here— *Ramón was brave and Ramón was stupid?*"

She caught Santiago's attention.

"My husband would agree with you, I think. It explains why he is so meticulous now. He takes his role as a healer seriously. You can see it in his face."

The image of the pagans gathering for their queen shimmered, as if it was changing.

"He is brilliant. He loves books on science and healing of all kinds. When he discovers something new that excites him, he'll spend whole hours bouncing around telling me about it. He takes his duty so seriously and puts the lives of his charges above everything. There's a reason he's my partner," Vienna explained. She never really shared this with anyone, but Santiago would understand better than anyone. "He's powerful as hell, too. He can harness the energy of the earth without bleeding her dry. We are opposites, really. I am more a being of faith. I work with the stars, the spirits, and the gods. I look like the ambitious one, but he is the visionary. He is my rock."

Santiago averted his eyes because who she was describing was too familiar.

Vienna sighed, "He is a healer, he can't… if a single soul is harmed by him, it wipes him out for a whole month."

That same voice echoed through… exhausted and defeated…

*I am a healer, Santiago. What we did was horrible.*

"Please stop," Santiago begged Vienna.

"That didn't come from me."

Santiago shook his head, his eyes closed.

"He's right."

He looked up at Vienna.

"It's not a vision you keep having. It's a memory. It's a story."

"It is a hoax,"

"Ramón, the dog, and your mother," Vienna replied.

A cold rage grew inside him as he demanded through his teeth, "What of them?"

"What can you tell me about them?"

"They are all…" he hesitated for a moment before forcing himself to say, "*sinners.*"

"That's not a similarity. It is a subjective view and it's not one that actually counts," Vienna retorted, losing her patience. "The similarity between all of them is that you love them."

Santiago's face twitched. "To love a sinner is a great virtue."

"That is what you tell yourself, yet you've been conflicted all your life. But Ramón seems to have made up his mind."

Santiago was growing impatient with this witch and how she spoke to him as if she knew him. "Ramón was stupid," Santiago retorted.

"His *method* was stupid. His reasons were not." Vienna then asked, "The vision you have? That community is standing with their grieving queen for the same reason Ramón did what he did. How can a vision like that be evil?"

"The devil is a master manipulator. He'll find a way."

"Was the devil going to manipulate you through a dog? Through a skittish puppy who just came up to you for protection?"

"To… to question God's will—"

"It's not a vision, Santiago. It's a memory."

Ramón's voice echoed again. *It's a story.*

Santiago, finally, dropped the façade. Panicked, he demanded, "How could he possibly know that? *No one* knows about that dream. That was my *secret* that was meant for *me alone.* How could Ramón know about it? How could he know more than me about it?"

Both of them inhaled, and as if on cue, they both heard a voice. It was not Ramón and it was not Remus. It was not their own. It was a distant voice, feminine and kind, one that inspired forgotten impressions of comfort, love, and warmth within Santiago. His eyes widened, welling with tears, "Momma…"

Somehow, she had found Ramón.

Santiago could feel it. Vienna could feel it too.

What Santiago didn't know was that his mother's voice sounded exactly like Vienna's and it took all her might not to shake just like he was.

She shared her own memory, just the voice of her mother telling her the story of the goddess Brigid sobbing over the death of her son, and all her people standing outside her castle to bear her grief with her. Her voice was the same as Santiago's mother's. She told the story just like his had and her soul echoed the same.

They could both hear it in the warmth of her words.

Santiago's tears fell. He sobbed.

It was not a vision. It was a memory.

"Who am I, Santiago?" Vienna asked softly.

Santiago averted his gaze.

"Look at me," she said firmly, catching his eye. "Who am I?"

He fell quiet as he looked upon her. The entire time, he

had been avoiding looking at her directly for the sole reason that she was a temptress. But something inside of him, it just… he looked up. He looked at her, with her thick, black hair and olive skin. The face looking back at him was distant but familiar, the same one he had seen in the mirror for the first eighteen years of his life, before his own had been burned. His eyes were the same sage-green as hers.

It was her face… it was his face.

She whispered, "He is the best person we will ever know."

A small sob left his lips.

"Don't leave him behind. *Please*." A tear spilled down Vienna's cheek.

He could feel her love like it was his own. He collapsed to the ground, holding his head in despair.

He'd heard enough. He slowly disappeared.

But Vienna knew he would remember all of it.

Vienna felt Remus's hand on her arm and she turned back to her life, walking into the arms of her lover. He held her close and pressed a kiss to her head. "Are you okay?" He asked. She could feel his heart and she loved it every time; it was soft and kind, like a summer's breeze.

She hugged him tighter as her tears poured down her cheeks, "I will be."

"Do you think you'll be able to change the past?"

She sighed and pressed a kiss to his chest, "That's my hope."

"Vi, you aren't him. Not anymore."

She gazed back wryly, "What are you talking about? We're just bros, Ramón." Despite her humor, her tears still fell.

Remus chuckled and kissed away her tears. They embraced each other tighter and held one another, for just… a little while.

# The True Bony Medusa
By Maureen O'Leary

I am the true bony now

I shiver and burn

My own body as fuel.

What comes of watching a leg getting carved by flame?

I can't tell if I am stronger now

Or just more pissed off.

If I want to be beautiful,

Or to pack a punch and run.

The ridge between my shoulder and neck

Holds a muscle that bulges a yoke.

My mother views the cracked and rippling flesh of me,

calculating its disappearance,

Striking matches and burning,

Setting fire to the wood at the stake.

My wrists are lithe as a dancer.

My hands are the heads of two vipers.

My tongue is glossy with truth and need and blood.

# The Perfect Li(n)e
By Desiree DiFabio

Violet liked many things to be positive. Comments from her trainer at the gym. Reports from her daughter's school. Outlook for their stock investments.

Not pregnancy tests.

Especially not one that came on the heels of her husband's push to "spice it up in the bedroom." Especially not one that came on the heels of Violet taking that push a little too far.

"Vi? Where are you babe? We have to leave!" Evan's voice sounded far away, like a distant memory of her life before, calling out to her.

"Coming!" She responded brightly.

The little stick, the hateful little stick that in the span of three minutes had changed everything, glowed with electric pink lines. Two of them, soldiers standing at attention next to each other.

"Ugh!" Frustrated, she snatched the test from the corner of the sink, wrapped it in toilet paper several times, and shoved it deep into the tampon box where Evan would never look.

Violet checked herself in the mirror, brushed an invisible wrinkle off the shoulder of her Lily Pulitzer Sophiletta shift, and pinched her cheeks. One quick, well-practiced smile in the vanity mirror and she was ready. She pulled the door shut as she went out to join her family.

*** 

Violet scrolled through roughly thirty pictures of her husband and daughter holding hands, walking down granite steps with the marble three-tiered fountain in the background. Evan's dirty-blonde hair lazily flopped over one eyebrow. Gracie's fingers, the tiny pink nails like little seashells, protected in the palm of her daddy's big hand. She gazed up at him adoringly, and he back down at her. #DaddyDaughterDance #BeStillMyHeart #MyTwoGreatLoves.

She scrolled through her feed while she waited for the first few likes. *57 in ten seconds.* Violet meant to pop on and off, but she got sucked in by her social adversary, Shelia. After a month of silence, Shelia was back in action, posting a batch of family pics at the sunflower farm in which she wore a dangerously low-cut shirt with full cleavage on display.

*Violet snorted. Boob job. She never looked that good in a halter top.*

She wasn't jealous—Shelia could never hold a candle to Violet in looks or any other department—it just annoyed her the way a pesky fly does when it buzzes around your head at a cookout. She wanted to reach through her screen and flatten Shelia with a swatter. Instead, she made sure to beat her in the who-comments-first game. #SoCuteShells #FamGoals.

Feeling satisfied with herself, Violet leaned back against the pristine white slats of the handmade Adirondack chair, one of a set of four decorating their large, low-country wraparound porch. Her 2021 Mercedes-Benz E-Class All-Terrain SUV gleamed, also white, on their newly paved driveway. Their gardener, James, finished loading equipment into his truck bed and raised his hand in a friendly goodbye. The grass was green and soft as velvet. The violets were in full bloom, adding the loveliest splash of purple to the already perfect backdrop. The welcome mat at the front door professed Violet's message to all: "Home Sweet Home." That phrase represented all that mattered to Violet – her home was a place people smiled at when they drove by, felt comfortable in when they came for a visit, and wished the life of the beautiful, yet understated, family within could be their own.

Violet had everything she ever wanted.

She closed her eyes.

Little pink lines bloomed behind her eyelids, reminding her that was no longer true.

Her thoughts turned to the night ahead. Evan and Gracie would be gone to the father-daughter dance for a few hours. Her toes tapped a slow one, two, three, one, two, three rhythm on the boards beneath her feet. She glanced at the phone in her lap every few seconds, waiting. After what seemed an eternity, her message notification pinged.

*Free?*

She knew, deep down in the places where she protected her most precious thoughts, that she should say no.

*Completely.*

The three bubbles appeared, then disappeared, then appeared again. She waited.

*I won't waste another second.*

Violet smiled at her lap. She couldn't help it. As she started to tap a response, a car door clicked shut across the street. She looked up. He was already there.

Careful, always, not to pique her neighbor's curiosity, she looked past him and down the road. A minute later she stretched her arms above her head, stood, and unhurriedly walked through her front door. She went straight up the curving staircase to the second level which housed Gracie's bedroom, Gracie's playroom, her own office, and a guest room. The master suite was on the main floor. As she walked past an oval-gilded frame mirror, she glanced at her reflection. Not a hair out of place. She went into the guest room and climbed onto the four-poster canopy bed she found at an estate sale, fulfilling her childhood princess fantasy.

Not more than a breath later, he was there. At the door. In the room. On the bed. On her.

\*\*\*

That was the last time she let him into her home.

For the next month she thought about how she had ended up here – thirty-seven, in the best shape of her life, plenty of money, a beautiful child, a handsome husband, and pregnant. Evan was as much to blame as she—of that Violet was certain. They had celebrated their seventh anniversary earlier that year with champagne and a Tiffany bracelet while sipping Veuve Clicquot. (#BubblyOnOurAnni #OnlyTheBestForMyMan) Evan casually suggested they "keep things fresh and exciting" by inviting an additional partner to their bed. To show that he wasn't looking for an excuse to be with another woman, he offered that it be a man. "For you," he said.

Violet surprised herself with how fast she agreed. Evan was sexy. He was successful. He was a good father. They had their woes like any other married couple, and they certainly weren't *swinging* from the chandeliers like they had in their twenties, but overall, life was good. Easy. Enviable to those outside looking in. So when he proposed the idea and she said yes, it gave her pause.

*Were they unhappy?*

*Was he bored with her?*

No, she decided. They were a cosmopolitan couple who

understood that happy marriages were not boring marriages.

It happened fast. It was exciting. Violet relished the attention from two gorgeous men, proving, in her own mind, that desire had nothing to do with age. The original plan was for him to come into their lives for a night, spark passion in the bedroom, and then disappear into the background, never to be spoken of again.

Violet had not followed the plan.

***

Another month went by during which nothing changed in their lives. Violet went to church and taught Sunday school every week. She hosted girls' night for the moms in Gracie's class, an evening of canapes and cocktails that put Shelia to shame. She made love to her husband at least three times a week. All the while, she carried around her little secret growing in size through a poppyseed, a raspberry, a plum. *#MommysHidingSomething.*

The morning she woke up and slipped into her Dolce & Gabbana Jeans only to realize she could no longer button them over her slightly protruding belly, she knew her time was up.

Until that point, Violet mostly didn't think about it. She took the situation off the shelf every now and again, held it in her hands, and viewed it from different angles, inevitably putting it away with no solution in mind. It was cut and dry as far as she was concerned – making it go away was not an option. Violet was a believer that what you did in this life counted toward whatever came after. She wasn't about to give up her ticket to *The Good Place.* And it would be a cold day in hell before she ever admitted how that little plum got into her belly.

Doors one and two were both firmly closed. It took her another week, but Violet finally figured out the key to door number three.

***

The front door closed softly. She heard Evan drop his keys on the entry table and stride through to the kitchen where she waited. Gracie was going to his parents' house for the night. Violet found a poetic justice in this conversation happening between the two of them over a glass of champagne (#DateNight #MyMan #ThankfulForGrampsAndGran), even if she only pretended to drink it.

"Hi handsome," she said, smile in place as she handed him a bubbling glass.

"Where's yours?" Evan asked. He leaned over and kissed her cheek, accepting the glass at the same time. As he loosened the tie around his neck, he visibly relaxed. Investment banking was lucrative but also incredibly demanding. "What's the occasion?"

"Sit down, tell me about your day." Violet deflected the question, not ready to answer yet.

"You know, the usual. Kicking ass and taking names." He grinned. This was normal foreplay between them. She thrived on his success. He thrived on her craving for it. On a regular date night, banter like this would lead them to the bedroom before the dinner table.

Evan moved around the island as he said it, slipping strong arms around her waist and nuzzling her neck. Violet tensed, worried that he would feel the slight roundness of her middle that had popped up overnight.

"Not quite yet, babe. We need to talk." She gently slipped from his arms and stepped back a few paces to put some space between them.

He didn't speak. Only looked at her blankly. Violet wasn't sure if she had ever said the words "we need to talk" to him before. They didn't talk. They performed.

"I'm pregnant."

Evan's face lit up with delight, then dropped in confusion, then settled on some form of resentment. It took less than a second.

"How?" He spat the word at her. Evan radiated confidence in the most stressful of situations, often to her irritation. For a moment, she saw it slip.

"Do I really need to answer that question? Do you really want me to say it out loud? To ruin all this," Violet flung her arm out in a large sweep, "for a mistake you brought into our lives?"

Evan followed the path of her arm. His chiseled cheek twitched, the only sign he felt anything. He knew as well as she that the answer to that simple question could bring it all crashing down around them."But…people would know. Our friends, our family, our church. What will they think if we announce you're pregnant?"

"If we keep a united front, *nobody* ever has to know." He blinked slowly, digesting her words. As the enormity of the situation hit, he deflated like a balloon two weeks after the party.

"It's our lives, our story. We decide how to tell it. Nobody would ever question us. Not if we stick together." Taking a deep breath, she relaxed her facial muscles. She would not allow worry lines to crease her forehead over this.

"Now, it's up to you. What are we going to do?" Violet folded her hands together, as if in prayer, then lowered them to her lap.

Time froze. Evan had the power to ruin them. Their fate was in his hands. If he didn't agree, the people she loved would turn against her. Including her daughter.

"You won't ever see him again?" Evan might be a pretty boy whose looks got him where he was in life, but he was nobody's fool.

She knew this was the most important moment of her acting career as wife. If he didn't believe in her, in them, it was all over.

"I haven't seen him since the day the pregnancy test turned positive." That much was true. That she had seen him *after* the test, well, Evan didn't need to know that.

She waited.

He looked at her, unblinking.

She looked back, unsmiling.

She watched him war with his desire to be admired against his feelings of inadequacy as a husband. Deep down, she knew. She knew which side would win out.

"Fine. I'm in. What do we have to do?"

She nodded once and got up to retrieve her phone from the docking station. Over her shoulder she saw Evan, now decided, sipping his champagne, relaxed, in his chair. He would assume the narrative so quickly that, from this point forward, it would be as if this conversation never happened.

Violet brought her phone, and the pregnancy test with those two pink lines standing at attention, over to her husband. She settled herself into his lap. Held the selfie stick up in one hand. The pregnancy test in the other.

"Smile," she commanded. She didn't have to look to know he had. She felt it down to her soul.

***

Chiming Instagram notifications woke Violet from a deep sleep. Their picture had already been liked 4,997 times since she posted it not even twelve hours ago. She smiled in anticipation of the congratulations she'd surely received overnight.

#ChangeofHeart #ReverseVasectomyBaby #ReadMyBlogForOurFertilityJourneyAt37

Evan snored softly from somewhere to her left in their oversized-king platform bed. She stretched long, low, and feline-like with appreciation as her naked skin slid across the Egyptian cotton sheets. Rolling over on her back, one hand cupping the tiny swell of her belly, Violet began responding to her followers.

# Revolution
By Wolf S. Helms

A man named Howard Korsakoff stood upon the tail-gate of a pickup truck within a large warehouse. Workers stood around him in solemn slouching arcs, their emaciation apparent. This was the revolution's second step, the first was getting into the warehouse.

The process of getting in had primarily consisted of the crumpling nose of the old pickup and tearing free its mirrors whilst coating the driver in small amounts of glass which was broken loose from the window. The guards stationed outside the rollup door fled upon seeing the truck with its unsafe speed and trajectory, they neglected to return after they had been beaten by knots of bludgeon-wielding factory workers. The guards had a chance to draw their pistols before placing them in postures, yet they would have been incapable of defending themselves. Even if they had shot before being surrounded in the first place, they would not have had enough bullets to take the lives of the eager men, women, and children of the iron works all willing to take a few blasts of hot lead to nobly exempt them from any future work.

This man, Howard Korsakoff, was known to most of the persons there as being an eighteen-wheeler driver. This was how he had learned of the cache of weapons within the warehouse. It was also why he was wearing adequate protection from the subzero weather of the city, whilst the other workers swathed themselves in whatever material they could find as they jogged in place to attempt to attain warmth.

Howard began, "We all know what feats of technology have been produced in the West: computers capable of managing paperwork, ordering necessary equipment, and supplying statistics, mechanical equipment called 'robots'. What does this suggest? That we are at the point of the ancient Marxist system of economics at which point non-restrictive communism or socialism should be instituted to lift the burdens from our shoulders and help us enjoy our lives instead of continuing to work with the capitalist system we have now, in which we are the majority, thrust down by those rich people who have slips of paper stating their ownership of shit! We the people begin step two, removing the government forcibly due to their inactivity. The time of working with them has been rebuked by their infernal old-minded mindsets. Let them burn!"

As he looked across the warehouse at the crowd, Howard continued, "The first row contains MP-P-3 millimeter light plasma repeating guns, contact barrels, and no guards, so the coolant systems are exposed, so watch yourselves. In the third, I believe, there are several kinds of grenades ranging from common fragmentation to the brand-new fusion sticks which have seven-second fuses and an indication bar light showing their timer. The seven seconds may be extended due to the cold. I don't know what else is in the other crates, but feel free to check. Thank you for saving the generations to come from slaving away when it is entirely unnecessary."

Howard jumped down with a crowbar in hand and began

assisting in opening the crates. He selected one of the aforementioned plasma guns from a box and filled a satchel with several hydrogen tanks. The gun he chose was modeled off the MP-40, but with a much wider body and longer barrel with outwards fluted muzzle. The entire barrel was surrounded by cooling fins and a triad of metal fins mounted to a rotating ring which surrounded the barrel and acted as the weapon's fan,

He forced one of the canister's nozzles into the lowest section of the rear grip, just as you would a $CO_2$ tank attached to a Tipmen 98. Howard snapped off the safety and a small fusion reactor within the rearmost section of the body began to heat up, filling with ionized hydrogen before its Gatling-gun-like mechanism began. The fusion commenced providing torque in the manner of a, well if I wish to patent this I suppose there is no point to suggest methods to my competition. Suffice it to say, the instrument was fully powered. Its boar began to leak steam from within until all the liquid was eliminated from within the body, as the entire firing mechanism began to warm.

Someone shouted the enemies were forming a circumference of the building, and thus, the third step unfolded. Everyone placed their guns in the direction of the wall which had been painted with a red can of spray paint. An order was given to fire and over fifty weapons left a scorched ring in the wall with a center that had become devoid of metal. It was filled with revolutionaries in a crouch allowing the persons behind them to fire over their heads. Streams of red and white plasma spewed forth forcing the few loyal soldiers back and some opposing shots to be fired, yet none were well aimed. The persons in the revolutionary army rapidly filed out in a line ten wide. Those on the outer edges fired into nearby streets to prevent any fool from attempting to break cover without thinking twice and deserting for safer waters. When their guns began to run low of fuel, they stepped into the center of the line with others taking their place.

This way, there was nearly no resistance between them, in their slow methodical march through the factory sector, into the rich sections of the city where houses were ignited and cars scorched.

The target was apparent, a large structure constructed in the ancient Grecian style, which held the five-man executive counsel of the country. Was there no resistance, no, but the resistance figuratively and physically melted away as they approached. That was until they entered a space directly between two large imposing houses of two of the executives. Both of the homes were constructed from marble and sandstone, producing a wall the plasma guns could not penetrate. Someone threw a few fusion grenades and their hot plasmas were induced to fuse with the sudden, great constriction of their container. The total mass of the gasses issued forth was lesser than were originally contained, yet the concussion was immense and masonry fell sporadically.

Somewhere a bell tolled off its hour and munitions flooded the street. Howard was struck in the ankle by a bolt, melting through his flesh and charring his bone to an extent that, upon falling, the appendage tore free, without his realizing its absence, for the pain persisted as if there was no notable damage.

Howard rolled over, withdrawing his gun from beneath him, and attempted to sit up, but the pain was too great. He lay on the ground firing in whichever direction the enemy bolts came from. The pain was not what subsided, but it was eliminated partly by adrenaline. As the old saying goes, intimacy breeds contempt.

When Howard reached his feet, he saw the carnage of struck and burned bodies. Soldiers picked through the ruins, firing upon all who were yet alive. A soldier beside him looked up from his grueling work and saw Howard, which was his death warrant. After that, Howard began firing indiscriminately in a swelling arc before falling upon his back. He continued his arc to make a three-hundred-and-sixty-degree arc of fire cutting down all around him, thanks to there not being near cover, or having time to redirect their aim rapidly enough to fire after they had notated their danger, Howard was the last man on the battlefield.

Whether by luck or cosmic jest, he would never know, for luck doesn't talk and the cosmos was, and will always be, devoid of meaningful answers explicitly stated allowing any individual to put together inconsequentially to produce evidence for any thought they could ever contain.

Howard refused to be held down by his injury but continued slowly walking toward the greater location. A soldier stepped from around a corner, gun raised, and prepared to fire with a perfect bead upon the exposed man in the middle of a broad thoroughfare. The soldier fired, and yet his plasma struck an obstruction in the form of a body wearing a black cloak, leaning upon a cane in the form of a baseball bat, the upper end being the one held. The baseball bat itself was prodigious. The shoulder of the body either belied the size of the person within or the person was a hunched-over giant with a minimum height of twelve feet. The obstructed plasma spread out and dissipated the same way water would, for plasma acted as a compressible liquid upon the macro scale and a gas upon the particulate scale.

The figure smoothly took three steps, nearing the soldier, and stood straight, yanking upwards upon the bat and sliding its black-gloved hand along the shaft, until the knob at the base of the instrument was reached. The full height was assuredly of twelve feet. The bat, with its prodigious size, was a mere child's toy in the hands of its master who brought it down in a sudden, powerful arc whilst also losing four feet to its accustomed hunch. The metal instrument shattered the soldier's cold steel helmet and blew the material of the man's skull and brain in all directions, continuing down, obviously shattering the spine. The bat warped and folded, whiplike into a form where the head of the weapon seemingly punctured the man's rib cage from behind. The figure within the cloak then released the bat. Howard suddenly didn't wish to see what entity was before him as a hand clasped his shirt. He was drawn through a place of stars and space.

The creature did not turn, yet Howard fell, not knowing what was reality, as a hand clasped his shirt. He was drawn through a place of stars and space, into a place where only the sun ruled, beating down through clouds, and blasting itself into the sands. An Aryan man waited before him holding a large needle and a surgical saw. A computer sat upon a folding table next to a mass of small filaments, all connected to needles and various other implements. To those who don't understand, neurosurgery was about to commence, in the form of the implementation of long sought-after additions to the human body, which would only result in the exhaustive revisitation of conspiracy theories. The wind susurrated and a shadow fell, leaving only the sight of two large red eyes as if Howard was looking into a void that dug its claws deep into his mind, leaving no need for the neurosurgical devices, though they would still be implemented for better notation of actions, the true finesse had commenced even before the shadow fell or the desert world became the reality.

It, with only nominal assistance, took a minimal amount of time to turn one man's wish for a fundamental and fair society to transform him into what was effectively a gardener of humanity, culling entire planets due to their "unredeemability" in the sideways servitude of an organization, Howard was not aware of, and would not have been capable of comprehending, due to its sheer magnitude. In most places, he was pleased with his higher grades of technology, but his disgust with the rich and privileged led to slaughters upon the battlefields between his woefully unequipped men and his adversaries far smaller, yet better equipped, men. He was a total success, for those who removed his sins of defeat, knowledge of his prior conditions leaving only his emotion to drive him ineffectively off a cliff into the oblivion of being subservient, through a great dream, to those who wished only to conquer, create something far stronger, only to break it down for entertainment.

\*\*\*

### Author's Note:

This narrative was partially based up on the Russian and French Revolutions.

# Corrosion
By Wolf S. Helms

I regret needing to add this notation even before my next, but this is an important detail. This story is written in an archaic manner which demands much of the reader's attention in piecing together details as if they were attempting to solve a mystery, though they are obtaining the information which the narrator's companion already knows. You, due to you not being capable of actually fulfilling the character's role, must deduce the information yourself. Furthermore, the narrator, by necessity of the narrative, is the kind of person who feels it necessary to recount every happening immediately to the person next to him. I hope you enjoy it.

For those who wish to neglect the notation feel free to continue with the next two paragraphs, which merely include locality without notable action. Otherwise, there will be only negligible losses in understanding, which will be alleviated - theoretically - before the end of the narrative. This bypasses this sidestepping of contemplation:

The narrator sat in what was effectively a U-shaped outdoor auditorium, formed of wood with crude, cast iron nails suggestive of the the early date of the narrative. Though its existence was permitted through nonsingular means, suggesting - temporarily, all bets are off.

A hangman's noose upon a platform stood at the center of the U-shape just before the position where the stage would typically have been constructed. The clothing was approximately that which would be found in an Arthur Conan Doyle book, though there were a few cloaked figures included.

"Ah, Sir, I recall sitting alongside you during that fateful trial of the man who will soon find himself on the gallows platform. You were a witness to your uncle's demise? Well, I am right, so sorry to hear. Though I assume, since it was so long ago, all wounds are as nearly healed as they ever will be. I must say, slaying his own tutor of the rapier, foul and low. And I was even a witness as to his digging your skull up when I awakened knowing something-"

"You refute my 'fictionalization' and demand that I 'confine any speech I make to a purely analytical and strictly scientific air.' Well, fine then.

"When I was awakened, presumably by my obnoxious dog's barking or presumably at a noise my damn horses made in their sleep, I went to my window with a candle. I intended to open it and shout at my dog to, 'shut the hell up,' yet, that attempt entirely failed.

"I dropped the candle on the wooden flooring upon seeing the sight from the window, in an act of providence which burned my foot whilst perhaps saving my face from a revolver shot. For I saw one of those revolutionary weapons, in a holster, at one of the men's hips. He was an abnormally large, broad-shouldered, tall man, perhaps a monstrous eight and a half feet in height, just above that of your uncle's by the half.

Thus, tallying almost exactly to the man soon to step

upon the gallows platform. My eyes were not quite awake at that time, and so the inconsequential inconsistency was readily explained.

"He was wearing a very bulky and flowing pair of cloaks which seemed to have been formed of an ornamental shawl, like priests wore, placed under a large, almost floor length - it most certainly brushed the close-cropped grass, with an out- ward flow produced by the wind. The fancy priest's hood was up, but the other was flowing outward from an undercurrent of wind.

"As I said, that holstered pistol was strapped to an ornate leather, gold cord wrought belt, peculiarly looped around the body with the end becoming two strands. One strand was draped over the holster, while the other was tied in a knot holding the holster. The other tail in perfect rigidness in an ornate fashion. The men were in the church laying yard, on the other side of the street from my bedroom window, and they had the grave of your uncle upturned. One of the three normal-sized bruisers, that is to say, big and strong but not a giant like your uncle and the man we will see hung soon, stood on your uncle's very coffin and threw loose dirt out of the hole with a small shovel.

"After a while, one man handed down a long crowbar which another positioned so the coffin lid could be forced open before climbing out of the hole. With a crack I easily heard; it broke open. Thank God the preacher is nearly stone deaf, or he would have been slain assuredly, either by the pistol of the brute or by his accursed sword to which many thousands of honest men have fallen.

"The lid was drawn fully open and some of the men looked in before one of them jumped down and lifted the corpse, and its sword, from the casket. The sword appeared corroded and clotted with some black material of some hellish form of degradation wrought by the charnel atmosphere, hiding the once gleaming metal and standing out thickly along the thin blade and handle. Your uncle's scabbard was still attached to his body by that stoutest of belts, which he always wore into battle over his chain mail in all his gallantry. Peculiar how he carried a weapon of finesse instead of a heavy, armor-cleaving blade.

"A moment later, I saw the pistol sweep from its holster and two shots rang out in the dark, leaving the two men out of the tomb dead on the ground. The prisoner suddenly knelt, forcing the other man's hand around the pistol and using his finger to pull the trigger, placing a third slug within the unfortunate's skull, before dropping the arm and gun, both of which fell solidly into the coffin, whose lid clapped down upon its new occupant in a deadly comic manner.

"You mislike my jest… A new humanist thinker, are you? I should have known with your excessive disdain for traditional superstitions.

"Well, somehow that evil man disappeared with the sword of your uncle without my noticing. Funny, I don't think he had a scabbard or sword apart from the wreck that became of your uncle's. Perhaps he lost his old one and needed a tried-and-true blade. Hellish dog!"

We ceased our speaking as we stood before the crowd in a great open-roofed theater that normally never saw anything but a mock execution but had been borrowed due to the magnitude of the crimes the man committed. He was known to have committed over seven hundred sixty-three murders among the longest list of thefts that anyone had ever seen over a criminal career spanning twenty years. Though unlawful dueling seemed to be his prevue with sixty confirmed cases of his hunting down and dueling the greatest fighters of the world, allegedly to prevent them from being amassed to slay him instead. It had taken several days for him to admit to every single one of the accusations read off of the list, thus nullifying any need for a fair trial which would have only allied with the noose's hunger being satiated with the pale neck of the greatest bandit who ever lived.

"His swordplay was, is unmatched. All those foes who had come against him with great sword and full armor had fallen by the wayside, with a swift puncture by the infinitely dexterous sword of the master swordsman the links of chainmail were split and bodies bled. His weapon was capable of easily breaking the links in chain mail when its point was forced inwards but, with the greater need for mobility caused by peace. His blade only needed to pierce leather armor or be jabbed through the visor of a foe's helm.

"When an equal weapon and a man thought to have equal skill stepped before him, he slew them with infinite suddenness and proficiency. The width of the blade, though not the length, made it seem as if he were welding a toothpick. By my evidence, it was also proven that he was a brilliant shot, outclassing anyone else ever seen.

"Here he comes, we can hear the mocking even from his guards. Aha. See, it takes four knights in shining armor to bring a single, bound man to the gallows. The creaking of the steps is audible even over the tumultuous noise of the crowd shrieking for the brute's doom.

"What, the, hell? Did you see that?! A man just appeared amidst the knights, with garb identical to that ghoul I saw! Is this the man himself come to save his double with some necromantic cloak of invisibility? I swear that is how he got about, never mind science.

"What did he just do? That suggestive flash of silver of the prisoner's own blade welded as if the stranger were faster than the prisoner.

"Well shit! All four knights have fallen with blood leaking from helms and beneath their chest plates. Those were masterful thrusts I must say, slipping upwards with the immense strength of the man's hidden legs, driving the flexible, yet well-organized, point into the chainmail in a manner that warps and then breaks the first and only link that must be broken before reaching the target. Only a skilled wielder of the blade could manage such a thing too many times without snapping the blade as the foe fell. What are they saying? All I hear is silence as the cloaked figure holds up one finger in his black-gloved hand for silence.

"I never heard that voice before, growling, fluid, guttural, and jaggedly drawling with a lisp upon all words, requiring the lips come into contact with the teeth or perform any action apart from the most basic of openness or its antonym, 'Trever, I absolve you from the penalty which confronts you, yet at a price; you must tax my skills or I will draw you to whence I come. Through the vortex, which these three moons you call planets orbit, whilst also orbiting a planet I know as "Joul-par-tar" and you call the "Land of Dreams." If I must draw you thither, beyond the rim of the vortex and deep within unto my world, you will know not for I will perform things unto your body and mind that would force you to wish to be hung a thousand, billion times over. Hung with a rope made of the thinnest of cables. Your garments of pins and needles, all being battered against your body by vindictive and rightfully vengeful men, in spite of the disturbance of the grave of your slain master not being your action. Which did not necessarily prove I had misaccused him.'

"With the conclusion of this speech, the challenger stuck the ex-prisoner's rapier through his bindings, severing them before driving its point deep into the boards of the gallows platform.

"What did Trever begin saying? 'I would wish to see the face of my challenger before stripping it of its flesh'? Ha, pathetic stalling, before the clank of his sword being jerked free by his hands pierced our and everyone else's ears with that carrying pitch of a warbling, singing blade.

"'I hope your ambitions carry through young man.' ha

ha, how stereotypical."

"As the necromancer drew back the dark blue hood of his priest-like robe, eliciting a gasp from all the people in the room, Trever released a shriek. Trever turned and fled, bloody coward, swinging his sword wildly around him as he stumbled down the steps four at a time. The necromancer's head was revealed to be that of a night-colored wolf or demon.

"You say it must have come through the portal from Hell and do not recall the fact any necromancer can assume any form he wishes. No? You believe transfiguration is not possible, though telekinesis, as we witness now, is obviously proven. Good god man! The necromancer just lifted Trever from the steps and forced him back onto the platform as he swept back his over cloak to disclose the same belt and draw a, a, a, O God. I falsely accused a man, a criminal man, but yet I falsely accused him. Oh God, please help me out of my catholic plight. Oh, I bemoan my not being a protestant without the necessity of work and the ability to atone for every evil action I commit! That is the corroded blade I saw that bestial necromancer jerk from your dead and rotten uncle's hand and, God! That beast could have slain your uncle as well and not this wrongly accused Trever. No one saw the deed and Trever fled with a sword corresponding to the one used to kill the great man.

"The demonic entity is speaking in its hellish, unnatural, and assumed tones once again, 'When I found your master inferior to my desires, I told you to learn from his mistakes and practice, so that I would not have to punish you when I returned for my sparing match with you. You tried to get out quickly without committing suicide to adhere to your more brutal religion of the night, and yet escape my test of your talents when I yearn, so for a fight which truly taxes me, and if you could slay me, I would be infinitely content. For you would have burst the thoughts of self-superiority over all living things which are forming now though, you must understand that you can never make me stay dead.'

"Holy god on high! Keep it down before that necromantic beast comes for us next. If that thing is telling the truth, it slew the greatest swordsman who ever lived, and this poor Trever, who was slaying in fear of his own life, yet perhaps is even still inferior to his first master. In the time that was left between the exiting and reentry of that witness of the murder of that master, the fight was so evilly short. We are screwed if you open your mouth again, especially insulting the creature's necromantic abilities. Now quiet, and let me watch the fight which may well be the last fight any of us here may see.

"Trever ceased to look hesitant and is now ready to put up a fight, crossing blades against that resurrected one of your uncle's. A brief clack. The new swordsman repulsed Trever's first swing with the angle of the guard and the blade before demanding more from this defender by sliding the blunt side of the sword down Trever's body from shoulder to the inner side of his left knee, striping some of the black mass free from the armament disclosing the most gorgeous of undamaged of silver edges. Another clack from a parry forced by Trever, before the challenger powers through and taps the tip against his foe's ankle, indicating the damage he could have done. He thrusted Trever away to stumble against the lever which released the trap doors in the floor before almost falling in himself. That push caught him off guard but gave him the anger necessary to actually fight, a foe he was deeply scared of, in reminiscence of his master, and in vengeance for his loss.

"The briefest of flurries of silver against a barely moving black blade as its corruption was removed by a ringing concussion. The challenger seemed to be using the brutal attacks, not just to make the sword gleam but to furthermore sharpen its tip upon the blade of his foe's sword, in a shocking series of dexterous motions before forcing the offensive in an attempt to prompt his foe's improvement of form and methodology.

"Now for every two clacks of the challenger's peculiar methods of nonchalant and rapid blocking, there was a loud reverberant clang of Trever's sword being used to deflect a brutal spontaneous motion of the challenger.

"A shocking flurry suddenly abounded, bringing Trever's garment down to an extreme, near indecency, caused by the challenger's deftest of careless, effortless motions with a blade which seemed amply sharp enough without any more additions to the edge's potency. The most shocking thing was there was not a drop of blood spilled by the onslaught.

"A new offensive by Trever rapidly began to force slightly greater motions by the challenger's sword until the necromancer was fully forced to move the tip from the near vertical it had been to obstruct, a hacking slash made for the challenger's legs. The challenger, even then though, was acting as if he had the least of concerns until he nonchalantly began to skin the man alive, still standing, still capable of landing blows, and still capable of blocking, among other things, which seemed to be the demand of the attack. Each slash produced another inch of expertly removed skin hanging from the remainder.

"A desperate continuation ensued before the challenger cleanly gutted the boy without puncturing any of the organs, save the already ruined integument, and began the process of Trever's bleeding out as the challenger removed the meat from between Trever's ribs, puncturing both lungs, and felling his foe, but until the very second Trever's heart ceased to still feebly beat and blood ceased to feebly trickle from the wounds the once corroded blade had inflicted the precise cleaning of the bones which continued even extending to the scalping of the skull and the complete removal of the face.

"Upon completion of the challenger's task, he looked

at the blade and began, 'This relic belongs in a museum after its last contemptible battle. My threat was not idle, and yet I have not tortured this man, for I know two things: he had a kind heart and he was doing his best towards the last, thus, I will answer my threat not so much physically to the man, but physically in all actuality and spiritually with such an entity retains the ability to witness occurrences instead of merely remaining idly as an abnormally shaped sphere of energy and material matter cannot effect or be effected by.'

"Granted, I am about to break my own advisory, or order to you, with my outburst of, 'What the hell do you mean and be damned once you answer," to your obvious feelings of consternation.'

"The necromancer laughed at me, the jackass, 'I am going to accelerate these three moon's orbits just as the others, as I empower the vortex until a balance is reached and yet there is enough gravity to suck away the atmospheres of your world and actually rip free portions of your moons. Though the husks will eventually lose enough matter to the vortex, which acts as a sun to your worlds, providing illumination and heat whilst instead being created by the working together of the six moons, for it to decline. I will in essence cause the means to your life to be sucked out of your reach into the mock atmosphere that is the vortex and begin the process of causing these moons to all eventually escape their orbits, close the vertex, and let them fly spinning off into the deepest, darkness of space where they belong.

"And with that, our adversary disappeared. We both looked up through the open ceiling to see the vortex suddenly grow larger and faster as the land of dreams began to whirl around at a visible rate. We all screamed for we knew that old law of the necromancer: They can never lie. It takes a mortal to care to lie, whilst the necromancer is so powerful that lying feels boring and is so unnecessary that their abilities to effectively do so are nullified with disuse. He said our planet, or moon, would lose its atmosphere in some distant age, only measured by the necromancer, from an elder eons older other world would be shattered."

# The Drumming Man
By Wolf S. Helms

It was a cold night, five years after World War I in a small town called Innsmouth. It's being the predecessor to that abhorrent location produced by H. P. Lovecraft in *Shadow Over Innsmouth*.

This small, decadent town had no resident with blood ties to any beast of the sea, nor was its bountiful harbor induced to bountifulness by intelligent amphibious vermin, but natural phenomenon, yet the drumbeat sounded hollow from afar. It permeated the night with darkening power.

The unknown drummer beat his insistent army poundings into the night with unvarying precision. His impacts were accompanied by disappearances with statistics suggesting those not tied to their bedframes were most likely to vanish. Whilst the very young and old were nearly exempt. None knew the reasons the unknown drummer beat, nor why every night with a new moon he did, people disappeared.

Though there were exceptions where none were taken. While the people of Innsmouth tied themselves down, three old men sat around a hearth fire, within a library, unbound. One possessed a revolver, which was slipped into his pocket. It had one empty chamber for safety he had said.

The drums had not yet sounded, for the night not yet descended upon the town, which hung in decrepitude within the swampy lands just west of Devil's Reef. Many a ship had sunk and disappeared into the unfathomable depths on the seaward side of that accursed chunk of porous rock, which became a quasi-island upon an exceedingly low tide.

One theory as to why the drumming man plagued the place was because his vessel had struck Devil's Reef and sunk with him before he could return to steal the children. Particularly children of any persons who could have built a lighthouse to protect him and other persons who could and would eventually meet their fate upon the reef.

The three old men continued to read as one of them glanced up sporadically at the skyline, paying close attention to the potential for devastation.

Soon this man said, "It is about to begin again," eliciting no response from the others, but setting them at rest, for it was the thing he had said countless times before.

When the first shot went off the pair across from the man, who had been watching the horizon, jumped, one with blood pouring from his chest, the lack of a click proving the one man a liar, whilst the other clutched his book to his chest before attempting to flee.

The second round placed him back within his chair, though, before the last light of the sun in the sky began to rapidly wane and disappear from the man's lap, where his dusty copy of ancient text lay, blood leaking upon its peculiarly thin, dark, leather cover, which seemed to greedily soak up the viscous material into the pages and bindings. A mere fifteen minutes later, the drums began to beat ominously in the distance.

A tall, dark-skinned man in dark blue military dress with a large drum strapped to his chest appeared. The man's uniform was pristine, his eyes glowing white from within, and determined the drumming man extracted the old man's inner workings, producing an intonation of endless sadness within a string of slowly spoken words. This induced the old man to draw his gun anew and fire upon the drummer, yet even as the drummer spoke, every chamber clicked empty in spite of them all containing loads.

"You have committed acts and plan to commit more," said the drumming man.

And with the completion of the intonation, the drummer disappeared. All of the chambers clicked upon fired in a manner that caused two of the rounds to lodge between their individual chambers and the frame of the gun inducing an explosion that ripped backward and flung shrapnel into the old man's right hand and left side, eliciting a slow viscous flow of blood.

The old man could no longer hold his gun. Regardless, it would have meant nothing even if he could retain the grip, for it was ruined. Besides, the tangible apparition had promptly vanished.

The old man lifted the candelabra, which he had been reading by the light of, and proceeded from the library. He had intended to find assistance from one of the persons he had planned to kill, and the plan had not changed, but only grown more complicated.

When the door creaked open, he expected to see the drummer standing there with some malicious purpose. Unsure of whether it be to him or his victims, he had not fully decided. Only the landscape met him, yet it was not wholly the landscape he knew, yet he somehow recognized every detail.

The hills seemed oddly fuzzy and the landscape slightly darker, even for a new moon night. Thus, the old man took off his reading glasses in hopes that his superb long vision would be capable of perceiving what was so wrong with the hills. He found every tree of every kind devoid of leaves. The old man dropped his gaze to the grass at either side of the path and saw only darkened blades, but when he brushed at them, they crumbled. As if dried out for all of eternity, or as if the entire world had been sucked dry.

The drums were unrivaled in the spaces and yet, his turn to the ocean elicited a sight of the most crystalline and calm of waters which were nonetheless dead. Normally such a sight would be gratifying.

Resigned, the old man walked toward the doctor and opened the door, knowing it would have to be unlocked to allow his entrance in the morning. The doctor was not within, but the band of cable to bind her to her bedpost was absent of the occupant, yet tightly tied as if with fear and proficiency.

With the knowledge he could not find any life to sadistically raze or obtain assistance from, the old man touched the candelabrum to the curtains, and even these, with their perfect dryness, were dead and refused to catch.

The old man sat upon the physician's bed and lay back, dying of blood loss, knowing that he was gone and wondered: would his bones lie in this form of hell or would they turn to dust to cover the floor of the room?

The next morning and afternoon, people in the town found themselves still not free. They were in need of a child's salvation due to their ability to slip free of their bonds. They rescued their parents who then commenced freeing the other persons of the town. After that task was completed, they found the dead men in the library. Their blood spattered upon the books they had been reading.

It was seen that one had been reading a battered copy of *Borealis*, bound in the skin of an African man. Shortly after, they were interred with the people's assumption the drumming man had changed tack and shot two of the men as he attempted to disappear. The other assumption, though, was endless tales of the drumming man disappearing random persons before the eyes of other people and never being seen. The question went unasked, for it was assumed the supernatural acted in illogical ways. Whilst, what is magic but unexplained science?

The town's people all vowed they would no longer permit the drumming man to pose a threat, and thus they marched in a devastating swarm. With fire, ax, and revolver with wood to construct a pier for the unknown man. They later marched toward the sounds of the drums on the next new moon.

The way was long, yet they found themselves upon a crag-like hill with trees receding from a central well. From it putridity flowed from which lifelessness expanded in the form of brown or even blackened grass. Several persons attempted to look into the well but were driven back or felled by the fumes. One man threw his well-made torch into the space. This somehow produced a violent flash from below as fire rose from within before subsiding to the powerful drumbeats, obviously coming from deep within the encircled well.

Impact after impact rained until a tall drummer, who appeared a pale and exceedingly strong, soldierly African American, stood upon the lip of the well, eyes glowing white. His military haircut glinted in the flickering torch light, actually overpowered by the light of an electric flashlight.

"You have come with one group purpose: murder. I ask you why. As a man slain, what does this bring to your infernal hearts?" Asked the drumming man.

And once again, he disappeared, leaving only the beats of his drum. These base impacts did not rise from a location but were all pervadingly omnipresent and seemingly omnipotent. Only bones stood around the well, all holding their weapons or lights and shouting angrily or with great fear at one another.

There were cries over the certainty that the skeleton's children would be left orphaned or that their ailing parents would die of the lack of protection. Most commonly, they screamed with the certainty that they were in the land of feinds and would die of hunger, thirst, or the poisoning of the waters which they saw putridly not to flow within the stagnant air around them.

Still, the drumbeats hammered on everlastingly powerful and irrevocably devastating as they rose to a crescendo; with the time when commonly clocks struck 7 a.m. when the sun rose above the skyline, and yet only greater darkness came to those trapped within the drumming man's spell.

At that same approximate time, the mail truck arrived and found the environs abnormally quiet. For normally there would have been other vehicles driving along the streets or horses being used to draw their carriages and drivers on errands of archaic import.

Soon, the mailman applied his brakes and slowed the truck before cutting off its engine to sit in the peculiar silence. He tried to understand the meaning of the absolute deadness. Shortly, he heard the shouting of an unknown person from within a house. When it had driven itself into the mailman's already rankled nerves, he vacated his vehicle and hammered upon the door eliciting only cries for help.

The mailman took two long strides back before charging and driving both polished boot heels into the door directly beside the handle in an attempt to rip out the jam. The door failed to give much and the man fell back upon the hard-packed ground. He realized he should first have rattled the handle. He stood from his position and did so to find it unlocked. He gained easy admittance.

The mailman found a child shrieking over the presumed theft of his mother by the drumming man. The mailman took the child out to his van and restarted its engine before peeling out for the fire department, in the absence of a police department. Only to find there was no one in attendance, but a phone line was available.

The mailman called for the police from a neighboring town. It took two hours to free the children from their bonds, after which a search began.

It was quickly noticed that a fire was rising from a high hill north of the town. After examination started and concluded, once the fire was put out with the use of several engines and aid of the cold dampness of winter to quench the fire, warped and blackened instruments were found randomly dropped around a low well, which was untouched. No one could understand what had occurred, yet they felt it their duty to dig out whatever was within the well with its particularly warm draft of abnormally sickly-sweet smell.

Once the bottom of the well was dug out to a slight extent, the brass fittings for a drum were found. After that, a body. An autopsy was performed finding the man had been brutally stabbed in the back a multitude of times. All of which had left obvious marks upon the skeleton of the nearly decayed man.

After further investigation, the man was found to have the name of Calihan C. Ford and had disappeared shortly after a military precession on the heels of the victory in Europe. It appeared he had been murdered and dumped within the well, but the connection to the disappearances and to the dead drummer was deemed non-existent in spite of the children's grim tales of the man who drummed in the night. The moral, normally, was to never be naughty, though in this instance it was, "Tie oneself to the bedpost and hope he doesn't come for you in spite of the greater difficulty."

These disappearances were the reason Lovecraft wrote his story some fifteen years later. Though, he was drastically wrong. Yet, his narrative was ample and wording well organized with precise detailing as to potential actions of the persons included in the narrative. There was no mention of any person of African descent, primarily due to the fact racism on that day was too great to place the two pieces of particular information on the front page, in spite of the connections. Placing the more important one, to understanding the secondary, was nearly omitted entirely and only saved by an empty space on the last page, as stated, due to the prejudiced ideology of the era.

# Sensitive People
By Devora Gray

I have a splinter in my toe.

My body sends signals: Foreign. Invader. Reject.

I'm looking for the pinprick of dark matter as I prop my foot on the bathroom counter where the light is good.

I see nothing.

When I run my thumbnail against the pink skin, it doesn't hurt. If it's a real splinter, I'd feel the hard intrusion lodged in my soft flesh. This is a best-case scenario for tweezers. Except, I can't find them or any sharp implement which might be used against me.

It's okay if it isn't real. It's okay if it's just in my head. I'm used to it.

For a moment, I remember who I used to be. Some called me a healer, shaman, and sin-eater. Most of them called me "sensitive." There was a time I didn't care what label they used because I knew I could help. I could reach into a person and touch their pain with my thoughts. If they let me, I could pull it from them like a tapeworm. But it got to be too much, and some of the bad thoughts, they weren't human in origin. The pain was too big to swallow, and I ran out of room to store sorrow and trauma. It left me fragile and unable to stand without reaching for a support beam.

I'll have to ask *the man* to look for the splinter. Examining with his critical eye, his brow will dip and crease. Lips pulled thin, he'll stop breathing, so engrossed in the fragile creature that is me.

Currently, he is lighting candles. Older, wiser, a man of smiles and intense stares, drawing me a bath as his favorite part of the day. We mustn't disrupt the schedule, not for any excuse. I will have to ask him to look for the splinter later if I have the strength.

The bathroom is warm. Misty. *The man* is a man without a name because he is only human, by all accounts. I'm told by others *the man* cares for me more than anything else in the world. His world.

He puts his heavy hand on my shoulder and says, "I exist to keep you safe."

Every night, he runs a bath, sprinkles the water with rose oil, and tells me, "Relax, you've had a hard day."

I have mousy brown hair and dimpled knees. My back is strong, but my bones are brittle.

I think, *Have I had a hard day? Thank goodness the man is here to take care of me.*

The water is the perfect temperature, just below burning. I disrobe, climb into the tub, and settle down as if sudden movement will disrupt a balance of which I am unaware. When the water is smooth and windowless, I close my eyes, clarity sinking to the bottom of my mind like streams of India ink.

I return to my favorite idea; I am a living, breathing house. Specifically, a two-story Victorian painted robin's egg blue. I have yellow roof shingles, white trim, and a wrap-around porch. The liquid embrace eases stiff planks and tight seams. Archaic, noble, filled with tiny rooms and strange angles, it is enough for a house of my limited ability to survive.

*The man* is humming. He's a shadow behind my eyelids. The melting candle wax smells like fire. In my house, there is an attic with a steep ladder. The steps require the use of both hands. Only a child with a child's unlimited energy could scale this height which equates to a giant beanstalk.

Before *the man*, I could get into the attic and rummage through dusty toys, costumes from playdates, and expired text-books. Most of the material was mine and familiar, but occasionally, I'd run across objects belonging to others. So far, I've found a thick pair of wool hunting socks, a bracelet not belonging to my grandmother, and a bear claw the length of my palm.

I am the house, but maybe someone lived here before? I am left to assume nothing is lost. They, the others who visited while I was away, must not feel the need to retrieve the items. I had friends once, and I tried to tell them about the attic. They reacted as the visions of their dead threatened to tell their secrets. I tried to explain, the dead have nothing new to explain. They just want us to remember we're alive and they are not. I don't have friends now. I have neighbors and family members who look upon my relationship with *the man* as the ultimate fairy-tale.

"Look at the way he dotes on you," they sigh. What they mean is, "You are in need of protection. Preservation. He does this because you are precious, and we are incapable of under-standing why you are so different."

Precious could also mean flammable.

I'm not afraid of heights, but I've become comfortable with *the man*. In the beginning of our relations, I was insane, or so everyone said. He held the blueprints for my recovery. When I explained I had an attic, he leaned forward. The veins in his arms slipped and slithered with tension. He was concerned for me.

"Don't go in the attic," he said. "It can offer nothing but pain, and I'm here to take the pain away."

I'm sure he must be right, but I always thought attics were like red phonebooths. They are for giving and receiving information, sometimes in the privacy of broad daylight. I'm not supposed to listen to the whispers because I'm too sensitive. *The man* says I have a disorder. He protects me from myself. Maybe he's right to do so.

If *the man* draws me a bath, and he knows how delicate I am, how sensitive to light and information and feelings, surely his care of me is justified. I have been sensitive all my life. I've heard voices and talked to people who weren't there. I've traveled to strange lands and inhabited strange bodies. I knew things I wasn't supposed to know, having never acquired a celestial passport.

The part of me living in the attic doesn't have a name, but I call it The Knowing. Everyone has The Knowing, but they keep their attics locked and boarded with nails. They don't know pain is part of The Knowing, a reminder only the living care about keeping secrets.

I stay out of the attic as he says I must, but The Knowing has been persistent of late. I hear voices in my sleep. Before *the man,* I tried to get rid of the voices. I cut myself. I broke glass. I raged. Everyone said they were make-believe, but they are real voices. Stumbling, falling, I'm mostly asleep, and the air is dizzy with power, but when I look in the mirror, my reflection is hazy. HE is erasing you, says a woman I can't remember. *Come to the attic.* I will help.

I can hear her best when I'm in water. *Come to the attic.* Yes, that's a good idea. Before *the man* climbs into the tub with me, I'm an entity unto myself. Open to belief. Susceptible to matches. I put hand and foot to the rungs of the stairs, intent on pulling myself into the crawlspace.

*The man* doesn't want me snooping around, it's not what's best for me, but I have missed my shingles. My weathervanes. The creaky floorboards. I long to watch the floating dust show me how stars die. If *the man* finds out, he will not be pleased. He will withhold things from me like food and confidence.

Confidence could also mean rage.

I don't have much time, but when I'm in the water, I'm stronger. I can float. I begin to climb the attic stairs. Halfway up, it gets easier to move freely. Of course, it's wrong. I know it's wrong. The closer I get to my friendly darkness, a place *the man* told me was sinful and the root of my suffering, the more alive I feel. My head is nearing the top. It's poking into the dark—

I hear them. The whispers. Scratching, nibbling, tiny feet in the walls of my house. I should be afraid. They don't belong to me or the woman I can't remember. They belong to two little boys, no more than eight years old.

The boys are trapped. Not in my attic. Not in *any* attic. The Knowing says they aren't being punished for breaking a vase or throwing eggs at a neighbor's front door. They stumbled into a prison of sorts, a holding cell. They're scared, and it's a terrible fear, because they know no one is coming to save them.

I've got my head and my heart past the landing. This is what I see.

The boys, one skinny, one lumpy, both dirty, trapped in a box that doesn't look like any box a human has seen. It's a blank white canvas. There are no windows, walls, or doors. There's barely a floor. They huddle together in a place that is neither hot nor cold.

The skinny boy has a gift. He's sensitive. He knows things he shouldn't know, sees things he shouldn't see, and talks to people who aren't there. He's learned to keep his secret. It's easy to play along, let others think what they need to think, while he picks up his Knowing, puts it back down, and knocks it over with his foot. It can be a dictator for a day, and tomorrow a bit of loose change his mother won't miss.

The lumpy boy comforts himself by thinking about chocolate milk. He doesn't understand The Knowing and doesn't try. He thinks his friend is special, and special things should be taken care of. The lumpy boy also has a gift. He has a heart the size of a Universe and has never told his sensitive friend, "It's just your imagination."

The boys don't know I'm listening to their thoughts. I get the impression they were playing in the woods. Pretending they were on a grand adventure where magic was rare but accessible. They stumbled into a sinkhole or a cave, I'm not sure.

The walls feel smooth, dark, and glittery as obsidian. The lumpy one trips, the sensitive one tries to catch him, but this is their undoing. Stronger together, they open a door into another world, and they fall into the white holding cell.

I strain to see, hear, feel the captors. Alien. Foreign. Wrong. So, wrong. Human, by all accounts, but ancient and banished from the light.

The boys understand they will be tested, poked, and prodded like specimens for dissection by creatures that are hungry for The Knowing. Since there's nowhere to run, no place to hide, they wait. They don't know if the tests will hurt, but can't imagine they will feel good.

The boys' captors don't know which one has The Knowing. It's a worst-case scenario kind of thing. The sensitive boy says nothing, but he's thinking, "I'm so sorry I'm like this. Why do I have to be like this?"

The Knowing tells me one of them is supposed to be eaten, slowly.

My eyes are closed, but I feel *the man's* foot break the surface of our bath. The water stirs. His invasion displaces my thoughts, scattering them like dry leaves. I have seconds to watch, listen, and understand.

Cobweb or spider?

Real or imaginary?

Safe or unsafe?

The Knowing speaks for itself. When it's awake and alive, it shakes the rafters and crumbles foundations. It scares people. The ones that aren't scared, covet. They want it for themselves. *The man* wants it for himself.

No. Don't think about him. Think of the boys.

The lumpy one is a conductor for The Knowing. He can channel it and absorb some of the burden. He doesn't know he has this power. He does, however, know they are coming for him first. They will test him, and he will fail their test. This makes him sad, not because he wants to win, but because he'll leave his friend all alone in the horrible place.

I hear his voice, clear as a fire alarm muffled under floodwaters. He says, leaning his head on the sensitive boy's shoulder, "It's my turn to be dead, isn't it?"

There might be a way I can help. I've been to places like this prison, but they were different. They weren't traps. My special place was more like a snow globe, and I could visit, coming, and going as I pleased. Instead of a blank canvas, I could walk on a sandy beach and sit under a palm tree. I didn't mind being alone. It was peaceful. I couldn't see the waves, but I could hear them. They weren't hungry.

I met a woman on one of my trips. She had skin the color of moist soil and a large pillowy chest. Her hair was braided down her back in streaks of gray, the color of turtle doves. Sitting under the palm tree with her, The Knowing lived beneath her skin and pulsed like baby galaxies. I didn't have to say a word, and wasn't that nice, not to be confused about what I am or what I'm supposed to do as a sensitive person. It's been so long since we met, I'm not sure I know her voice if she remembers me at all.

*Don't be foolish, girl, she says into my attic. I can hear you. That man isn't supposed to take what isn't his. You need to do better. The children don't have much time.*

I know her name, I know I do. It's something about houses and colors. A Victorian house has three colors and is called– Yes! She's The Painted Lady.

"What do you mean?" I ask. "There's nothing I can do."

The Painted Lady says, *That's a bit of nonsense. You're a whole house, aren't you? You have more to offer than just an attic.*

I used to be able to leap into the attic without the use of stairs, I was that strong. I say, "Tell me what to do."

*There is a crack in the floor of the prison,* The Painted Lady says. *Tell the boys to shrink into tiny mice and crawl into the crack.*

"Where will it take them?"

*Into your walls. They're small enough, you can hide them, but it won't last long. You must keep it from the MAN. He's worse than all of them.*

"And if I fail?"

Silence. Darkness. Not the friendly kind. Then she says into my attic, *The sweeter the sheep, the sharper the teeth.*

No time, no time at all, because *the man* has slipped completely into the bath. The water sloshes, slapping against my chin. My Knowing flutters, wavers. The ripples disperse my ink thoughts. I'm a kite that's lost its tail. The tail has baby blue knots the color of robin's eggs, and it continues to soar into space while the main body, my body, comes spinning down and back into the water.

*The man's* body is warm. Real. Animal. He's a magnet, and he covers me like a pregnant cloud that's decided, "No. I'm not going to share my power. I'd much rather drink and drink and drink some more."

So, he does.

"Let me take care of you," he murmurs. I feel his weight on my knees and thighs and belly and chest. He drinks me up, takes my energy. The Knowing is drawn out of me and into him where he collects it for his own purposes.

When we first met, he drained me dry. I could be a normal human, numb around the edges. He has done this every day for many years. If it weren't for those little boys—What little boys?—I'd be convinced there's nothing more special than *the man's* intimacy.

My attic is just a box, and they're just voices, after all. Cobwebs of thought. Maybe I shouldn't disturb them. No one wants their hard work dismantled by a sensitive person who has lost her way. But a box is supposed to hold something precious, a gift or a toy. I think of the lumpy one, he's a real boy, and he is precious. Not just as a conduit to make his friend stronger, but as a gift that exceeds the limits of imagination.

Surely, if what I am is so bad, it would pollute *the man*. Poison him. Hurt him. His care for me would be about love and sacrifice, but he keeps drinking, and it makes him thirstier. He wants my energy. My attic. My Knowing. Maybe he's not the caretaker of my house. Maybe, *the man* is a colony of termites eating away at my soul. Maybe, I'm a sensitive person for a reason.

Sensitive could also mean immensely powerful.

But, too late, the attic fades. I'm a stranger looking at a pretty blue house with white trim. I have mousy brown hair. It's dark inside, but I peek through the windows, knocking softly on the panes of glass.

*Please, won't someone let me in.*

Right before *the man* puts his mouth over mine, I can see down the hall. A door is open. There's a set of stairs. They lead to the basement. The furnace lives in the basement. It's glowing red. Pulsing, fiery red. It's a wave rising like a tide from the pit of my house.

Yes. I am a house. I have skin the color of a robin's egg, yellow hair, and downstairs in the basement, a raging furnace. My hunger is real.

Hunger could also mean ravenous.

*The man* continues to drink me, but I'm being quiet as a mouse. I've slipped and slithered into the cracks of my house. I remember myself and other sensitive people. They smile with their whole faces. They cry alone in the dark with no one to hold them. They are brittle, sometimes breakable, but if they see someone in pain, they rise up and let the fire do its job.

The Knowing tells me how to reach the boys. In my attic, while I still have time, I pop my head into their holding cell.

"Both of you, listen carefully. You must shrink like me."

As if it were natural, as if sensitive were just another word for magic, I transform into a mouse.

"Be small and quiet and follow me."

They are terrified, but the sensitive one nods. He knows me. We are the same. He grabs his friend's hands, tells him to close his eyes, and the pair shrink into bite-sized mice. They scamper toward the hole I've made in the floor, but the aliens have heard us. They are coming. The white shakes. A whiny, rendering force reaches for their tiny tails.

I open my mouth and scream. It is not a small sound made by a weak woman. It is a hurricane that rips the holding cell to shreds. The boy mice drop quietly, neatly into my hands. They are shaking and crying, but they are brave. Clamoring down the attic stairs, I can barely stand or hold on to The Knowing.
Placing them on the floor, I whisper, "Hide. There is one more, and HE is the worst of all."

What *the man* has been doing to me is wrong. Alien. Foreign— I need to feed the furnace. The Knowing says, *INVADE HIM.*

In the bath, my arms come up. They twine around *the man*'s neck and drip with inky thoughts. I look into his eyes.

I say, "You're so good to me. How can I repay you for your care?"

He freezes. I should be exhausted. Empty. I should be numb around the edges instead of glowing, smiling, pulling us under the water where my sensitive thoughts have open arms and sharp teeth. *The man*'s not concerned any longer. He's scared. Maybe he sees my eyes have gone red. Maybe he's an animal caught in my make-believe trap. Maybe The Knowing will drown us both.

Right before our heads dip under the water, I lean my head on his shoulder.

I whisper, "I need you so much. Lie still for me. There's something in my house I need you to see."

The furnace roars, feeds, and he's just a man drowning in my arms.

I wiggle my toe. There is a splinter.

# Beef & Lube
By Glenna Hartwell

Effie and I hung out by the snack bar, now shuttered, with her crumpled soda can and my cold, limp cheese fries. Our mom was late picking us up. Par for the course. Naturally, she couldn't be reached by phone. My messages dead-ended in her voicemail graveyard. The coaches couldn't get a hold of her either. All the other kids had piled into a rush of SUVs driven by normal parents who picked them up on time. Cars crunched and pattered on the gravel lot one after another, then pulled out. I checked each one to see if it was Mom's.

Soon the sun would set. Our coaches, Mrs. Guchie and Mrs. Reed had packed away the bats and softballs long ago. They made a halfhearted attempt to hide their annoyance from Effie and me. Mrs. Reed searched up and down the country road as if her glare could make my mom's car appear.

I knew what they were thinking. It happened a lot.

Once, after rehearsal for the winter play, Effie and I stood outside the auditorium for an hour in six-degree weather.

The music teacher finally emerged, locked the doors, then passed us on his way to the parking lot.

"Mara. Effie. You two still here? Who's supposed to pick you up?" He asked.

"My mom," I said, but it came out, "Ma moh," because my lips were stiff from the cold.

"You can't stay here. You guys will freeze to death!" He offered us a lift in his Mini Cooper.

I was happy to get a ride. But, to my horror, he dropped us at the police station instead of home. You would think our mom's embarrassment at having to explain herself to the local PD would have cured her tardiness. But she was full of excuses: single working mom, boss made her stay overtime. On it went. She even threw us under the bus by telling the desk officer that we hadn't said what time rehearsal was supposed to end.

As I said, it happened a lot—teachers and coaches got tired of waiting for our mom, and at a certain point, the police station began to seem like a nice alternative. Mrs. Reed's foot was already tapping, so the wheels were probably turning.

I didn't feel like facing that officer again. Who wanted to be known as the town's neglected kids? Effie was only twelve and still in elementary school, so she probably wasn't too aware of stuff like that. But I had my ninth-grade reputation to keep up. If I got taken to the cops again, my friends would surely find out, and my popularity would drop faster than last month's TikTok challenge.

I shook off the memory. "You can just leave us here," I suggested. "I'm sure she'll be along soon."

"We can't leave you," said Coach Guchie. "It's against the law to leave underage children alone." The huff in her voice was as obvious as her frosty breath.

"Go on and head home, Anne," said Coach Reed. It was always weird to hear adults call each other by their first names.

"I'll stay with them. There's a restaurant just over there—" she pointed to the woods beyond the softball field— "where we can wait until their mom comes."

"Or until you decide on other arrangements," Coach Guchie said before leaving.

That was code for cops.

***

We walked up the road, past the quiet field. The approach of evening chilled my bare arms. Up ahead, garish light filtered through tall pines and spilled onto the gravel. Birds settled in for the night, their chirping overtaken by rumbling motors and loud voices, like disturbing elements intruding on a pleasant dream. A sign came into view: *Beef & Lube*. It was a tavern, rimmed in a green neon strip surrounded by scuffed cement posts that probably kept drunk drivers from crashing into the building.

Engine fumes mixed with the scent of pine. Motorcycles, pickups, and the people who belonged to them clogged the lot. Thick-necked men with shaved heads wore jeans and leather vests stretched over their broad torsos. They mingled with guys in baseball caps and denim jackets with the sleeves ripped off. Women of all shapes and sizes smoked and gestured to each other, flashing painted nails and dyed blonde hair. Everywhere motorcycle chrome reflected the green neon. Exhaust billowed from vibrating tailpipes, drifting across the lot like fog.

Inside, all traces of the summer night's freshness disappeared. I almost gagged on cigarette smoke and the smell of beer and pee.

"There's a table over there, girls," Coach Reed said.

I didn't know how she saw it through all the smoke. The tavern's interior was dark and warm like an animal's lair. The bass from heavy-metal music thumped through the dimness as we made our way to a wobbly table. When I sat down on the sticky seats, I imagined germs crawling up my bare legs. Coach Reed looked over a menu. She seemed at ease, but Effie held her head so far down I thought it would disappear into her neck.

A long-haired bartender wiped circles on the counter with a rag. "What can I get you, ladies?"

"Coke okay?" Coach Reed asked us, and Effie gave a tiny nod.

"Diet Coke," I said.

"Two Cokes and a Diet," she told the bartender. At least she wasn't ordering alcohol. He reached under the bar for glasses and got bottles from the refrigerator behind him. "Try your mom again," she was saying when he brought everything over. She nodded a "thanks," and he winked.

I extracted my phone from my backpack and hit the number.

"You've reached…" mom's voicemail began. I waited until the beep and told her where we were.

"Hey, honey," a man called out. He sat three tables down. "Them your daughters? You don't look old enough to have kids." He wiped his mouth with a filthy, fingerless glove. His greasy hair was long and shot with gray.

Coach Reed half-turned in her seat. "Mind your business," she said, but when she turned back, she had a hint of a smile on her face.

"Hah! She's got some spunk to 'er. Right?" he said, elbowing a man beside him.

"And them girls is cute," said his friend. He looked at Effie and me. "Hey, sweet things!"

It was like when truckers honked their horns at us when we walked home from the bus stop, but this was up close and personal. Effie sucked down her Coke, pretending not to hear. I studied the walls. Under the table, I clenched the fingers of my left hand so hard they hurt.

The place was plastered with beer ads, yellowed posters

of rock bands, and faded photos of sexy women posed on motorcycles. Behind the bar, a plate-sized pentagram was carved into the wall next to shelves of albums—actual record albums—aged and dusty as if they hadn't been taken from their sleeves since CD players were invented. Reflective material like ruined foil balloons covered the ceiling, purple bar light rippling across it and adding to the glow from Christmas lights strung haphazardly from one raunchy photo to the next. Oversized, fake plastic cans of beer hung from the ceiling. They swayed in the air every time the door opened as if they danced to the blaring music. The bar would be a living nightmare for someone with OCD.

Was it even legal for us to be in this place? The people weren't like any I had met before. They made me nervous. Coach Reed might even get in trouble for bringing us.

Effie's eyes darted all around. "Do you think you should just take us to the police station?" She said.

"I want my Coke, though," I lied. *Please, no police station.* "And I'm starving." Another lie since cheese fries from the snack bar lay congealing in my stomach.

"Let's get something to eat, then we'll leave," Coach said. She caught the bartender's eye. "Can we have some fries, please?" Her voice had a flirty sound that she never used while coaching our softball team. It made me cringe big-time. I was getting a bellyache. Soon I'd have even more fries in there to make it worse.

Soon I'd have even more fries in there to make it worse.

A guy shoved past our table, a wallet chain and bandana spilling from his back pocket. He ordered, then turned and leaned back, elbows propped on the bar and one boot hooked on the footrail. He looked us over. I mean, *really* looked us over.

"Hi, sugar," he said to me. "We don't have any dancers tonight. Maybe you and your girlfriend can fill in?"

"She's my sister," I said, looking into my soda glass so he

wouldn't see my frightened eyes. "Leave us alone.

"Ooh, listen to her! Uppity little lady! How 'bout you, then?" He asked Coach Reed. "You're pretty hot."

She still had that little smile on her face, but at least she shook her head, *no*. I was beginning to think my coach was a regular here.

He rambled away with his order, unsteady on his feet.

The bartender brought our fries. A grinning, devil-face tattoo leered up at me from his forearm when he set down the greasy basket.

"Hurry up," Effie said. She saw it, too. "I'd rather wait outside in the dark than here."

"Help me eat, then." I gave her a fry. She dipped it in the little paper cup of ketchup. The purple lights over the bar lit her blonde hair and gave her elfin features an otherworldly glow when she bowed her head.

A guy tapped Coach Reed's shoulder and asked for the salt and pepper. But it was just an excuse because he struck up a conversation as soon as she handed them over. She didn't seem to mind and even shifted in her seat so she could talk to the guy. I tried not to pay attention, but Effie gave me a look when he asked where we were from. I rolled my eyes when she actually told him.

Then the guy who wanted us to dance was back. He'd brought reinforcements: two drunk buddies, their arms draped over his shoulders. One gave a little wave with his fingers. The other stuck out his tongue like the Rolling Stones logo and wiggled it. The three bodies weaved, and one of the men stumbled. They stank like sweat. Still yukking it up with her new pal, Coach Reed didn't notice. The bartender poured drinks at the other end of the bar.

"I insist these ladies get up and dance! What do you say?" The guy yelled over the throbbing music. His drunken voice carried to the back of the room, and some of the crowd answered him with whistles and clapping.

I grabbed Effie's arm. "We've got to get out of here. Come on."

We skirted around the men, but one of them snagged my sleeve.

"Let me go!"

"What's your rush, hon? Gimme a kiss." He pulled me toward him.

The bartender appeared as if out of nowhere and pulled my arm free. "What's the matter with you, Dave? Can't you see they're kids?"

"Fuck you, man. If they was kids, they wouldn't be in here." Dave reached for me again.

"Leave 'em alone," the bartender warned.

Dave's friend threw a sloppy punch, catching the bartender on the side of the mouth.

"You're outta here!" He wiped a trickle of blood from his lip, seized the drunk by his collar and belt, and frog-marched him toward the door.

All eyes were on us. People had stopped drinking. Some cheered, others shouted, "Dance! Dance!"

The bartender shoved Dave's buddy outside. I figured Effie and I would follow, but someone threw another punch, and the bartender went down this time. Dave kicked and stomped him to more cheers and clapping. Rough hands forced me and Effie through the crowd, other hands pawing us as we passed. The whites of Effie's eyes reflected the Christmas lights. We were practically body surfing by the time my back hit the bar–that hurt a lot–and then I was hoisted onto it.

Dave jumped up, too, and yanked me to my feet. "Get the other one!"

Then Effie was beside me, stricken. My little sister. What

if *dancing* didn't mean dancing in a place like this?

Coach Reed stared at us, her hand to her mouth.

"Call 911!" I screamed over the roaring crowd and the music that someone had turned up. She did nothing and still wore that stupid smile. *Damn her.*

The crowd had grown, people coming in from outside, a sea of faces with eager, hungry eyes.

Dave pushed me forward with a hand to the middle of my back. "Dance!"

The crowd cheered.

"Okay. We'll dance," I said in a quiet voice.

Dave eased back and stopped pushing.

I took Effie's hand and gritted my teeth. "Do it."

She gave a single nod. Our eyes locked.

The room grew dim as we concentrated, the cries of "Dance, dance!" fading away. Mom would've told us not to go any further. Before, I had always listened. But not now, she had left us alone and vulnerable.

It didn't have to be that way.

I let myself fall away. My outer appearance felt unzipped, as though I were stepping out of a costume. Effie lifted her chin. The gesture made her look like nobility. Quiet Effie. Her eyes lit with a yellow-green fire. Her blonde hair turned platinum, and her skin vibrated an incandescent blue more intense than the purple lights overhead. Static electricity buzzed around us. The corners of the posters lifted.

I felt the fiery incandescence on my skin, too. It flowed through my skin toward my hands and gathered in my fingertips. Then it burst free, a current too strong to hold in. The people in the room seemed to shrink as my strength increased. Effie and I rose over the bar.

Below us, Dave scrambled and half-fell.

"Down," I commanded.

Every one of them hit the floor. Dave fell off the bar. Everyone, including the men who had tried to force us to dance, fell into the stillness of sleep. At least, from the outside, it looked like sleep. They were aware, but prisoners inside their bodies, unable to move. Our prisoners. The *Beef & Lube* had grown silent as a tomb.

Effie let her radium gaze roam across the people on her side of the room. I did the same on my side.

"Not the bartender," I whispered. "He was nice."

I sent nightmares coursing out through the current blazing from my eyes and fingers. A waking dream shot into the mind of every scumbag in the room. I spared no one who hadn't helped us. They lay on the floor, paralyzed, while I drenched them in deep dread and demonic horrors. For Dave, a special dream: Effie, severing his limbs one by one, walking patiently behind him as he wriggled away, trailing blood until all he could do was use his chin to drag himself. He would dream it every night for as long as I wanted. That would be a long time.

The door opened, letting in the last of the blood-red sunset. Our mom stepped in, hands on her hips, silhouetted against the crimson sky.

"Girls! What have I told you about showing yourselves in your *mare* form?"

"Mom, we had no choice. Maybe try being on time for once."

She was late, but I was relieved to see her. She was our mom, after all. She had taught us everything we knew about fitting in. And everything we knew about who we really were: the *mare*. We were demons. But I didn't see that as bad. The ones in the bar were the bad guys.

"I can't believe we used to actually have to touch these smelly creeps to do this," I said.

Effie wrinkled her nose. "Like, literally, sit on their chests while they sleep."

"I'm proud of you girls for trying it this way," Mom said.

"Yay us," I said.

I relished the feeling of taking on an entire room. Especially when it was so justly deserved.

"Well, do you need help?" she said.

I shook my head. We were nearly finished sealing the *Beef & Lube* in a tomb of horror when Effie asked, "What about Coach Reed?"

"Did she help us?"

"No. But she bought us Cokes and fries."

Coach lay on the sticky floor, a flirty smile frozen on her lips.

"Fry the bitch," I said.

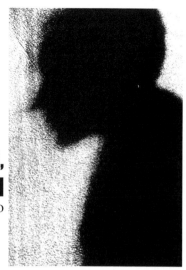

# I'm not the Villain, I'm Misunderstood
By Dexter Amoroso

The greatest people in history were so often self-critical
Thinking themselves as failures, worthless, or over-analytical.
However, the reverse is true, I shall remind
History's biggest losers, its greatest villains,
saw themselves as God's very gift to mankind.

It's all fine, to believe in a nice, sweet, rosy world,
Maybe someday it will be, or at least in your dream world.
But if those who believe in such, would just remove their glasses,
They might see the truth - this universe would kick their asses.

But I'm not the Villain, I'm misunderstood.
I'm a soul whose intentions are all that's good.
To give myself some credit, for surviving it all.
To do that shows I have some guts, some courage, and gumption after all.

This does not in any way romanticize villainy,
'cause its heroism that saves us literally.
"Joker" wasn't a feel-good movie, by no means.
The end will never justify the means.

# They're Just Little Wolves

By Melissa R. Mendelson

**5:30 a.m.**

The room was pitch black. The shades were pulled down, the door closed and locked. Only the alarm clock dared to shine. A faint, violet light lifted upward over the small black box as the light grew brighter. A blinding purple now filled the room, pulling the darkness down, and screamed, "It's six a.m. Wake up."
A hand slid from beneath the covers. A groan following close behind as a finger hit the snooze button.

The alarm clock screeched, "You have work today. No time to be late."

A body jolted from the bed, groaning against the wailing sound that had erupted throughout the room. Silencing the alarm, the purple light disappeared from the room.

"Lights on. Dim," Ashley said.

She flinched, falling back onto the bed as the alarm clock continued to buzz.

"I'm up, you stupid robot." Ashley pulled herself from the bed.

"Leave the lights on dim?"

"Yes. Please." Ashley moved over to the closet door and slid it open. She had disabled the camera so she could not be seen or recorded. But she left everything else on. It would be suspicious if she turned everything off. With her job, she didn't want to trip any alarms.

"I'm taking a shower," she announced to the room. "In case anyone was listening." She was never sure if someone was.

**6:30 a.m.**

Ashley parked her car in the commuter lot. She hoped the line at the bagel store wasn't long. Last week the line was ridiculous and she had to skip breakfast. She checked her watch. There was only fifteen minutes left to catch the train. Otherwise, she would have to wait a half hour for the next one, making her late for work. One more strike and she would be fired. Nobody would want to hire her after what she did.

Ashley glanced at the bagel store over the rim of her black sunglasses. There was a line, but it was a short one. Quickly taking her spot in line and ignoring the stares at her sunglasses, she moved her hair in front of her face. Three years and two strikes. Technically work didn't start until 8:30 a.m. and she was always plugged in on time. But her new boss wanted her there at 8 a.m. Her boss was punishing her for some reason, and if not for her boss's boss, she would have already been fired.

"Order?" The young man stared at her sunglasses. He was not amused. "What do you want?"

"Everything bagel with cream cheese. Coffee. Black."

"You're the only one that comes here, asking for black coffee." He got her order. He wanted her out of there as soon as possible, as if her very presence bothered him. "Four-eighty."

Ashley handed him a five-dollar-bill and grabbed her breakfast, "Keep the change."

She heard him mutter something under his breath, but she didn't care. The familiar pain in her right hand caused her to flinch. It had been three years since she got that horrible scar across the palm of her hand. It never healed properly.

"Five minutes left," she muttered as she checked her watch and headed to work.

Because of her job, Ashley had a reserved spot right near the train station. She hated for people to know what she did. Her commuter car had been keyed multiple times. Someone even threw a rock through her windshield once. When she could find another spot, she would try and park there, but most mornings the lot was already full.

Ashley could hear the train coming as she bolted up the steps. She moved faster. This was usually how she got her exercise in. She never had time to walk or run afterward. She was always plugged in at a table. Then she was either at home sitting on a couch or in bed. She did too much sitting, so she moved herself up the stairs and hopped into the train just as the doors closed.

Again, people stared at her, looking at her sunglasses, but she didn't care. They did their job, hiding the marks on her temples. She had to be discreet because if they knew what she did, then she would never get to work on time, and there was no seat. She tucked the bagel under one arm and drank her coffee. All while keeping her balance as the train lurched forward.

She stared at the ground. If she had thought to look behind her, she would have seen a man charging toward her, bumping into her, and trying to make her drop the coffee. She dropped the sunglasses instead, giving him the perfect view of the marks on her right and left temples.

"Oh, I'm sorry. I didn't know what you were. I thought it would just be funny to make you spill your coffee."

"Why would that be funny?" Ashley asked as she

grabbed her sunglasses off the floor.

The train came to a sudden stop. Almost losing her balance, she spilled some of the coffee on her black shoes.

"Is that funny?" She asked the man.

"No. I just wanted you to spill coffee on her."

Ashley followed his gaze to a woman sitting nearby wearing a pale, yellow dress. The woman was obviously not wearing a bra, but Ashley hoped she was at least wearing underwear. It took a moment for the woman to realize some coffee had splashed across her sandals and manicured feet.

"Really?" The woman hissed at Ashley. "Some fucking people."

She jumped out of her seat and hurried off the train.

"It wasn't me." Ashley looked back at the man who bumped into her, but he had already returned to his friends, laughing at his small victory. "Fucking minor crimes," Ashley muttered as she sat down in the now vacant seat.

**8:01 a.m.**

The facial recognition wasn't working again. There was a line from the metal detectors back toward the entrance doors. Employees grumbled as security manually scanned the palm of everyone's hand. This was always an issue for Ashley. The scar made it almost impossible to get an accurate read, and most of the time, would lead to a swab from a nurse to confirm her D.N.A. Ashley understood the protocols, but they were a pain in the ass. And so was her boss, who was standing by the elevators waiting for her.

"No swab today?" Ashley asked, surprised after security scanned her hand, the light beamed red and they waved her through. "Don't you want to make sure it's me?"

"Not today." They gestured toward the man behind her. "Go ahead. Your boss is waiting for you."

"Shit." Ashley almost threw her bagel into a nearby garbage can. She had already discarded the empty cup of coffee. She sighed, thinking she could chew on the bagel on the way home, crying to herself that she got fired. Then, she would return to her apartment, pack her things, and go back to her parents' house.

"I'm sorry I'm late," she said to the blonde lady who looked irritable, arms crossed over her chest.

"Save it," she snapped as Ashley stared down at her feet. "Can you take off those fucking sunglasses, or have you gone blind?"

"I'm not blind." Ashley took off the sunglasses. "I'm photosensitive."

"Whatever. We had a meltdown."

"Susan?" Ashley asked.

"She killed herself last night." Ashley's boss coldly watched her wipe a tear away. "For fuck's sake, she was a five-yearer. What do you think will happen to you in two years if you're not fired or blind?"

"Maybe you should fire me," Ashley blurted out, but then regretted her words.

"I would love to, but I can't. Janine is a five-yearer too, and we don't know when she will crack. That leaves you, because you have three years in, and Bob."

"Bob is a two-yearer."

"I know what Bob is," Ashley's boss snapped. "At least we get another round of new recruits today. Maybe this time half of them will make it." She checked her watch. "You need to plug in soon, so let's go." She pushed the button for the elevator. "You going to eat your bagel?"

Ashley tossed her bagel into a garbage can. "No, I'm not hungry."

"Suit yourself." Her boss seemed satisfied with the small

victory. "We saw the cracks with Susan."

"I didn't see any cracks with Susan. I should have had dinner with her last weekend, but I didn't."

"I'm waiting for you to crack," her boss said.

Ashley went to the bathroom. She had ten minutes to get herself ready for work. She needed to focus but hearing about Susan rattled her.

She liked Susan, and Susan had seemed a bit scattered lately. But Susan didn't show any of the signs of those who had done this job for five years. Her death was unexpected. Maybe it could have even been avoided.

Ashley's office was literally a gray square. The only door was behind her. The chair was comfortable, but the table was flat and cold with a jellyfish-like keyboard. There were two pieces of paper on the table she was required to read every day before she started her work.

The first paper stated to focus on Major Crimes that ranged from trafficking, which included people, drugs, and weapons, to murder, on to serial rapists, and then terrorism.

The second paper was much shorter, only stating, "We do not focus on Minor Crimes."

Ashley thought back to the incident on the train.

She took off the sunglasses, dropped her pocketbook at her feet, and winced against the fluorescent lights overhead. With her sunglasses on the table, Ashley lifted the viewer nearby.

The viewer reminded her of those old virtual reality headsets. They were outlawed a few years after becoming available to the public. People could not tell the difference between reality and fiction, and some did terrible things. But the government utilized the headsets when they created this program.

Ashley slid the viewer over her head, covering her eyes. The band around her head was always tight, but that wasn't the worst part. The worst part was the little, robotic arms that unfolded themselves, and plunged their way into her temples, linking her to the network.

The network was boosted by an app downloaded onto computers and cell phones. Even the new car radios had them. Most people were unaware of it until they started to catch on, but a lot shook it off. Who could believe there was technology that allowed access into the human mind? Granted, it was limited access, only offering up the short-term memory. Anything in long-term memory was inaccessible, at least to most people. Ashley was able to scratch at that surface.

She quickly checked on her target, but only briefly. If she focused too long on them, the network would take notice, and she didn't want that. She started running through people's minds. It was kind of like a sprint, stretching her legs, seeing what was out there, and apparently, there was a big shipment coming in at the docks. The kid slipped up while calling his girl for a booty call, thinking of the information in his short-term memory. It was all she needed as her hands moved along the jellyfish-like keyboard, typing in the information.

"I could call it a day."

She was eager to get home. She knew where her target would be. Tonight was the night, and she was excited. The last time people noticed her excited about something, she had to lie and say it was a big date, which was also another lie. It was actually one hell of a kill.

## 12 p.m.

A siren blasted into Ashley's gray square. Someone's mean joke of a lunch alarm. Ashley was surprised she hadn't gone deaf by now, but it was her eyes that were going.

The doctor assured her that her sight hadn't changed. It was just affected by light. What was the difference? At some point, the sunglasses would become permanent, making the hunt harder. Maybe more fun. She liked the idea of killing in the dark, but with this job, it was either the mind that went or the body. She preferred the body.

As she slipped on the sunglasses and stepped outside to stretch her legs, she walked into Bob. He was a tall, thin man, grinning like the cat that ate the canary. Without saying a word, he grabbed her hand and led her over to the training room where the new recruits would do their first plug in. A young woman lay on her back with her eyes closed, gasping and moaning. Her body writhed and the instructor could not make her stop.

"What the hell happened to her?" Ashley asked.

"Who knows? Maybe she got into the mind of a pedophile, rapist, or someone thinking of sex. She's locked in there, even with the helmet off."

"That's terrible. And we're all watching her?"

She watched Bob shrug.

"You're awful."

"Hey, another one threw up on the floor even before the helmet went on their head," Bob said.

"I tell you the new recruits lately are failing miserably."

"Not that one over there." He pointed to a short redhead. "She's as good as you, and I think she's in. Probably the only one who is."

"Excuse me?"

A man wearing a white uniform, similar to a hazmat suit, stood across from them holding a metal suitcase. He glared at them through his narrow glasses and slipped into the training room, moving over to the young woman on the floor.

"He's not going to do what I think he's going to do, right?"

"Oh, yes he is, Ashley. He's going to shock her. It's the only way."

Ashley heard the hum from the suitcase and flinched, "I

can't watch. Lunchtime is almost over."

"You're hungry?"

"Not anymore. No thanks to you, Bob."

She moved away from him.

"You heard about Susan, right?" He called after her. "Damn shame."

"Be careful, Bob. Some turn into toast even at two years."

Ashley stormed away from him, heading for the bathroom.

"You're the Black Dagger Killer," Ashley heard whispered as she pushed open the door of the women's restroom.

She froze, looking around the bathroom. Was someone in here with her? There was no movement from the stalls, and she didn't want to touch the floor. Too many people throw up after a day's work, and it was usually on the floor. She only threw up in the beginning, but luckily, that stopped. She also always made it to the toilet except once or twice, and if anyone knew the truth about her, then it was all over.

"You're the Black Dagger Killer."

Before Ashley could respond, someone said, "No. No, I'm not, but she is. I know she is. She's too good at her job. No, you're the Black Dagger Killer."

"Hello?" Ashley approached one of the stalls, pushing the door open, but it was empty. "Anyone there?"

"You idiot, she heard you. Why don't you just kill her, or did you forget your black dagger?"

"I can hear you. Janine?"

"Shit. Shit. Don't call the police. She should call the police. It's her. No, it's me."

"Janine, you know the rule. If you're having a meltdown, I need to report it."

Now Ashley had really lost her appetite. "I have to report it," she said, stepping away from the stall.

"Ashley, don't," Janine said as she came out of the stall. She was a short, round woman, and always made people laugh. It was kind of odd doing that here with the seriousness of their job, but it was also good to have someone make them laugh, unlike Bob. "Please, don't. I'm okay. I just needed to get it out of my system. That's all."

"Janine, you were talking to yourself, and what you were saying was-"

"I know. I know. The Black Dagger Killer. We all know who it is." She laughed nervously and looked at Ashley. "Am I right? It's always the quiet ones."

"Okay, now I am reporting you." Ashley stormed away, but Janine grabbed her by the arm. "Janine, let go of my arm, or I will scream."

"I could cut your throat. No, no, I didn't mean that. I'm kidding. Ha ha."

"Look, I don't have time for this. If you can't pull yourself together–,"

"I can. I'm fine. I'm sorry." She touched Ashley's shoulder. "I'm fine. Are we good?"

"You know if Susan didn't–,"

"I know."

"You keep interrupting me."

"I'm sorry, Ashley. I think I'm almost done here, but I just need a little more time. Are we good?" Ashley sighed as the poor woman looked back at her, pleading for her not to push the alarm that was right outside the bathroom door. That alarm was exactly for this kind of situation, a meltdown. "Okay."

Janine surprised Ashley with a hug.

"Okay," Ashley repeated. "We have to get back to work."

"Thank you, Ashley. Thank you."

Janine hurried out of the bathroom.

"Fucking hell," Ashley blurted.

She went to use the bathroom, not caring if she was late getting back to work. Today was just out of control. All she wanted to do was go home and get ready for her kill.

She had barely stepped outside the bathroom when she walked into what felt like a wall. She noticed the badge hanging off his waist before looking at his face and recognizing him. Detective Hunter Knight was pursuing the Black Dagger Killer.

"Excuse me." He had a nice voice, but why was he standing outside the bathroom? "Bright in here?" He gestured toward the sunglasses, and Ashley took them off, flinching as she looked at him. "Side effect of the job?"

"Yeah." Ashley looked down at the sunglasses. How much did he hear before, or was he just walking by now? "You're out of your jurisdiction, detective."

He glanced down at his badge.

"Trying something different. Narrowing the field." She didn't like that, and he noticed by her expression. "We're getting close. Real close."

"To finding the Black Dagger Killer?" He wasn't surprised at her words. "I've seen you on the news. I guess we still need detectives."

"Your system isn't full-proof, and there's enough evidence of that. But most crime is down."

"That's good. I have to get back to work."

Before she could move away, he said, "Thank you."

"For what?"

"For doing what you do. Thanks to you, there's not too many serial killers around. The ones that are, well, I guess they know how to avoid the system."

She met his gaze, knowing he was waiting for her to say something.

"I'm late to plug in," Ashley said as she hurried away.

"See you around." She didn't like that either. "By the way, what's your name?"

Ashley pretended not to hear him. He probably knew anyway.

"Shit. Shit." Now, she sounded like Janine. "Fuck."

## 12:33 p.m.

She sat down in her chair, trying to calm herself, and saw the scar on her right hand. The last time she was this worked up was with her first kill, and she didn't mean to kill him. Well, he was trying to kill her when she confronted him in the alleyway. That broken bottle had saved her life, despite cutting her hand open.

"Calm down, or the system will detect you," Ashley whispered to herself.

There were a lot of glitches that first year. It was amazing she still had her job and didn't go to prison. The killing got easier afterward.

She hummed a soft tune and her mind calmed. The walls went up. Yeah, she learned how to get around the system. That's why nobody broke her door down. How did he catch onto her, though? Did she make a mistake somewhere? She was usually so careful, and the victims never knew each other. They never had anything in common and were killed in random places at different times. What gave her away? If she thought like that anymore then he would be waiting for her right outside the door.

"Back to work."

The little robotic arms unfolded themselves and plunged their way into her temples, linking her back to the network.

The afternoon passed by, but she found a few small fish. Nothing like her big catch that morning, but it was usually how it worked. A lot of little fish, or a lot of nothing. Or one big win, and maybe some extra to go with it. At least the week was almost done, and she allowed her mind to slip toward later that night.

She knew the time, but that was the only detail she left out in the open, tucking the rest behind an invisible wall. Should she even dare with that detective lurking around?

## 4 p.m.

It was time to go home. The robotic arms removed themselves from her head, folding back into the viewer which she placed on the table. Her fingers were sticky from the jellyfish-like keyboard, and she adjusted the two pieces of paper where she had found them earlier. The one noting Minor Crimes stuck to her finger.

At night, there was only one or two people doing the monitoring, and there were a lot of blind spots. If you were going to commit a crime, it was always best to wait until after seven. The cops would be doing their patrols, and the detectives their hunting. But there were gaps, and she knew how to slip in-between them. At eight-thirty p.m. tonight, her black dagger would find its next victim.

She stepped out of the gray square and heard, "I'm the Black Dagger Killer."

"Jesus, not again," she muttered but then saw a doctor moving down the hall past her.

She turned to see two security guards restraining Janine. "Janine lost her shit."

Of course, Bob was standing behind her. He moved like a cat. "And she thinks she's the serial killer."

Ashley looked past him to see the detective standing nearby. He wasn't staring at Janine. He was looking at her. Ashley turned around and adjusted her sunglasses.

"It could be a woman," she said to Bob.

"Yeah, and you can hardly see."

Ashley watched the doctor give Janine a shot before she

slumped to the floor. "First, Susan. Then, that new recruit. Now, Janine."

"Yeah, it's just you, me, and the redhead." He noted Ashley's surprise. "She starts tomorrow."

"That was fast."

"Yeah, don't trip on the way out, and I'll see you tomorrow."

"I'm not blind, Bob," Ashley yelled after him.

She glanced toward where the detective stood, but he had walked away. She was sure he was watching her. Maybe, she should lay off the killing.

The ride home was quiet, but she felt unsettled, almost as if someone were watching her. But there was no sign of the detective, and luckily, no more minor crimes. At the station, as she headed for her car, a pair of teenagers ran around trying to knock people over, especially those who were elderly. One of them decided to start with her, but she pushed her hair back, revealing the marks on her temples. He froze mid-step.

She got to her car, and yes, there was another scratch made by somebody on the driver-side door.

"Fucking minor crimes," she muttered.

**5 p.m.**

She had three hours to kill.

She made herself a tuna fish sandwich and drank a cup of tea. Then, she sat on the couch and forced herself to relax. The lights were still on dim, but she closed her eyes, playing music in her head.

"Alert me at 7:30 p.m."

"Timer set for 7:30 p.m," a computer replied.

She could never tell if someone was probing her mind, but she didn't keep her devices near her. Her cell phone was in her pocketbook. Her parents knew she only called them on the weekends. There was no one else for her to talk to.

She used her computer randomly, always deleting her search history which probably didn't matter. If anyone went through it, they really wouldn't find anything except maybe an old search history on black daggers.

In her second year at work, when she was finally sure nobody was coming to arrest her for that first kill, she went to a fair where she saw this man who made handcrafted black daggers. No one was interested in them except for her. She bought them all, promising herself she would use them wisely. They were sharp. Sharp enough to cut the femoral artery. That's how she killed her prey.

There was a knock on her door. Usually, it would be the food service deliveries who would knock on her door. Maybe, occasionally, a next-door neighbor. She was almost sure once of being seen, coming home with bloody clothes. Again, nothing happened.

"What time is it?" She heard the alarm go off. "Shit. I need to get ready." Another knock was heard. "Coming," Ashley said as she jumped off the couch and opened the door. Detective Hunter Knight waited outside. "Detective, what are you doing here?"

"Can I come in, or are you going somewhere?" He seemed to already know that answer.

"No, come in."

Ashley held the door open for him, watching him walk inside. She had the black daggers hidden inside a flex wall within the bedroom closet. She caught herself thinking about it, but then relaxed. It was after seven p.m.

"Can I get some water?"

"Sure. Yeah. Um… Have a seat and I'll get it."

She gestured toward the couch and turned her back on him, which was probably a mistake.

"We never finished our conversation." She heard the click of his gun. "Do you want to know what you did? Where you screwed up?"

Ashley sighed as she turned around, looking from him to the gun in his hand.

"You going to shoot me?"

"Where are the daggers?"

"What daggers, detective?"

"I found the man that made them for you. Well, actually you bought all of them from him."

So that's how they found her.

"I don't know what you're talking about. You want some water?"

"You know the law, Ashley. Murderers and serial killers get the red light, so I have the right to shoot you. And I won't have to defend my actions, but I have to applaud you, really. It was brilliant using the network to find your kills, those committing minor crimes."

"They're just little wolves, detective. Little wolves terrorizing people who are trying to live their lives. Some of their crimes are not minor."

"So, you're what? Little Red Riding Hood with a black dagger?"

"Something like that." Ashley stared at the gun. "I know the law, yes, so if you are going to shoot me, then do it. What are you waiting for?" She watched him walk over to the apartment door. "What are you doing?"

The detective opened the apartment door, and a man in a dark suit waited outside. He smelled like government, but the part that you never talk about or want anything to do with. He stepped inside, and the detective holstered his gun.

"I don't want to see her again," the detective said. "If I do, I won't hesitate to shoot her."

"I understand," the man in the dark suit said.

"Hey, I'm standing right here." She watched the detective leave. "Hello? What the fuck is going on?"

"You have two choices, Ashley."

"Uh, excuse you, but I don't know you. You can get out of my apartment."

"You might not know me, but I know you." The man stepped closer, making her cringe. "I know everything about you."

"Who are you?"

"While you were at work, plugged into the network, you caught my attention. While you were monitoring others for information, I was digging through your mind, your long-term memories."

"No, I would've felt that, and that's not possible to access long-term memories."

"Oh, come on, Ashley. I know you can do that too."

"Who are you?"

"You have two choices."

"You said that before."

"Yes, I did. Choice one, kill yourself tonight." He stood in front of her. "Don't think it won't happen because it will." He watched her flinch at his words.

"Did you kill Susan?" He shrugged in response. "Why?"

"Because she was protecting you. She knew, Ashley, and she was a loose end."

Ashley backed away. Her mind already spiraling in terror. Did she have time to run into her room and get her black daggers? Something inside told her, no. "The second choice?"

"You come with me."

"Where?"

"Somewhere you will never be seen again. You will be alive, inside the network."

"Inside the network? What does that mean?"

"It means that you will still be alive, and you could still hunt your little wolves. You'll just be killing them differently." He stared into her eyes. "You would like that, wouldn't you?"

"My parents?" She watched him shake his head.

"I'm on the clock, so…". He clapped his hands together, making her jump. "Which choice, Ashley?"

Ashley looked toward her bedroom. Her head turned toward the man who stood an inch from her face. It was almost like death stared her down, and she did not want to die.

"2," she said. "Choice 2," and he suddenly buried a syringe into Ashley's neck. "But– But you said that you wouldn't kill me."

"I'm not going to kill you, but I am going to transport you to the real network, your permanent home." He watched her lose consciousness. "And trust me when I say, after a period of time, you'll forget you were ever human."

# Challenging Perception
By Sehra Dylan Nikol

There was not a knife sharp enough that could cut the tension between Sandy and me. This wasn't our first fight and it wouldn't be our last, but I'd had enough. I couldn't hold it in anymore.

"I can't believe you!" I said opening the door to the house we called home. Although it didn't feel like that anymore. The door slammed shut behind me.

"It's not my fault you got the schedule mixed up." Sandy said, nonchalantly shrugging his shoulders as if to say 'So What.'

"But that's the thing. I didn't. You did and instead of talking to me about it, you reversed all of my nightmares and gave everyone dreams."

I sat down on the bench next to the door to take off my black Doc Martens. The simple act of untying the shoelaces allowed me to recenter my focus, calm me down, and think more rationally.

I sighed before I said, "We've talked about this. There's a

balance; people's perception of the world has to be balanced."

I could tell he wasn't paying any attention to what I was saying, so I headed upstairs to get some rest. But this is how it always was. Sandy never paid any regard for how his actions would affect me. It absolutely infuriated me that he didn't seem to care. The only thing worse was our parents didn't seem to care either.

I was always painted as the villain or a complete and utter outcast. But I'm not the villain, I'm just misunderstood. Please, just listen to my side of the story, and maybe it'll challenge your perception. There are two sides to every story, and this is mine.

See, the thing with my family is… my mother is Mother Nature. Yes, THE Mother Nature. And my father is… Father Time. So, if you connect the dots, all of the legendary figures are my siblings. Santa Claus, Tooth Fairy, Easter Bunny (spoiler alert, he isn't actually a bunny), Jack Frost, Cupid, and you've already met my youngest brother, Sandman. And, that would make me… You guessed it. I'm the Bogeyman. But I prefer to go by B.

I woke up just after sunrise came and went. We, me and all of my siblings, were called to an emergency family meeting. I begrudgingly got out of bed and got dressed. I was not looking forward to this at all, but I couldn't keep prolonging the inevitable. I stalled long enough, drug myself downstairs, and walked straight into the dining room where my family waited for me. I slouched in my chair, my head in my hands. I know this meeting was going to be about what happened last night between me and Sandy. I sat up as Mother audibly clapped her hands to get our attention.

"I think we all know why we're here." Mother said in a gentle but firm voice as she made direct eye contact with me. I couldn't meet her gaze, forcing myself to look at the floor.

"B, Sandy, will you please tell us your sides of this story, so we can get to the bottom of this." Sandy was about to speak up when she held up one finger to silence him. Well, that's a new one. "I want to hear from B first."

I sighed and stood. "Sandy isn't following the schedule of who receives dreams and who receives nightmares. He got it mixed up, reversed all of my nightmares, and gave everyone dreams instead of double checking with me first."

I looked around the room for support, but I was only met with judgemental faces. I sat down when Sandy stood.

"What can I say? Mistakes happen. B didn't have to lash out at me like that."

My jaw dropped. He just completely dismissed me when I had calmed down and wanted to talk about what had happened last night.

Mom and Dad shared a look, having a silent conversation with their eyes. They nodded in agreement. Dad spoke this time.

"Sandy is absolutely right. You shouldn't have lashed out at him. Now, apologize to your brother," he said in a calm, gentle voice I normally found very comforting.

Right now, it was agonizingly vexing. I felt so defeated. My mouth fell open once again. Me? Apologize to him!? My hands started to shake. My whole body practically trembled where I sat. I couldn't believe this. They took his side. AGAIN.

Why do they always take his side? It's because I'm the eldest. I'm supposed to be perfect. I can't do anything right. Why? Why can't I ever do anything right?! Why wasn't I good enough?! Just once, I'd like for them to take my side. Just once! What's wrong with me!? Why am I always placed second?! Not even second, more like last.

I couldn't take this mental agony, so I snapped, screaming at the top of my lungs, "That's it!"

I stood up, slamming my trembling fists on the table, causing my chair to fall over, and trying, but failing, not to cry.

"I can't take it anymore. Why am I even here?!" I wiped

the tears from my eyes as I pulled on my black Doc Martens, snapped my fingers, and poof! I was gone.

It wasn't long before I couldn't stand on my own. A month. That's all it took before I was too weak to stand on my own two feet. I had to lean on walls in order to keep going. The longer I was away from home, the more ghostly I felt, my presence beginning to fade away.

I was stumbling around in the shadows and watched the sky grow dark. Then the wind picked up. Rain poured down. The smell of fresh rain reminded me of my mother. I know it may sound cliche', but my mother's moods affected the weather.

I slipped but somehow managed to catch myself on the windowsill of someone's house. I was about to leave when I heard a voice coming from inside. They couldn't see me. No human could. Unless we allowed ourselves to be seen, and the only time that happened was if our guard was down.

"Mom, I don't want to go to bed," A young teen, her tone lacking enthusiasm, said.
Her voice sounded so melancholy with disdain when she said, "It's always the same… I don't enjoy them anymore. Dreams were always the best part about going to bed."

"I know your dreams aren't what they used to be. But you need to get some sleep."

An older woman, presumably the young teen's mother said, trying to coax her teen daughter to bed. I watched from the window as they went to that young teen's bedroom.

The older woman turned the light out. "Goodnight, don't let the bed bugs bite."

I thought everyone was better off without me. I thought maybe Sandy was right, that everyone wanted to be happy. I felt so heartbroken seeing that young teen so lost and hopeless. Was I really helping them? Or was I hurting them? I thought that I was only hurting myself.

A wave of guilt washed over me. More than anything, I wanted to reach out to that young teen, and do whatever I could to make her feel better. How could I continue to hurt them? I had to make this right.

I took a deep breath and mustered up the rest of my strength. I snapped my fingers and poof! I was in the young teen's bedroom.

I sat down on the bed next to her, touching her shoulder to obtain some of her essence. Creating a nightmare for younger humans was simpler than creating a nightmare for adult humans. It required less manipulation of the human essence.

I held her essence in my hands, closed my eyes, and channeled the surrounding shadows. When I opened my eyes, her essence was manipulated just enough so she would receive a small nightmare. I placed my open palm on her forehead, gently easing the nightmare into her mind. She tensed up, but only for a second. After that brief second, she became relaxed. I felt a little bit of strength return.

Just enough I could find my brother. I slowly stood, staring off into the distance in order to hone in on Sandy and I's connection. A by-product of both of us having to feed off of the energy sleeping humans gave off while experiencing a dream or nightmare. I've hated our connection for as long as I could remember, but right now? That didn't matter. The only thing that mattered was finding him. A sudden rush of strength took over my body and shook my senses back into reality. I knew where he was.

He was in someone's apartment, about to give them a dream. I took a deep breath and closed my eyes, drawing the last drops of strength I could harness into my being. I raked my pale, slender fingers through my dark, jet-black hair flecked with silver which stood opposite of my brother's golden strands, seemingly full of life and light. I had to stop hesitating. I snapped both of my middle fingers against my palms as I brought my hands down to my sides. The sound echoed for a moment and then poof! I was gone.

I appeared in the apartment. My shadows enveloped the bright light my brother carried within him.

I locked eyes with Sandy in complete desperation. I had to stop him. I had to fix this. I couldn't let this continue. Not after I saw what had happened to that young teen.

"You have to let me give them a nightmare."

"No, I don't. Dreams make people happy. People always want to be happy."

I was about to speak when the person who was asleep on the couch across from us woke up.

My brother and I locked eyes in shock. Both of our guards were down.

The man got up and rubbed his eyes. He looked at the two of us for what felt like an eternity before he finally said "You must be the Bogeyman and that would make you the Sandman." He gestured to both of us before ruffling his wicked cobalt blue hair that's shaved on the sides. It remained voluminous on top and hung slightly in his eyes before he finished with "I knew it! I knew Legendary Figures were real."

He let out a sigh riddled with confusion that ended with a laugh. His forehead was sweating as he wiped it off with the back of his hand. After that, he chewed on his thumbnail, unsure of what to do or say next.

Without allowing the man time to process what was going on around him, Sandy spoke up, blatantly ignoring the anxiety and distress written all over the man's face.

"We need you to settle something for us. You've only been having dreams for the last what? Month-ish? You decide... your options are to dream and keep being happy or to have a nightmare and become filled with such pure horror and gripping paranoia whenever you see your own shadow?"

He looked at Sandy, and then took a step toward me, meeting my gaze in a silent plea. I knew what his decision was before he could even say a word, but I wanted Sandy to hear it, too.

"Please give me a nightmare. Please, I'm sick of dreams. I want to feel something other than happy for once. And, if it causes me to become filled with pure horror and gripping paranoia whenever I see my own shadow, then so be it. I don't care. Just please give me a nightmare."

He grasped my hands in his. They shook so badly that he lost his grip on mine more than a few times. I hoped he would be on my side, but for him to so willingly look past the unwelcoming appearance my body held, and still hold my hands so desperately as he had. I didn't know my actions would have much deeper and darker consequences than I originally had anticipated. I felt a twinge of pain in my chest, the same pain I felt for that young teenage girl. I couldn't leave him like this.

I tried to conceal my feelings of guilt, as I said "Okay." As soon as I said that one simple word, the man's dull eyes lit up with relief and a renewed sense of hope. He let go of my hands and laid back down on the couch.

I sat down on the opposite end of the couch, "You'll have to close your eyes, take a couple of slow deep breaths, and then you'll start to fall asleep, but you won't be completely out of it. When I give you a nightmare, your natural response is going to be to fight it, but you're going to have to ignore that instinct. Let the nightmare enter your mind and play through."

He nodded and said, "Thank you… for giving me a nightmare. My name is Belvue by the way."

As I stood, I gave a slight smile. "Always."

His eyes closed and his breathing slowed as he entered into a deep sleep. I touched his shoulder. When I opened my hand, his essence was there. I threw it into midair and then...

I twisted my fingers into my palm, my thumb on top. The shadows pulled his essence to me. Once I held it in my palm again, I took a deep breath. I had to brush his hair aside before slowly pushing his essence into his mind.

He tossed and turned. I knew he was trying to fight it, but it looked like he was fighting himself more. Was he actually listening to me? No one ever listened to me.

The tossing and turning ceased, and I felt it. A rush of energy meant the nightmare had entered his mind. I exhaled a sigh of relief. My strength was coming back.

If you thought giving people nightmares was easy, you'd be dead wrong. I don't enjoy giving people nightmares. But I have to. It is physically taxing. The mental and emotional toll that it takes on me forced me into a dark place within my own mind. A place I don't like to be. One I have no control over.

My brother and I went our separate ways. Once the sun started to rise, we made our way home. If I could even call it that.

The silence between my brother and I was deafening. Not a word was spoken as I opened the door, and we went inside. After I closed the door, I sat on the bench, becoming lost in my thoughts.

Sandy wouldn't meet my gaze. He appeared to be lost in his thoughts, too. Was he angry about what happened with Belvue? Should I ask him what's going on? I didn't want him to shrug me off like he always did. He sat beside me to take his shoes off. Now, I know something is wrong. He doesn't like being around me. So, why would he sit next to me?

He slipped off his white Vans and locked eyes with me. He looked so defeated as he said, "You were right. And I'm sorry."

I didn't know how to react. I couldn't believe what I was

hearing. Before I could even open my mouth to respond, he hugged me. I hugged him back. Our hug only lasted a moment before he pulled away, sighed, and ruffled his hair with his hand.

After that, he stood and said, "I'm gonna go to bed. Um... sleep well?"

I smiled. It felt so unnatural. I haven't had a genuine smile on my face for... I can't even remember the last time. "Thanks. You too."

***

I woke up the next day with my sense of self restored. I finally felt the way that I've always wanted. I felt like things between me, my brother, and our parents may finally have a chance to change for the better and stay that way.

I got out of bed and pulled on a pair of high-waisted dark-wash ripped denim jeans. I threw on my favorite T-shirt, which, ironically enough, was white, and had a bright yellow smiley face on it. It was my favorite T-shirt because Sandy gave it to me a long time ago. I haven't worn it since things between the two of us took a turn for the worst. The last thing I did was put on a pair of long, thick, heather-gray socks. I smiled at my reflection before I left my room and went downstairs.

I walked toward the dining room where my family waited for me. I expected the worst. To be yelled at for being gone so long, almost dying, and preventing Sandy from doling out more dreams that made everyone happy. I hesitated to step into the room. I was met with acceptance instead of judgment. I sat in the same chair as last time. Sandy was the first to speak.

"This was all my fault." He paused, putting his head in his hands for a brief second, before continuing, "I've convinced all of you that Bogeyman was the villain, an outcast, the second choice. When in reality, he was right, there is a balance. I tipped the balance in favor of myself, believing that everyone wanted to always be happy. But that is far from the truth. Now, I understand I was the toxic one. Not him."

He came over and pulled me to my feet. We had a silent conversation with just our eyes before he finally said, "I know I don't deserve it, but can you please forgive me?"

I gave him a shy smile and said, "I forgive you."

We may not have always seen eye to eye, but he was still my brother. Things weren't perfect, far from it. But they were getting better. And that's all that matters.

Before I knew it, it was time to deliver nightmares and dreams to the world. Everyone said their goodnights while I pulled on my black Doc Martens and Sandy pulled on his white Vans. We stepped outside our house where I finally felt I could call home and it was then I noticed something.

"You're wearing the T-shirt I gave you," I said, looking at Sandy's T-shirt. It was almost identical to mine, except his was black, and instead of a yellow happy face, it had a purple upside-down happy face. We got them for each other when we started developing our connection.

He chuckled as he said, "It's my favorite T-shirt."

\*\*\*

I'm always seen as the villain, an outcast because I inspire fear, but I only ever truly wanted everyone to be happy. My nightmares allow people to cherish their good dreams. Which is all I ever wanted.

# Mary

By William Connell

Bridget Burr looked up into the darkness at the top of the stairway. The great Queen Anne-two-story house on Main Street was empty. She does approve of them at all. Her father and mother were attending a reception at Armory Hall being given by John Stubbs, the second richest man in Warren. Elizabeth, Bridget's younger sister, was with her friends at their uncle and aunt's house. Bridget looked down at the items she had gathered that sat on the hallway table. A compact mirror, a long wax candle, a small hammer from her father's tool shed, and a stick match all sat together on a white lace doily. The last, which Bridget thought was the oddest, was the book. The one that the librarian had told her she must never read. Her sister's molar tooth, which had fallen out two days ago.

\*\*\*

She sits quietly in a quarter-sawn oak armchair. The seat is upholstered with a purple brocade made of silk. It is quite comfortable. Her body leans forward, her hands clasped in front of her. Pale, willowy, wearing a white body-length sheath dress with thin straps on the shoulders. Of course, one could be forgiven for not thinking she was pale, or her dress white, as she is covered with wide swathes of blood. A variety of mirrors are nearby. A French oval ormolu dressing mirror, sitting atop a small end table. A tall freestanding ornate giltwood and composition mirror. A triple plate dressing mirror framed with brown teakwood. Many more. The "walls" of her abode are an ever-present gray mist that surrounds her. This is her home. The World of Reflections.

Some might see her as a lonely figure, but they would be mistaken. Other souls exist in the gray. There is the small oriental girl, the closest she has to someone you might think of as a friend. Yet there is so much pain and anger in the oriental girl, that it interferes with their relationship. She does not approve of the oriental girl's violence when she is summoned, but she does understand. They are both subject to forces they cannot (always) control. They comprehend each other. They accept each other.

There are others. Others who relish the giving of pain. They are not like those who are forced to. They are those who choose to.

She does approve of *them* at all.

For the most part, though, her thoughts keep her company. She is quite content with them in the silence of the gray.

\*\*\*

Bridget placed the molar on the doily. This seemed most odd, but the book had said this was part of the ritual. Sneaking into Elizabeth's room after dark to retrieve the tooth that had been carefully wrapped in tissue paper and placed under the pillow had left Bridget with some guilt. She reasoned that when her mother came later that night to retrieve the tooth, mother would just assume it had fallen and was lost under the bed, and she would quietly place a coin under the pillow anyway. Elizabeth would get her coin. Mother might be mildly perplexed. And

Bridget would find out what she had to know.

Just two months ago her life's story was in place. Bridget had set her sights on William Waterman when they were both at the Market Street School. They had dated since they were both sixteen. He, the son of the wealthiest family in Warren, and one of the wealthiest in New England, the owners of the massive waterfront textile mills. Oh, how her friends and others had been envious of her. Years had passed quickly, and though William had a wandering eye, and friends "confided" to her that he had other dalliances, everyone knew that she was his girl. Her parents had mentioned that she was not getting younger. It did not matter. William was working very hard building his family's business and was required to go on long trips. He had assured her they would be married, and she would be the wife of the son of the owner of the Warren Manufacturing Company, the largest textile factory on the Atlantic seacoast.

Then he announced that he was going to marry a girl from Boston, Dora Tulley. Five years Bridget's junior, and the daughter of the famous shipping family.

Bridget found herself alone. And now the subject of old maid jokes amongst many of her friends, so-called.

So, she had to know.

Who would she marry?

So she had looked at the book that fool librarian, old Ms. Baker had told her never to read. But Bridget had found the book and had read it, and now she was doing what it said.

She took the hammer and tapped Elizabeth's molar tooth. It would not break.

She tried again, and it still would not break.

"You're harder than I thought," she thought.

She got onto her hands and knees and placed the tooth and the doily on the hardwood floor. She struck harder with the hammer, three times.

The tooth was crushed.

Bridget wrapped the pieces of the tooth in a doily and stood up against the table. She struck the match and lit the candle. She placed the compact mirror and the doily in the pocket of her dress. Then she turned off the gas lighting dial. The flames in the lamps went down and the entire stairwell was covered in darkness, save for the one candle she held. She walked over to the stairs and looked up. Eighteen steps to the landing, which then turned to the left and rose another three steps to the second-floor landing. Bridged turned around and felt for the compact mirror. Then she held it up and opened it and saw see her reflection. She stepped out of her shoes.

For a moment, she recalled Ms. Baker's words.

*"Do not mess with these things. In the spirit world, there is divination and sorcery, and one can turn into the other very quickly. Especially to someone who is not wise and experienced with both. And you are far too young and foolish to try."*

"Too young and foolish," Bridget said with a snort. Well, what did Ms. Baker know? She was ancient and poor and had never married, and probably happy that is how her life turned out. But Bridget's family worked hard. The Burr family was respected throughout Warren. Bridget needed to find someone who fit her station.

And the book had told her what to do. What spirit to conjure, who could reveal her future husband?

Gingerly she took a bare step backward and upwards onto the first step. She twisted a little to the side as she pushed up but did not lose her balance. After a pause and a deep breath, she took another step back, the second time more confident than the first. Then another. This would work.

After counting nine steps - halfway up - she said, "Bloody Mary."

Bridget Burr felt a slight chill, but she heard nothing. After a momentary startle, she smiled. In the shadowy recess of the hallway at the foot of the stairs, outside the candlelight, a figure who had been observing Bridget Burr also smiled.

\*\*\*

She hears her name echoing through the air. She is being summoned. From her home in the World of Reflections. This has happened many times before. With a sigh, she rises from her chair and walks to the giltwood and composition mirror. It is one of her favorites. She runs her fingers over the glass and then touches the winged cherubs that sit atop the mirror. For a moment, she hesitates and breathes in the cool air. Something is wrong.

Quickly she sets on her way. To the Land Beyond the Mirrors.

\*\*\*

Bridget ascended two more steps. Then – her heart jumped, and she fumbled with the mirror, but held it. Her body was shaking.

She remembered the book's warning.

*If there is no husband to be, then the spirit may be conjured.*

She almost – almost – opened her eyes. The book was resolute on this point. Do not open your eyes until you are at the top, or the ritual would be broken.

In the darkness there was still only silence. She took another step backward and as before, said "Bloody Mary."

\*\*\*

She waits in the darkness on the landing at the top of the eighteen stairs. Not fully formed. Still a shadow. Still in the land of gray mist, but right on the precipice with the other world. The

Land Beyond the Mirrors. She cannot speak, not with an oral voice. She makes a sweep with her right hand and looks on as the gray mist starts to swirl in a circle over the second-floor landing.

\*\*\*

The book had said one had to be just before the top of the stairs before making the final incantation. Bridget had counted seventeen steps. She felt with one bare foot and sensed she was right at the top.

"Bloody Mary," she said, a third time.

\*\*\*

Mary looks at the mist. The spinning fog begins to open up a hole in the center, through which an image is forming. Mary watches it take shape.

A tombstone. "Bridget Burr – Beloved daughter" carefully etched thereon. No date. She has seen this many times before as well. Not with this name, but with many other names. Those young women who will never marry. There is no husband to reveal. So, Mary can only reveal herself. And hope the young women does not act too rashly.

\*\*\*

Bridget Burr looked into the mirror and — a figure appeared in the reflection.
Her heart stopped.

It was not the face of a strapping well-dressed gentleman as she had hoped, but rather a woman. A pale-faced woman, with long stringy dark hair falling over a white countenance. Deep-set eyes with dark circles beneath them (though if Bridget were not so horrified she might think the eyes were more sad than evil). The figure's head was cocked to the side. The face and body were splashed with crimson.

Bridget was frozen.

And the World of Reflections and the Land Beyond the Mirrors intersect.

\*\*\*

The figure cannot voice anything. She can communicate but one way.

In the mirror, Bridget Burr sees the figure's hand reach toward her shoulder. Bridget is too terrified to see the letters "D-O" drawn in blood in the reflection of the mirror. She whirls around and comes face to face with the woman.

The woman starts to reach for Bridget's face. Bridget screams and recoils from the bloody figure, and her left heel steps back. Bridget Burr falls and as she does, she has one chance to reach for the wood railing on the staircase, but she still has the mirror in her hand and is unable to grab a hold. Now her feet become twisted and both slip out beneath her, and she is tumbling backward. The mirror and candle fall. Her body tumbles over itself. The back of her head lands squarely on the eighth step. Bridget hears her second and then the third vertebrae break. Then all goes black as her body cartwheels downward before reaching the bottom landing. She finally careens across the landing and hits the house wall with such force that she cracks the oak wood walls.

Bridget Burr lies at the foot of the stairs, wedged into the corner of the hallway. Her head is draped across her chest at an impossibly acute angle.

The candle fell to the hallway floor. The compact mirror lies on the fifth step.

She is conscious. She can hear. But she cannot move. She cannot feel anything beneath her chest. She can open her mouth. She tries to take in air, but she cannot. It is as if a heavy weight sits on her chest, squeezing out her air. There is no weight, but the sensation is understandable as both her lungs have been punctured. She is not so much in pain as she is – numb.

Bridget hears a song being sung. From another side of the staircase. Bridget cannot move but she does hear the voice in a pleasant, sing-song voice.

*"A-tisket, a-tasket,*
*I lost my yellow basket,*
*I wrote a letter to my friend*
*and on the way I dropped it."*

The singer appears. Bridget cannot move her head, but she sees a pair of black boots dance in front of her.

The singer stops singing and says "Oh, dear, did we have a fall?"

Bridget spits up blood.

"I'm sorry my dear, let me get a good look at you."

The singer bends down. She is a woman, middle-aged, wearing a white and blue gingham dress. Golden hair speckled with silver, rolled up in a bun, under a bonnet. She is carrying a white wicker basket. But there is a – glow from her skin, from her clothes, an aura that forms around her.

"Don't worry, dear, I found a new basket."

She leans closer to Bridget's face. Bridget can see she is wearing a strange necklace.

The fair-haired woman touches the necklace and says "Oh, you like this? Well, have a closer look." She leans in.
Bridget sees the necklace. It is made of teeth, strung together on a chain.

"I collect these."

She puts the basket down and pulls out two silver utensils, one in each hand.

"This is called an elevator," she says, shaking a single long silver stick ending in a sharp fork. "And this is called a forceps extractor." She holds what looks like a set of silver tongs. She flexes her fingers, and the tips of the tongs clink together.

"These are the tools of my trade, my sweet. And I need to take what is mine. You see there are rules, and you know who

I am. You never should have crushed your sister's tooth. When a child loses a tooth, I need to get one. And if I can't get your sister's – which I can't since you crushed it – I have to get another one. And since you destroyed my tooth – you owe me one of yours."

The golden-haired woman knocks on the walls.

"These Queen Anne's are built well, with sturdy oak walls. They hold noises inside so well. You cannot find this timber today."

There is a creaking sound from Maplewood steps. Bridget can still see. She sees the Faerie turn to look up. The bloodied woman is halfway down the steps. Bridget cannot move her neck, but she can shift her eyes and she looks upward. The singing Faerie and the bloodied woman stare at each other for some moments.

"Oh, look honey, this one's head droops just like yours."

The bloodied woman takes another step down.

"Go back," the Faerie snarls, no longer in the singsong voice, but something much deeper. "You have no power over me, Mary. She crushed her sister's molar, and that was mine. You know the rules, as do I. I have the right to take from her what is rightfully mine. So long as I do it before she dies."

Bridget hears a calm voice say "You tricked her."

"The Faerie laughs and says "Oh that's just a technicality. She was summoning you, my dear, not me. And you came. And she had no future. That's not my doing."

"You arranged it," says the calmer voice.

The bloodied woman takes another step forward.

The Faerie's voice raises just a timbre and says "She summoned you. You saw no future for her. She lies here near death. You can do nothing to her." After a pause, the Faerie's voice added "Or to me."

The bloodied woman looks at Bridget Burr's broken

body. Bridget Burr is gurgling blood.

The Faerie laughingly says "That's right, go back to your mirrors. And let me do my work."

The one called Mary, her face shows a look of regret, but the Faerie is right. Mary recedes back up the stairs into the dark.

Now the Faerie's singsong voice returns and she calls, "Don't worry. They'll find the mirror and the candle, and they'll say it was a foolish accident, but those who know – They'll know. You'll get all the credit for this. Another victim for your tally. You did this. And as for me- "

the Faerie clinks the forceps again.

"I'm just taking a tooth."

The Faerie turns back to Bridget and crouches down in front of her.

"We finally got rid of her."

The Faerie reaches into her basked and resumes singing.

*I dropped it*
*I dropped it*
*Yes, on the way I dropped it*
*A little boy he picked it up*
*and put it in his pocket."*

The Faerie looks up into Bridget's rapidly shrinking pupils and sees the look of a question.

"I know," the Faerie says. "You followed the book's instructions. To a T. But you see, you were desperate and vulnerable, and I sense vulnerabilities. It is what I exist for. I enchanted the papers of the book you read. You never steel the tooth of a child and crush it. For it is mine. And if a child's tooth is destroyed, I have to retrieve another from the person who took my tooth. Somehow."

Bridget Burr's vision begins to fade out. She feels such fear that her body shudders. She tried to say something, but her mouth is too filled with blood, and now she cannot move anything other than her eyelids. The fairy reaches forward with her tools.

The last thing Bridget Burr hears is a soothing voice as the forceps reach into her mouth.

"My, you have such beautiful teeth. I may have to take a few."

\*\*\*

She watches her own reflection as she rocks ever so slowly. A figure in a white sheath dress, both covered with blood streaks. She rests on a Venetian rocking chair, with a seat and backrest carved like seashells. Everything the Faerie said was true. The girl may or may not have had a future, but the Faerie manipulated the girl's fate to achieve her ends. The Faerie is cunning and wise, very ancient, much more so than she. While the Faerie may fear what she can do, the Faerie knows the rules. As does she. But the Faerie is a far more skilled machinator than she is, and the Faerie knows this. For a period of time, she is indeed melancholy with these thoughts. But upon further reflection, her thoughts remind her that with great age can come great hubris. Hubris can lead to mistakes. Mistakes can cause the breaking of rules that must never be broken.

But when those rules are broken - different things can happen.

These thoughts bring her comfort.

She will bide her time.

# Be Careful What You Wish For

By William J. Connell

A tavern in the early evening. It is like many taverns in the region of southwestern France and northwestern Italy during the fourteenth century. A rectangular stone building isolated on a stretch of road, a small open space cut out of a dense forest. Just behind it is a two-story waddle and daub house, relatively solid, which serves as an inn. In the alley formed between the alehouse and the inn, there is a row for games such as bowling (or bocce, if you prefer). A few men play this game as a fire burns in the nearby firepit. Lovers are intertwined in the darkness along the tree line. Inside, many boards, what some would call tables, and forms, or benches, are scattered about, along with some cut-in-half wine barrels. On the side, there is a large hearth with a fire burning. This and candles provide the interior light. It is an oasis for travelers journeying through the dense and mountainous woods.

On this particular night, the alehouse is especially crowded with pilgrims and other wanderers. A large, somewhat corpulent man named Gianni is sitting on a cut barrel at a long table. This form is a long rectangle, like the building, and several people sit drinking at the table. This man's companion, Michele, younger, taller, and thinner than his companion, is drinking next to him on another cut barrel. Their drink is stout. They have another companion, Francesco, but he has found company with another woman in the tavern.

"This place stinks," says Gianni, spitting as he talks. He speaks with a broken, occitanian dialect.

"All taverns stink," Michele says, keeping his eyes on the table. "There's always too many people. Everyone here is a traveler. And they're all running from the plague in Florence. And they all come in from the road. Of course, they stink."

Both men drink some more.

"Look at the dog Francesco is with," Gianni says while pointing to the corner. The crowd makes it hard to see, but their third companion, a younger black-haired youth with olive skin named Francesco, is kissing a young woman wearing a red cape in a darkened corner of the room.

"That creature he's with looks like shit," Gianni says loudly over the din of noise. "And with the money we just found." Michele, keeping his eyes on his drink, admonishes "You talk too much."

"Who gives a rat's fuck? This place is awful. This beer is piss." Gianni looks back to the corner and said "Jees, I think that hag has only one eye."

"So what of it?" says a voice.

Both men look up. A red-haired woman wearing tight-fitted breeches, shining black leather boots, and a white linen shirt stands by their form. Michele waves her away, but Gianni says "What of it? He's our friend and he just got a lot of money and he can find a barmaid who will do better than that piece of shit he's with. That's the what of it."

"Shut up," Michele says through gritted teeth.

A man who has been sitting next to Gianni and quietly drinking his ale falls off the bench to the floor. The red-haired woman moves in and sits down in his place on the form. She rests her arms on the table, clasping her left hand over her right one.

"How did your friend get the money?" she asks. She speaks in the refined dialect of Middle French.

"A funny story," Gianni says. "Would you like to hear it?"

The red-haired woman leans closer and says, "Do tell."

"Shut up," Michele says again, more strident than before.

Gianni shoves Michele and says "Piss off."

Michele glares angrily at him, then gets up and stands over the woman. "Leave us," he commands. But when the woman turns her head ever so slightly and makes eye contact, Michele's face becomes pale. Quickly he grabs his stout and leaves. The woman turns back to Gianni and smiles

"What got into him?" Gianni asks, watching Michele leave. Then turning back to the woman he says "Ah you're nothing special but you're better than that one-eyed bitch."

"Thank you," says the woman.

Gianni spills stout on himself.

"Damn it," he yells. Then he asks "You're not drinking?"

"Not on an empty stomach," the woman answers. "But I will eat later."

Gianni eyes her with a little caution, but the woman brushes her fingers through her hair and says "Please tell me the story. I like to hear funny stories."

Gianni shrugs and continues. "Well, you see, Michele and Francesco – he's back there with that one-eyed hag."

"I saw them," the woman replies, keeping her eyes on Gianni. "I know that girl."

Gianni notices the woman has very red lips.

Gianni has a brief pause but is too drunk to feel more.

"You ain't mad or her friend are you?" He asks

She smiles at him and says "Pay no mind. Please go on with your story."

"Like I said" he continues through gulps of stout, "We were in a place like this yesterday morning. We trying to find work. I'm a metal worker, you know, and so are the others. Chains, nails, armor, we can make anything. But there aren't any furnaces working here. So we drink all day."

"The great pestilence has made life hard for all of us," the woman comments. "But please continue."

"Ah, we were drinking in a tavern like this, yesterday morning, and we heard one of our friends, another metal worker, he died from the plague. And I cursed god and man and everyone else I could. Another friend dead from the black death."

"The great mortality claims many," the woman says. "What else did you say?"

Gianni answers "I said I want to find death; I want to kill death. And we all agreed. Michele and Francesco and me. We drank a toast and wished to find death and kill it."

"To kill death is a noble ambition," the woman comments. "What happened next?"

"Arr, some old beggar man there told us he could tell us where to find death if we bought him a drink. And we laughed and I spat at him and told him to fuck off. But Michele says what the hell and buys one for him. The beggar man drinks half his glass and I say I'll kill him if he don't tell us. Then he stops drinking and says if we want to go find death, go one hour down the road and there's a path off the road by a dead maple tree. I said there are lots of dead trees around but he said we wouldn't miss this one."

"It is spring and the leaves are flowering," the woman observes.

"Yea well, you know your seasons," Gianni says. "Anyway this beggar, he said go down that path, and he described a tree, an oak in the shape of a damn perfect V, and we'd find death there. Well, we says, let's go. And we did. And by afternoon we found that path, and we go down it, and we find that oak tree. A perfect V, just like the old fart said. And you know what we found?"

The woman shook her head.

"I have no idea."

"Well, nothing at first. And we figures we'd been swindled out of a drink so we'd go back and we'd find the old bastard. Then Francesco says let's dig around the base. We starts digging until -" He takes a great big drink and belches. Then he looks slightly askance at the woman, and now he leans into her.

"You want my gold?" he asks. "Remember, I got two friends here with me."

"I swear on my soul, I have no interest in your money," she says quietly, making a cross sign over her heart. "Or in causing you any pain."

Gianni shrugs.

"We find gold. Gold coins. And Francesco, he says they are florins, the new coins they make in Florence. Worth more than a hundred deniers each. And we got three sacks of them!"

"Really?" The woman says enthusiastically.

"So at that point it dark, and we not stupid. We stay there all night and take watch, over our gold. Next day we take it and come down here and hide it."

He laughed and drinks some more, then adds "Someplace it can't be found."

The woman asks, "Why here?"

The man grabs a barkeep, places two glistening coins on her tray and takes a mug of ale. The barkeep's eyes widen, and she quickly grabs the coins and puts them in the fichet or slit within the front of her surcoat.

"Lots of places to hide things down here," Gianni says. Staring at her closely he says "And the woods here are dangerous. Lots of bad people 'round here, you know."

The red-haired woman leans on her elbows and smiles.

\*\*\*

Michele works his way through the crowd towards Francesco. The tavern is crammed with bodies, and he is being jostled. He had not noticed it until Gianni said it, but the crowd is especially smelly and dirty, even for a roadside tavern. People look pale and decrepit, and there is strange murmuring about. Michele catches a glimpse of Francesco. The girl wearing that red cape is straddling Francesco. covering most of his body.

"Sorry to do this but we need to leave," Michele calls, walking towards him.

\*\*\*

"You see," Gianni says, "that man, he thought he so smart. He thought we kill ourselves over the money. But we not so dumb. We not greedy. We agree to share and we put it where only we know it."

"You are a smart man," the red-haired woman says, "A brave one too. When one seeks death, one often finds it."

The man drinks. "I still here, no?"

"Yes you are," the woman answers, nodding. "You certainly are."

\*\*\*

Michele sees the back of the skinny waif's head moving all over Francesco's face. *He's having a good time*, Michele thinks. Then the woman's head moves further down his body, and Michele has a good look at Francisco's face. Francisco's eyes and his mouth are open, but his body is shaking. He – something is wrong.

Michele gets by some more people and calls Francesco's name.

The woman turns around. She has one glazed eye and one empty socket, and an open bloodied mouth. She is chewing on something, something fat and bloodied and throbbing that has a string of flesh still tied to Francesco. There is a fist-sized hole in Francesco's chest over where his heart would be. If the woman was not eating it.

Michele runs for the nearest way out.

*** 

"You," Gianni says. "Let's go to one of the rooms. I want to know you better. Inside and out."

He leers at her and drops a pair of florins on the table.

"I can make it worth your while."

"That's funny," the woman says. "I want to know you too. Inside and out."

She stands up. Gianni stands as well but sways and says "Let's go. There's a house with rooms back there."

"Oh no, right here will do," the woman says.

Gianni looks puzzled. Then, swaying, he says "Sure, right here." He starts to fall forward but catches himself by putting his hand out on the board. The woman firmly pushes him back up with her left hand. She holds up her right hand and Gianni notices how long and sharp her nails look. She wraps her left hand around his neck and pulls herself up over his ample waist, and kisses him. Gianni feels her right hand reach into his trousers and slide down to his groin. Gianni is so intoxicated that he barely feels her hand.

She pulls back from her embrace, her right hand still groping him below.

"My name is Elizabeth," she says, breathing heavily. "And the girl back with Francesco is Nicola. She was once my lady in waiting."

Gianni's lips feel strange.

"I – don't feel right," Giannis mutters. "What's with your

mouth?"

The woman kisses Gianni again with more intensity.

Then she draws her right hand up, and her nails slice from the base of Gianni's protruding belly to the sternum. The woman steps back.

Gianni looks down. His belly is bulging forward. There is a deep cut, and his abdominal wall is exposed, barely holding in its contents.

"I do want to know you, inside and out," the woman named Elizabeth says. She makes one more wave of her nails along the cut on Gianni's torso.. A mixture of entrails and body fluids burst onto the table. Gianni makes some gagging noises and shakes his hands wildly. He grabs at his intestines in a futile effort to contain them, but the cut is perfect, and in seconds almost all his bowels have spilled onto the board.

He collapses to his knees and stares forward. He feels no pain. It is more a numbness.

Blood has splattered onto Elizabeth's white shirt. No wonder, as she is consuming part of Gianni's organs.

No one comes to his aid. No one can. They are either feeding or being fed upon.

***

Michele makes it out of a doorway into the back alley. The men who were playing bocce are being eaten. Flesh eaters are all over the bodies, an orgy of blood and viscera. Michele runs down the alley between the ale house and the inn, and directly into a tall, broad-shouldered man wearing the remnants of military clothes. His name is Janosz Ujvary, and he is a former mercenary from German lands, who fought with the Archpriest himself, Arnaud de Cervole, as part of an army called the Great Company. But that is not needed for this story. The military man wraps two large hands around Michele's skull, lifts him off the ground, and with a shift of his wrist, he wrenches Michele's neck.

Michele's body twitches and spasms. The military man holds Michele aloft with one hand, wraps an arm around Michele's neck, then rips off Michele's head. Janosz drops Michele's body, takes the head, and bashes it against the stone wall of the tavern until the skull cracks. The flesh easter pulls back the cranial bones to reveal the brain, still pulsating. He begins to feast.

Two smaller flesh eaters pounce on Michele's discarded remains.

\*\*\*

In the tavern, Elizabeth slices Gianni's intestines into multiple pieces with her sharp nails and tosses parts to others – *her others* - in the tavern. They tear into it hungrily and devour it. Gianni slumped to his side on the stone floor, shuddering, but still alive. He sees the barmaid's partially dismembered torso atop a barrel, being consumed. He makes gurgling noises – he feels cold overtaking him. Elizabeth kneels by him. She sees his pupils have not faded yet. They look out at her, questioning.

She lowers her head, getting close to his ear.

"I suppose a few words are in order," she states quietly. "First, it is true, I have no interest in your money. And second, I am not causing you pain. You are too drunk to feel anything. Like many of the others here. I don't want to hurt you. But we need to feed, and you are our food. And lastly, you can know that your wish was granted."

Elizabeth pauses. She sees Gianni's pupils are fading,

"That old man was probably an oracle. You wanted to find death. And you did."

Waiving bloodied nails at him, she adds, "You need to be more careful what you wish for."

As he takes his last breath, Gianni realizes she is right.

# The Battle of Tours
By William J. Connell

*October 9, 732 A.D. The northeastern province of France is known as the Duchy of Aquitaine. A massive expeditionary force has crossed over the Pyrenees Mountains and stormed its way across the Kingdom of France. Under the command of the Umayyad Caliph, Governor Abd al-Rahman, this army smashed its way through every opposition it encountered with devastating strength and ferocity. The city of Paris is within their sight. The land of Gaul, as western Europe is known, trembles in fear. The governor seeks to engage the only military force remaining to oppose him. It is a combination of regular soldiers and an assortment of farmers, tradespersons, and other civilians who have volunteered or been conscripted by the Frankish warlord, Charles "the Hammer" Martel. For the prior three days, the armies have sought each other out, with skirmishes taking place between scouting groups. But tonight, both leaders know their armies are close to one another. We look in, somewhere between the cities of Tours and Poitiers.*

Charles Martel peered through his helmet from atop his gray courser at the still smoking ruins. Duke Eudes, similarly armored, was beside Martel, on his mount, a black palfrey.

"The Saracens are efficient," Martel said to his companion. "They've found and destroyed this monastery, Saint Hilaire de Grande. very quickly. Yet we cannot find them."

"You commit our forces to the plains of Moussais-la-Bataille," the Duke responded.

"Don't worry, my Duke," Martel said. "The governor of Cordoba will be there tomorrow."

"You must not do this," warned Duke Eudes. "It is blasphemy."

Martel smiled and said, "Perhaps it is. That is why we have come here under cover of night with such a small group." He gestured back to the eight other fighting men who sat atop their horses a respectful distance behind them.

"We should not do this," Eudes repeated.

Martel gazed at the burning building in silence.

"We must fall back," Eudes stammered. "We cannot fight Al-Rahman's forces here. We are mere mortals!

Martel smiled and said, "Wait for me here." He kicked his mount with his heels and rode towards the burnt remains of the church.

*\*\**

As there was a full moon, along with some flames, there was enough light to allow sufficient navigation. Martel rode around the remains of the church's exterior. He saw the wooden roof had totally collapsed, of course, and most of the stone walls had been broken down. Those that still stood were scorched. As he approached what he thought was the entrance, he came upon several bodies on the ground. Even in the dark, he could see their throats had been slashed. A few peasant women were cleaning the corpses

Martel slowed his horse as he rode by a woman stooping over the remains of another woman. Though the field was filled with the disgusting odor of death, it was strangely silent.

"It's very quiet," Martel commented.

The kneeling woman said, "Because there must be living souls to make such sounds."

She added, "Survivors, there are none. Will you save anyone?"

Martel said nothing but rode to the gates of the church and dismounted. He paused at the remnants of two towers, just on the edge of the church.

He undid the strap under his chin and removed his domed spangenhelm helmet and put it on the ground along with his shield and his chain mail byrnie. Martel crossed the narthex and walked into what had once been the central aisle of the church called Saint Hilaire de Grande.

His footsteps on the stone floor seemed to echo as if the church still stood intact, and he looked back and forth as he walked. He reached the center transept and looked around.

To his right, he saw a woman on her hands and knees, scrubbing the ash-and-soot-covered stone floor with sponges. A wooden bucket was by her side. He approached her and saw she was wearing a stained linen tunic and a coif, and her arms were covered with black soot.

Martel said, "You should leave this place."

Still scrubbing the floor, the woman said, "You purport to tell me what to do, Charles Martel?"

Martel felt a chill of fear. He almost spoke but recalled the seer's words.

"You must not speak her name."

He dropped to one knee and bowed his head.

"There is no need to kneel," replied the woman.

Martel rose.

The woman never looked at him but continued sponging in wide circling motions. She asked, "Why are you here?"

Martel cleared his throat and gathered his thoughts.

"The Umayyads have crushed all the armies of North Africa and Iberia and al-Andalus. And Aquitaine. And now Abd Al-Rahman and his army are here. Near the field of Mousssais-la-Bataille, at the juncture of the Clain and Vienne Rivers."

"And your army, they are positioned between those two rivers," the woman noted. "You are certain the Umayyads will find you?"

Martel laughed.

"Their scouts are excellent. They will find us."

"Your back is cut off from retreat by the two rivers," the woman said. "A tactical error on your part?"

Martel laughed again and said, "You understand battle tactics, my lady. I call it a calculated risk."

The woman asked, "And you question the quality of your Frankish army?"

"My regulars? No. They can match the Umayyads. But nearly half of my army are stragglers, cobbled together from the dregs of the Carolingian Empire, such as it is." Martel shrugged. "They are brawlers. The Saracens outnumber us, but I have found where to fight them. Against men, we would have a chance."

He paused.

The woman waited some time for Martel to complete his thought, before asking "But what else?"

"The invaders have made a -- pact. Al-Rahman and his cavalry are vampires who feast on blood. They only form part of his army, maybe four thousand strong, but they are enough."

"Will not the sun weaken them?" the woman asked.

"They fight in the sun," Martel answered. "It will diminish their powers, but they still battle well in it."

The woman continued to clean the same spot on the floor with the sponge. Martel saw her entire body was caked with soot and ashes

She continued. "When Abd Al-Rahman defeats you to-morrow – which he will - there will be nothing to stop him. His armies will conquer not only Aquitaine but Neustria, then Burgundy, Austrasia, Lombardy, Swabia – even Frisia – and more." The woman stopped scrubbing, then added, "And I do not wish that to happen."

Martel thought before speaking again.

"Then why do you not strike Al-Rahman down?"

The woman explained, "There are rules, limitations, from a greater power that even I must follow. I cannot create history." She paused before adding "But I can influence it."

The woman dropped her sponge into the bucket and stood up. The soot slid from her body and clothing. Martel saw her clothes shimmer and transfigured into a flowing, immaculate purple tunic with long sleeves and gold trim. She put her hands to her lips indicating silence, then reached into one sleeve and produced a small glassine bottle which she laid on the spot of the stone where she had been washing. Then she began to walk upward, ascending a non-existent stairwell. When she was several times his height above him, she stopped and hovered.

"On the battlefield tomorrow, you must use all your skills to defeat the Saracens. And when during battle you are struck with a mortal wound, at the point of death, you must drink the contents of the bottle."

Martel started to reach for the bottle, then stopped.

"This is so small."

"My time is short," the woman said. "While your request is most interesting to me, it is not the only one, and I have other places to visit. Do you take my offer of assistance or not?" Martel grabbed the flask.

It felt like – a small vial of liquid.

"You do not ask the price," she commented.

Martel quietly responded.

"It will be exorbitant. But I must pay it."

"Even if the cost is your life?"

Martel paused before replying "Yes."

The woman smiled. Martel felt a chill as she said, "Then we have an agreement."

He saw the woman's image grow blurred. "If you win, you will see me again tomorrow."

The woman dematerialized. As her image disappeared, he heard the words, "Remember, only drink the liquid on the point of death."

\*\*\*

October 10, 732 A.D. Sunrise. Moussais-la-Battaille, a large field roughly wedged between the Clain and Vienne Rivers.

"Steady men!" Martel cried, riding along the front of his army, trailed by Duke Eudes and the same detachment that had accompanied him to Saint Hilaire. Martel rode his horse to the middle of his line and stopped about forty paces in front of all, so, he could be seen up and down the line.

"Front row, show your swords."

The men in the front row, kneeling on the thick grass, held their Carolingian swords up. Straight blades, narrow and tapered.

"Second row, raise your weapons!"

The men standing in the second row held up their spears, long handled with sharp metal ends, and their halberds, long poled weapons topped with an ax blade on one side and a spike on the other. Most of these men wore spangenhelm helmets, chain mail byrnies, and carried round wooden shields, covered in leather.

"Remember your training," he called again. "Listen to my commands."

His voice carried far over the completely silent line.

\*\*\*

On the other side of the field, within a tent from which flew four crescent flags, Abd Al-Rahman, Governor of the Iberian province of Cordoba, and his second in command, Tariq Musa, listened to the reports of the chief of scouts, while several other commanders sat in.

"So, Charles Martel finally chooses a place to fight," Al-Rahman noted. "Weapons and formations?"

"Four thousand men on foot, kneeling just atop the ridge," replied Zaid Jafar, the chief scout. "Behind them, a second line with four thousand men standing. And behind them are a larger group, a rabble. We estimate fifteen to eighteen thousand total."

Tariq Musa, Al-Rahman's second, added "Either number is less than our twenty-four thousand. Their men kneeling in the front stand three paces apart and are armed with swords. The second row of men stands two paces behind the first row, in the space between the men kneeling in the front line. They are armed with halberds and spears. All metal pole weapons. The men further in the rear have mostly swords, spears, and maces."

Al-Rahman turned to look at the field. Nodding his head, he said

"He has his best soldiers in the front. And he has a position on a plateau atop the field. It is not high, but we must ride it. The rivers to our far right and left will funnel us toward his lines."

Al-Rahman stroked his beard. "But they have iron weapons. And he shows no cavalry. And the rivers cut off his retreat."

He turned back to his men and gestured to the field.

"Martel is no fool," Al-Rahman said.

Turning to Tariq Musa, he asked "What is he thinking?"

The second studied the field before answering.

"The rise is slight and will slow our horse's stride, but not force us to stop," Musa said. "The first row is a feint. The pole weapons are in the second row. As soon as our horses are on the hill Martel's second row will move forward and try to knock our riders off our horses. Then the ones who are kneeling will engage our riders who break through and attack those knocked to the ground while they still scramble for footing."

Musa looked back to Al-Rahman and added, "He is using the field to funnel our attack to meet a line of his choosing."

Al-Rahman stroked his beard more as he pondered this assessment. The first rays of sunlight fell from the sky.

"Rain would be better," Al-Rahman thought.

"Governor, perhaps we should wait," Tariq Musa said.

On another day they might wait.

But not today.

"Have the men mount," Al-Rahman ordered. "Have my cavalry form a wedge behind me. The infantry shall follow. We shall approach slowly. When we see the first volley of arrows, we charge. We push our horses up the hill."

Al-Rahman turned. Fangs sprouted from his mouth. "We'll break through their ranks into the belly of their army and see how their iron weapons work against us."

***

Martel had only seen the ocean once in his life when he was eleven years old. He remembered being fascinated by the motion of waves, curling up, growing, and spreading in length, until they turned and crashed onto the shore. He thought of this as he, along with Duke Eudes, surveyed the Umayyad army's advance across Moussais-la-Battaille. The heavy scimitars of the Saracens glinted in the early morning sun. They formed a line longer than the tree line on the other side of Moussais-la-Battaille, where Martel's army waited. The Umayyads rode slowly atop beautiful Arabian stallions, a sea of grays and whites, with the morning sun reflecting off the Saracen's helmets and armor.

Martel adjusted the mail coif which he now wore with the battle imminent. He quipped, "They seem in no hurry, do they, my Duke?"

Duke Eudes did not respond.

"Of course, they have no need to," Martel continued, answering his own question. "Their horses are Andalusians. Beautiful animals, don't you think? And in the open field, even faster than our coursers. But I like our coursers and our rounceys in a fight."

Duke Eudes remained silent.

"I wonder, Duke, are we closer to Tours, to Poitiers?"

The Duke stammered "I – I – not...'

Martel raised a gauntlet-covered hand and said, "It doesn't really atter. Go back to the rear and do as I instructed." Martel ordered.

Eudes turned his palfrey and went back through the Frankish lines.

Looking across the field, Martel saw the hungry look in the eyes of the advancing Arabian cavalry. He felt a knot of fear in his stomach but quickly banished it. He spun his horse to the men, raised his sword, and slashed the air, yelling "EYES – DOWN."

In near unison, his soldiers bowed their heads.

\*\*\*

Even in the bright sun, Al-Rahman's eyesight was keen. He saw the heads of the men in Martel's first two lines look down.

"Interesting," the leader thought. The Moors' approach was designed to strike fear into the opposing forces. Martel was having his men ignore the oncoming cavalry.

"You can have your army avert our eyes," Al-Rahman said. "But you cannot close their ears."

Al-Rahman raised his silver scimitar and pointed at Martel's line, then it was his turn to slice the air with his sword.

The Umayyad cavalry charged.

***

Martel felt the ground beneath his horse shake, and the thirty thousand hoof beats pounding the field sounded like thunder. Martel pointed his sword to the far right and left. Arrows flew into the air and fell on the advancing Saracens. The arrows themselves did not strike many fatal blows, but they disrupted the rider or the horse enough to cause falls. Some riders fell, and riders behind them crashed. Still the waves kept coming. As the arrows from the second volley were still in the air the Saracen cavalry spread out, the front riders charging faster, while others slowed to create spaces between them. The Andalusian horses were quick and agile, and their riders skilled. The extra space allowed some riders to avoid an arrow or a fallen rider in front of them. The arrows did strike home on some, but fewer than the first volley. The vampire cavalry continued their ride. Behind them, the foot soldiers – mortals, but still great fighters – followed. A third volley went, and before it landed Martel rode back to the second line of his army.

Martel signaled for the fourth volley of arrows to be held.

The Saracen cavalry approached the Frankish army.

"HOLD YOUR POSITION!" Martel yelled.

The Umayyad cavalry had reached the rise. The riders pushed their horses up the incline.

"SWITCH!"

The kneeling soldiers dropped their swords and reached into the tall grass for wooden lances that they had lain there.

The cavalry drove forward up the hill and into the tree line.

Each of the kneeling men thrust the base of the lance into the small hole they had dug, clutched their lance with both hands, and raised the wooden tip of the lance skyward.

As the vampire cavalry reached the top of the rise, they ran into a row of wooden lance tips, all angled up. With no time to stop, many of the vampire cavalries rode into the lances. The wooden tips pierced their leather armor and impaled the vampire riders through the heart.

***

*October 10, 732 A.D. In the middle of Moussais-la-Battaille. Midday.*

The battle had waged for hours. Martel's maneuver had considerably reduced the Saracen vampires. More than half of the Umayyad front row had been skewered and killed or mortally wounded the moment they reached the front line. The speed of the Andalusian horses worked against the cavalry, for the second line had moved in and collided with many of the first wave of riders, as there was no room atop the rise to maneuver other than forward. Many of those riders in the front fell onto the second wave of riders. Many of those who tried to turn fell into the rider beside them.

Martel's scheme, although a success, had not won the battle; it had only removed a sizable portion of the Saracen cavalry. Foot soldiers from both sides moved onto the flat field, along with the remaining cavalry, and engaged in the brutal medieval combat that Charles had so much experience with. Dead and dying bodies along with severed limbs, torsos, and heads were so numerous that it was hard to move without falling. The Franks were fighting furiously, but Al-Rahman had rallied his men and organized a counter-offensive, with his surviving cavalry and the wave of foot soldiers on the plain. The Saracen, man for man, and the Frankish warriors were basically equal, but the vampires, now roughly a thousand in number, tipped the scales. In the closeness of battle, a vampire could be killed by being beheaded or having its heart ripped out. An especially strong Frankish warrior might give the vampire a battle, and a group of men could kill one. But in a single encounter, the vampire won more than he lost. As the battle continued, bodies dropped, and more open-air space appeared between the combatants, leading to more single encounters.

Martel clutched his sword. He stood on the plain. His horse had been killed after the first hour. His helmet and the mail coif were long gone. Blood ran down his face from a gash he had been given by the edge of a Saracen shield. The stench of death was everywhere.

"Martel!"

Martel turned.

Al-Rahman, still atop his horse, was looking down at him, holding a scimitar. Several of his vampire aides, including Tariq Musa and the scout, Zaid Jafar, were on horses behind him. Al-Rahman moved his stallion forward and motioned his vampires to stay back.

Martel glanced around for a shield or a battle axe but saw none. He clenched the hilt of his sword with both hands.

"You are a fine commander," Al-Rahman called out.

Martel spoke between heavy breaths.

"You speak -- Aquitaine -- very well, Governor."

Al-Rahman raised his curved sword and called out. "Remember, Charles, you must strike me in the heart or the head. That is the only way you will ever stop me."

Martel tightened the grip on his sword.

Al-Rahman charged.

They met.

Martel's swung his sword and gashed Al-Rahman above his heart and across his chest to his abdomen. Al-Rahman rode by and stopped his horse, looked at his wound, and coughed. He slid to the ground. For a moment, Martel thought he had killed him.

But then Al-Rahman stood up, blood pumping from his slit chest.

"A serious blow," Al-Rahman said, leaning on his horse and breathing heavily. "But not enough."

Martel's sword felt heavy in his hand. He saw it covered in blood – two different hues. Martel dropped it and felt his throat. Blood was leaking from his neck.

"Your artery," Al-Rahman said.

Martel collapsed onto his hands and knees. His vision grew dim. Around him he heard nothing. He fell onto his side and felt cold. Very cold. Then his eyes closed, or he lost his vision. It did not matter.

*The liquid.*

With his body stiffening, and his heartbeat racing, Martel reached under his mail and clutched the small wine sack he had wrapped the bottle in. Unable to see, he removed the cotton batting he had stuffed the bottle with and brought it to his lips.

He drank.

His heart beat two more times. Then it stopped. Then his vision went dark.

Then -

Martel could see. Not outside. Within. Within his body. He could see his heart. From his years on the battlefield, he had seen many of the body's inner parts and recognized what a heart looked like. He could see his heart stop beating.

"No," he thought.

And his heart began to beat.

He felt the bloodlines in his neck and saw the torn flesh around them. He – willed – the tubes to close. The muscle, scapular, and trapezoid (not that he knew the names but he recognized them from the battlefield) that had been cut – reassembled themselves. Slowly at first, then quicker. He made the muscles reform. He willed the tissue to reconnect. He felt blood gushing through his severed artery, and anywhere there was a wound, the blood flowed in, and he – *willed* the wounds to close. The skin healed, and there was no mark left.

He commanded his body.

Martel sprang to his feet and looked at Al-Rahman. At the governor's open chest wound. Martel could smell Al-Rahman's blood dripping out. More than before. Also, vampire blood had a tinge of green in it, a hue, which he had not noticed before. And more, he sensed into Al-Rahman's mind. There was – fear – at seeing that which he never had before.

"How?" Al-Rahman uttered.

Martel ran towards him with no weapon in hand.

Al-Rahman hesitated. Then he climbed back on his horse, held his scimitar and charged. He swung his scimitar in a low sweeping motion, but Martel dove under the blade and grabbed the Saracen's sword hand from behind. Al-Rahman was pulled off his horse and lost his weapon, but he quickly scrambled to his feet. He was partly hunched over and held his hand over the wounds on his chest that were still bleeding. Martel saw the blood being pumped by the heart and pushed through the vampire's wounds.

And he wanted it.

Al-Rahman looked at Martel and bared his fangs. Martel was looking at him with a hunger, a stronger hunger than a vampire had. But – Al-Rahman had sliced open Martel's throat moments ago. Most of his body armor had fallen, which exposed a torso that was now unblemished after hours of fighting. Al-Rahman reached down and picked up his scimitar.

"Your magic is powerful," he called.

Martel snarled at him and called back "Prepare yourself." Looking among the dead, he found a large battle ax which he picked up with one hand.

Al-Rahman needed both hands to hold his sword.

From their horses, Al-Rahman's second, Tariq Musa, and his officers saw the Frankish leader rush their governor. They could see Martel nimbly running over the bodies, springing over the bodies, showing no fatigue. Al-Rahman appeared ready to slice across Martel's chest, but at the last moment, he changed his grip and raised his sword overhead. He cut down, trying to split Martel in two. Martel jumped to the side, avoiding the scimitar, and swung his ax.

The ax blade severed Al-Rahman's head, which flew off in silence.

The Saracen leader's decapitated body stood erect for a moment, blood shooting up from the neck into the air, before crumpling to the ground.

The lieutenants who watched were stunned.

Charles Martel, however, was just starting. While the others stared at their leader's body, Martel ran across the field and swung his battle ax at Zaid Jafar. The chief vampire scout fell off his mount. Jafar jumped up quickly, but Martel was on him and bit deep into his throat. Jafar made a gasping cry, and his body rattled. Martel felt something inside himself being transferred to the scout. Then Martel let Jafar go. The scout staggered and bent over, but stayed on his feet.

Tariq Musa regained control while atop his horse, he raised his scimitar with his left hand, towards Martel and said "Destroy -".

He had intended to say "Him." Before he could finish, the bitten scout grabbed Musa's right leg and was gnawing into the femur. The Tariq Musa screamed as blood spurted. His sword was on the side of the horse opposite from where Jafar bit so he hit him with his gloved hand, but the scout would not release his jaws from Musa's leg. The others watched as the second's horse rose on its hind legs and threw his rider to the ground. After wrestling with each other, the scout stopped and looked at the other riders. Both Jafar and Musa got up. Their eyes were covered with a dull glaze.

One of the surviving scouts cried out "Kill them both!" He drove his horse towards the two, expecting others to follow, but he glanced back and saw no one came with him. His horse tripped over another of the many bodies on the field and both horse and rider fell to the ground. The horse struggled to get up, but its right front leg was broken. The rider lay pinned under his horse. He tried to wriggle out, but the animal's weight was too much.

Then Musa and the scout were on him.

A Saracen warrior, carrying only a spear, came out of a melee and ran towards Martel. Martel smiled. He was in the soldier's mind and could see from the soldier's perspective. In his mind, he saw the soldier's spear aimed at him.

Martel commanded "Stop," in the soldier's brain, and the soldier immediately did so.

Martel quietly walked over and bit into the bicep on the arm carrying the spear.

Martel liked its taste.

***

*October 10, 732 A.D. The middle of Moussais-la-Bataille. Approaching dusk.*

Martel sat on the battlefield. His body was saturated in the blood of others, but underneath that blood, his own body was pristine, save for one gash on his forearm that he was in the process of healing.

As he surveyed the area, he thought "It is an unusually quiet battlefield." There was not the usual cacophony of groans and cries of agony from dying men. No, those on the field who lay fallen lay dead. Bodies of dead men and horses were everywhere. Of course, the air reeked with the smells of the dead, which drew the women who came to clean the dead, and the men who came to pilfer.

Martel felt - invigorated.

He heard a familiar voice.

"You're thinking this is like the scene you saw outside the chapel where we met last night."

"Yes," Martel said, then added "and no. The dead here are my soldiers mixed with those of my enemy."

Looking up, he saw the woman, hovering a short way off the ground. She wore a pristine white tunic and a gold headdress adorned with glowing jewels.

"As a young bastard, a monk tried to teach me of the supposed Greek gods," he said. "You remind me of one."

"But I am not," the woman observed. Then she commented, "The Umayyads have withdrawn."

Martel chuckled. "I never studied math or science, but that same monk once tried to teach me that as well. I remember an idea. If one piece of something splits into two equal pieces, and then the two pieces split into four equal, and so on, then even though you have the same amount of wood, the number of pieces grows quickly. I thought it was meaningless information. Today I see the significance."

The woman continued. "I watched you. As a Saracen warrior was turned, that vampire or the occasional man turned on another, and so on. Some of the Saracens were eaten, but enough turned on the others. You were fortunate that most of the vampire army stayed near Al-Rahman. And you controlled them. Once they became flesh eaters. Which I foresaw. But you had Eudes take the smaller cavalry of the Franks and swim the horses across the Clain River. I had not foreseen that."

Martel shook slightly at the words. "Surprised the Duke didn't drown himself." Then he added, "But then again, palfreys, although they are not great war horses, they are great swimmers." The woman crossed her arms and continued. "Having them swing around and cross it farther up, a pincer movement around the battlefield to the Umayyad's camp. That was brilliant. And then Eudes' men – you had them release the Umayyad servants."

"Yes well. With the Saracens caught between us on one side and their newly freed servants on the other, with Eudes calvary support, in the rear – I don't think Al-Rahman saw that coming."

"I do have a question for you." the woman said. "You freed their servants, but you allowed much of the other Saracens to escape. Why?"

Martel breathed deeply before responding.

"Why not?"

Then he added. "Fear of the undead is quite strong. Fear of looting their treasure was even greater. They've fallen back with their spoils and are heading to their base in the Pyrenees."

Then he rose to his feet.

"So, I have lived to meet you again," he said. He felt very relaxed. "You must be here to claim your price. Do so."

The woman descended to the ground and encircled Martel as she walked.

"First, you have stopped the Saracen invasion of Neustria. That is your victory. It also works for my interests. But that victory is part of your price. You may not understand, but victory itself is a price to pay, sometimes even more than defeat."

Martel listened carefully before responding.

"Every victory has a cost. Go on."

"Second, you know the taste of flesh. And you experienced how to repair your body. Yet you shall never be able to use this power again. Oh, it will remain in you. Dormant, so to say, but present. You shall sire children, and they shall sire children, and the power will be passed down, but it will not appear as you have held it now. Not for many generations. Oh, occasionally a portion may be seen. You will have a grandson who you will not live to see, who shall have the greatest tactical mind the world has seen, even greater than yours. But he shall also be refined in a way you are not. He shall unite the Franks into an empire much greater than you can imagine, the largest of his day."

The woman laughed. "But it will not last. As I said, the powers will appear on occasion, but they shall not manifest themselves all the time. And your grandson's children will not exhibit the same brilliance as their father. The powers will be in your bloodline but diluted with each generation. Your lineage shall sire many, both legitimate and bastards, and this latent power in you will be diluted. And you shall know this, and that knowledge is a price."

Martel nodded.

"And?"

"Someday – far from now, very far from now – there will be a chance for another to be even more powerful than you. An aberration if you will. Your many crossed bloodlines will converge in her, purely by chance. She will be most interesting."

"She?" Martel asked.

The woman smiled as she nodded, and Martel saw a spark in her eyes.

"Yes, she. But to achieve the highest powers, she will need to find and conjoin with the blood of three others who will, like her, appear by chance as the next purest blood descendants. Another bastard like you, but a woman, and her two children, who may be a young girl and a boy. This will lead to a new and exciting game which may be – eventful."

"Eventful?" Martel questioned. "Maybe? You do not know?" You seem very interested, even happy about events so far in the future."

"I am not truly immortal, but my life is long," the woman

said. "I need to keep myself interested. And while I set things in motion, nothing is certain. I am not omnipotent. You cannot comprehend it all – thought to be, frank, I believe you understand more than I thought you would. Today we have put things in motion which may come to pass."

The woman stopped in front of Martel.

"Time is transient. For instance, the one to be born so far into the future, the one with the hunger for flesh that you had – she might hear us, even now."

The woman looked directly into Martel's eyes. For a moment he thought – no he sensed – another presence within her, like a shadow passing over her face.

Then it was gone.

A swirl of dust began to swirl around the woman's feet, and then began to rise, encircling her, blotting her from his view.

Martel heard her say "You are an interesting man, Charles Martel. Live well."

Then she was gone.

# The Power of Silver
By William J. Connell

*The time is 1350 A.D. The place is a forgotten village on the border between the Kingdom of France and the Italian city-states. The Black Death ravages across Europe. Nearly half of Europe's human population is decimated. The main struggle is to survive. People, however, are not the only victims. Animals, particularly nocturnal ones who feed on other living creatures, are also susceptible.*

*Even vampires.*

\*\*\*

Carmen Teresa stared up at the night sky. It was her fault, really. After spending three days at Castle Otranto, they rode for three nights toward the general direction of Toulon in southern France. They found shelter during the day. Once in an old mine, once in a cave, and once in the woods. She had thought they rested sufficiently at the castle, but she everyone too hard, even the horses and both had tired. Two of the nightmares died, and the rest were weakened.

The group was fortunate to come across a small hamlet that had been struck hard by the plague. They had ridden to the village's manor house, set off quite a walk from the other houses. Having found it mostly deserted, they entered and allowed their horses to rest in the adjoining stable. The few villagers still alive were too weak, or too afraid, to seek them out, so the vampires were left to themselves.

Carmen Teresa thought of the others. Bernardo, a wiry Tuscan. Federigo, the oldest of them by far, with a pointed bald head humans found especially fearful. He was also the only one Carmen Teresa knew well enough to trust. Raphael, the youngest of the group, black-haired, and olive-skinned. Miguel, a large Corsican and physically the strongest. Then Thomas, a vampire of average height and very quick reflexes, from Florence. Oh, and of course, their prisoner/guest, Cesare Borgia. She smiled at the many ways to describe him. Her former lover. The one who used potions. The most dangerous among them, by far. The creator of the great mortality.

Of the group was also the one who had recovered from his resurrection the quickest. He had been useful in going on food forages when the others rested. On the first night he found a woman in the village with a deep scar running from her jawline down onto her neck. It was not the scar of plague buboes, but more that of a vicious bite. Otherwise, she seemed to be free of the plague, and Raphael was able to lure her to the manor house. Everyone wanted to drink her blood, but Carmen Teresa forbade it. For the girl's smell was not right. Feeding on those whom the black death lived could lead to sickness and death for a weakened vampire. The woman was allowed to go. No one from the village came to the manor house the next day to inquire, either from fear or being too sick. Still, on this second evening in the manor house, Carmen Teresa ordered Raphael and Federigo to rely on animals and plants, as they had since leaving St. Michael's monastery.

Behind her, Cesare Borgia was stretched out upon a plush bed of goose feathers, his head propped on a down-filled pillow, drinking from a leather wine sack.

"What are you thinking, Carmen Teresa?" He asked. Carmen Teresa sat on the bed, overlooking Cesare. "So where is it?" She inquired.

Cesare shrugged his shoulders and continued drinking from the wine sack. He questioned back, "Where is what?"

Carmen Theresa spoke sternly. "You know me too well, Cesare. I have tired of your games. I won't keep asking."

Cesare laughed.

"Why don't we all leave, and I show you?" He asked.

"You're not well enough to travel yet," Carmen Teresa said. "And neither are the others, except maybe Raphael. We tried moving from Castle Otranto and look what happened, we lost two horses, and the others are exhausted. You all need to rest here a few days more."

She reached over, took the wine sack, and drank a swig.

"You did not res-ur-rect me, remember that," he said. Carmen Teresa smiled.

"No, I remember it. But you were holed up in a wall for nearly two years by the pontiff's guards. Trust me, you don't look so good." She observed, handing the wine sack back.

She grinned at him, allowing her upper fangs to extend.

Cesare shook his head as he took another drink.

"You bring me here, ju-ust for me to tell you where the lab-oratory is," he said quietly. "Then I tell you and you kill me, no? Or if I don't tell you, you kill me and bring me back. Like one of your mindless minions. Then I tell you everything, no? Is smart thing for you to do."

Cesare sat up and threw the wine sack aside.

Pointing a finger at her, he said, "But your plan, it has one fault. You bring me back, which you can, I know. But may-be I not remember some things. May-be I be no good to you." He leaned forward and snickered, "Then where you be?"

Then he coughed. Several times.

Carmen Teresa shook her head. "You sound well," she jested. Then she added, "But you misjudge the situation."

She rose and pressed her finger into Cesare's forehead saying "There is far, far too much information in that brain of yours to destroy it. We need you to find a cure to the menace you've created Cesare. We've sent other poisoners, assassins, killers, to the fleshers and they just don't come back."

Cesare brushed her finger aside and smirked.

"I no cre-ate them. I create your black death. Your great pestilence. Is what our leader wa-nted. And what their pope wa-nted. The flesh eaters, they rose on their own. From the black death, perhaps, but I not their father."

Carmen Teresa crouched in front of Cesare. "Created, spawned, birthed. Parse words as you will. We need you as you are. Tell me where the laboratory is. I will ride out to it and find the entrance. That is all I ask. I am sure you have it protected. I will then come back to get you."

"And then we will all go together," Cesare finished. "And I make antidote for you." He threw his head back and clapped his hands. "But Carmen Teresa, like you say – I walled up in two years in papal prison, and I not talk. Why you think I tell you?

Still crouched in front of Borgia, she looked into his eyes, saying,      "Because I am asking you." Her smile and fangs grew again as she added, "And you know I have other ways of making you feel pain."

Borgia waited a few beats, clapped his hands, and said, "Why not, Carmen Teresa. Why not."

He leaned forward and wrapped his hand around the back of Carmen Teresa's head. She resisted for a moment, then smiled, leaning in, and said "Why not?"

\*\*\*

The vampires, other than Cesare, gathered around an

interior room of the manor house.

"He gave us a location," Carmen Teresa said. "About two nights ride from here. Toward the Durance River. Raphael and I will go search for it. If and when we find it, or if we find nothing, we will return here. Either way, we will ride out and be back in five nights."

"You trust him?" inquired Federico, a pensive look on his face.

"Not at all," she said. "But he knows if he lies to me what I will do to him. I need you to watch him carefully."

"We should all go," said Miguel, and the Corsican pounded the table with his large hands.

"You need a few more days to rest, as do the nightmares" Carmen said. "I pushed too hard. We can't lose any more horses; they take too long to train."

"And we need to eat," Miguel grumbled.

"Do not touch the villagers here," Carmen Teresa said. "There's a smell of the plague in the air."

Thomas said, "Vampires are not prey to the black death."

"They are if they're weakened," Carmen Teresa retorted. "And you all are. The plague has hit this village. In a few days you will be able to eat and drink as you want."

"You question Carmen Teresa?" Federigo, spoke loudly. "You all agreed when you volunteered to follow her, no matter what. And do you, Thomas, think you know more about the resurrection process than her?"

Carmen Teresa smiled and said, "Your own personalities are coming back. That's good, but your bodies are still regenerating. Inside. You will stay here and keep Cesare company."

Miguel said, "You take Raphael, that runt?"

"He is the youngest," Carmen said. "He has returned the quickest. It is no shame on any of you, it is merely how these things work."

"Bah, I am ready," Miguel scowled

Carmen Teresa's hand shot out and slapped Miguel across the face. The Corsican stumbled back but caught himself on a table before falling. He rubbed his jaw, a trickle of blood flowing down. Carmen Teresa looked at the others.

"You forget who I am," she said, licking Miguel's blood off her fingers. "Any more questions?"

No one spoke. Miguel gave an angry glance to Carmen Teresa, but then looked down when she met his eyes.

"Good. Federigo is in charge while Raphael and I are gone. Watch Cesare in shifts. I think he is too weak to go far, but I want him in this manor house while we are gone. Don't trust him. At all. And do not feed on the villagers."

There were murmurings of agreement.

Outside in one of the adjoining rooms, Cesare Borgia listened to each word that was spoken. He held a small clay bowl, or mortar, in one hand and a pestle in the other.

He had seen Miguel's look.

*\*\**

Miguel sat at a table, watching a fire in the central hearth of the manor house. Borgia sat in a corner, pounding a powdered substance into paste with the pestle and mortar.

"How long since they left?" Cesare asked.

"What do you care" Miguel said, staring at the fire.

"I am hungry for real food," Cesare replied. "I have not fed on real food. Not for long time."

"That's your problem," Miguel retorted angrily.

Cesare said, "And yours."

Miguel shrugged and asked, "So what?"

"So, the woman Raphael brought here two nights ago was fine, that is what," Cesare said. "You feel fine, no? You look fine, no? She look fine, no?"

Miguel looked over at Cesare.

"What are you doing over there?" Miguel asked.

"This?" Cesare said holding his bowl up. "This help us eat."

Miguel walked over. Though the flames from the fireplace barely touched the corner, the contents in Cesare's bowl had a silver hued shine to it.

"It looks like silver shit," Miguel grunted. "You want us to eat that?"

Cesare laughed gruffly.

"Nooo," he said deliberately. "This you call shit? It detect the plague in people."

"Ehhhh?"

Cesare nodded.

"You rub this on the body. It turn black if person has black death. Is poetic, no?"

Cesare watched Miguel's eyes widen for a moment, then harden.

"Carmen Teresa told us to avoid eating from the village," Miguel said.

"And Carmen, she not here now, is she?" Cesare observed. "You and I, we go outside," Cesare said getting to his feet. "I find you some food that is safe. Bring Thomas. Bring the others. I show you." He added, "I saw where that girl lives."

\*\*\*

Carmen Teresa and Raphael rode the night mares gently along the moonlit path, one beside the other. Their destination was Rolliere's, a village several miles west of the Durance River, near the southwestern edge of the Alps. They sought another manor house, but with stone walls cut from marble. Unusual to find in any village. Further, there was a cave to be found near the marble house. Cesare had said to seek out the locals. They would know where it was because they avoided it.

"You seemed a bit troubled, Mistress," Raphael said.

"I don't like leaving Cesare with the others," Carmen Teresa commented.

"Miguel is strong, surely he can overcome Cesare?" Raphael asked.

Carmen Teresa smiled and said, "Miguel is strong. So are Bernardo and Thomas. And Federico is wise. But Cesare is crafty, very much so. He has outwitted popes and the vampire doge. He hung chained in a cell for two years without telling where the location of his workshop was. Yet he gave me the general location."

"He trusts you and knows you are honorable."

After laughing, Carmen Teresa said, "Ahh, young one, that is why you are with me. Cesare does nothing without something to gain. Do you like salt, Raphael?"

Puzzled, Raphael said, "It can be satisfying at times."

"When you dine at the table with Cesare," Carmen Teresa continued, "he won't pass you the salt without getting something greater in return."

Raphael took a drink from his wine sack.

Carmen Teresa noticed it before. It was the one Cesare had earlier.

\*\*\*

Margarita di Molese was on her knees, praying to the Virgin Mary. In the adjacent room, behind a blanket covered doorway, her husband of fifteen years, Talano di Molese, lay naked on a cot, sweating profusely. Talano was a decade older than Margarita, but his death would still be premature. Margarita had removed all blankets, but in the summer heat there was no relief. Talano had been fine only two days before, when he left their home at sunrise to work in the nearby field, he cultivated. He returned unexpectedly by late morning, complaining of general weakness. He went to lie down, and at mid-day when she checked, he was extremely hot and complained of a burning feeling. She gave him water and gingerly removed his tunic. Late in the day he still complained of heat. She peaked under his linen tights and saw his inner thigh and abdomen were marked with egg-shaped buboes. Terrified, she retreated to the other room.

Through the night she heard his fever induced moaning. At various times he begged her for help. Once, she mustered the courage to return to the room and remove his clothes, careful not to look too closely at the body. In the morning she peaked in again. The buboes were prominent and had swelled more overnight. A few had burst, oozing a mixture of blood and watery fluid. One had a chance of surviving these. But then Margarita saw the purplish splotches on the chest and neck of Talano.

"God's tokens," she whispered.

Indeed, these were signs that death was near.

She prayed for forgiveness. Forgiveness for not helping her husband more. As each hour passed, his condition had descended closer and closer to the end. A bloody cough had appeared late in the second day, followed by violent vomiting. The room stank. She wanted to help him more. God's tokens were clear. One was not going to survive. Margarita could not leave her husband, but she feared being around him, and she could not summon the courage to do more.

She also prayed for forgiveness for her transgressions. Only a few nights ago she was out walking when she recalled meeting a stranger, a virile young man who was thin but muscular in a wiry type of way, with sharp brown eyes. He said he was a pilgrim and passing on his way to Avignon. Had it really happened, or had it been a dream? She could not recall. Indeed, she could not recall anything thereafter. Perhaps she had committed a great sin, erasing the memory from her mind, but she had no clear recollection of what had happened to her or to the young man. But there were vague – thoughts? Images? Her in the manor house. Others around her. She was being stripped and looked at.

What was her greatest sin? That she liked the memory?

She could not help but like it. Years ago, her husband told her not to go out in the evening. Talano had spoken of a vision he experienced where she would be attacked that night by a great wolf. She ignored him and indeed, thought the worst of him. He left the house that night to seek out this wolf, but she, not trusting him, followed. She had to spy on him, thinking Talano was cheating on her.

In the woods she became disoriented, and just as Talano had predicted, she was attacked by a great wolf. She was rescued from death by a pair of passing shepherds and returned to her husband. Margarita recovered, but her deep scars from the attack ran from her jaw to her collarbone. People stared and winced when she walked by, and no man would ever look at her, save for Talano, who always loved her. So, this recent memory of men looking at her with desire, even if it were only a dream, gave her pleasure. And that was sinful.

Knock, knock, knock. It came from the door.

Margarita's heart jumped. Was this a sign?

There was a shove against the wooden door. It was barred with a solid maple plank. The plank held.

For a moment.

It split apart as the door swung open. Miguel and Thomas burst through first. Miguel followed, pulling Cesare by his tunic. Margarita cowered on the ground, screaming for the help. In the next room Talano vomited blood. He was beyond comprehending what was happening.

Miguel shook Cesare and said, "You said you could prove who was plague ridden. Now prove it."

Cesare smiled and said, "Just watch me."

*** 

Miles away, Raphael was doubled over in pain and gasping for breath on his nightmare.

"What's wrong with you?" Carmen asked urgently.

The young vampire slid out of his saddle and lay on a forest floor of clover. He continued to gasp and was clutching at his heart.

Carmen Teresa swung off her mount and went over to him. There was a glazed look in Raphael's eyes. He arched his back and shuddered. Carmen Teresa saw that wine sack he had been drinking from and grabbed it. She gave it a quick taste, then spat it out.

"Silver nitrate," she muttered. Quickly her fangs extended. She bit into the back of her forearm and sucked, drawing a good blood flow. She shoved her forearm into Raphael's gasping mouth. For a moment he resisted, but then she ordered, "Drink!"

The vampire began to suck blood from Carmen Teresa's arm.

***

The four vampires stood over Talano di Molese. He was on his side, trapped in his own excrement, and half slumped off his bed, a hand resting in a pool of blood and vomit.

"It stinks in here," said Thomas.

"These creatures are so weak, look at how the black death eats them," said Bernardo.

"This one has the purple patches," Miguel said. "He's already dead. Why do you show us him?"

"Waaatch," Cesare said. "He is close, is true, but not dead yet." Cesare poked at Talano. The old man groaned and shifted slightly. Cesare pulled a sack out from his tunic with the pestle. He then sprinkled the white-silver power on Talanao's arm. The other vampires were noticeably offput. Cesare took the pestle and rubbed it up and down Talano's skin, leaving a large white streak mark along his arm.

"You are crazy," Thomas said.

"Just watch," Cesare said in his deep voice.

As they stared, the powder on Talano's arm turned from silver to black.

"You see?" Cesare asked, pointing. "The powder reacts with his body. If it turns black, he has the black plague. Poetic, no?"

"This proves nothing," Bernardo said, storming out of the room.

Thomas silently followed.

Miguel pulled Cesare from of the room, threw him against the wall, and said, "So what, we all could see and smell. He has the plague. We don't need your magic for that."

"And what about her?" Cesare asked, gathering himself and gesturing to Margarita. "Does she have the smell of the plague about her?"

The other vampires went over and encircled her. Margarita stayed on the ground before Thomas pulled her up and licked her on the neck, the side not scarred.

"She seems all right," he said.

Margarita was repeating the Hail Mary over and over ,looking to the thatched roof of her cottage.

"Let me show you," Cesare said, again applying the white-silver powder to Margarita's bare arm as he had done to her husband. She moaned slightly.

"If she is without plague, it will turn to silver," Cesare said.

The vampires watched. In a minute, there was a very bright silver streak on Margarita's arm.

"You see?" Cesare asked. "Are you convinced now?"

Thomas grinned, but Miguel asked, "Why did Carmen Teresa tell us not to feed on her?"

Cesare stared right at Miguel and said, "Carmen Teresa know ma-ny things. But she not know the black plague as well as me. How it works. Or how to detect it. Is true."

"And you want us to eat silver?" Miguel bellowed down at Cesare. "You want to kill us."

Cesare looked at their hungry faces and calmly said, "You not feed at the arm."

Cesare sensed their desire to feed, but their fear of the silver.

"The silver on the skin, it no bother you," Cesare assured them. "You no believe me? Then watch."

Cesare took Margarita in his arms and, while she continued praying, he said, "Keep asking your Mary for help." Then he bit down her neck and drew blood.

\*\*\*

Margarita swooned into unconsciousness. Cesare handed her limp body to Bernardo, but Miguel pushed in drank. Bernardo began to feed from the scarred side of Margarita's neck. Thomas, the smallest of these three, held back, but when Miguel released his bite, Thomas moved in. They drank their fill from Margarita. She was unconscious the entire time and died after approximately one-half hour of this exchange.

A short while later, her husband expired in the room next door.

\*\*\*

Raphael sat on the ground, rubbing his forehead. Carmen Teresa was feeding straw to the nightmares.

"What happened?" Raphael asked.

"Silver poisoning," Carmen Teresa responded, walking toward him. She held up the wine sack he had been drinking from.

"You got this from Cesare?"

Raphael nodded, noticing her arm was bandaged.

"He gave it to me before we left, when we were getting provisions."

"Of course, he did." She threw the sack at him. "The

water has been laced with a silver nitrate. A very carefully ground powder, it almost disappears in water. It goes right to the heart and grips it."

Raphael shook his head and said, "I can't believe I didn't taste it."

Carmen Teresa tightened the saddles on the horses and said, "You can't taste it. It has a very faint odor, but Cesare knows how to disguise it. I can smell it, but you can't. It is hard to detect, and it might not kill a stronger vampire, but you were only resurrected a few days ago. Cesare knew that. He must have found some when we were in the cave."

He noticed her arm was bandaged.

"Thank you," he said apologetically.

"Don't thank me, I need your help. You may be my only companion left. Get ready to ride, we are heading back to the manor house."

"What about the marble house?" Raphael asked, rising to his feet.

"A ruse. Cesar wanted me gone."

They mounted the nightmares, though Raphael was a bit unsteady. Carmen Teresa threw a cloak over him. "Get your hood up, we're going to have to ride a little while in the daylight."

"What about you?"

Carmen Teresa went to her horse and said, "I have a blanket, that's all I need. Hate to risk the horses, but I am sure Cesare is making a move. I hope we find someone is still there."

***

Miguel was collapsed on his hands and knees just inside the manor house, heaving deeply and coughing up blood. His heart felt as if there were a steak in it. Bernardo and Thomas lay outside in the woods, dead.

When they drained the woman of her blood, they had felt filled. The four vampires left the house, leaving the old man to his fate, and his wife crumpled on the floor. Cesare had begun to walk away from the group, back to the manor house. The other three pursued, thinking they would run him down quickly. Bernardo dropped in mid-stride, dead. Thomas and Miguel felt pain in their hearts and stomach, pain that doubled them over. Thomas got within site of the manor house when he fell and convulsed for several moments before expiring. Miguel collapsed outside the manor house but had crawled far enough to get inside. The pressure on his heart was too great, so the blood coughing started.

Cesare walked into the room; several bags slung over his shoulder. Miguel grabbed his ankle. Cesare shook free easily, crouching down.

"I afraid I made mistake," Cesare said in a low voice. "The silver color means a person has plague. But not fully. You see, is strange. Some humans, they carry plague in their blood, but it not show in them. That woman, she must have gotten it long ago, but a weak strain. Maybe she feel a little sick for a day or two. But the great pestilence? No, she no show it. That type of plague very bad for vampire. People like her, they show silver. Person no have plague, their arm show white. I got confused. I sorry, Miguel."

Miguel coughed up more blood and said, "Help me."

Cesare said, "There no help for you now my large friend. Just lie here. It be over soon."

Cesare got to his feet and headed toward the door.

"You drank from her," Miguel spat out.

Cesare stopped and turned.

"When I was a guest at Saint Michael-du-Anjou my good host, Abbott Dom Felice, he feed me many things. Sometimes animals, maybe some dead humans, I not know, he not want me dead, but sometime I taste, I know the plague had been in the food. I ate it anyway. If I died, I died. But fun-ny thing happen.

I get sick, I was sick, but I no die. And then I get better. The plague no bother me now."

Miguel managed an "I'll kill you," before his hands and knees collapsed. As he hit the floor, he vomited blood.

"I think no," Cesare said, turning to leave. "I go now."

He paused at the doorway, then added "Don't worry about your friend Federigo, I take care of him. I also take all horses. I no think you need them. Adios."

***

Carmen Teresa and Raphael made it to the village less than two hours after sunrise. The road was heavily forested, providing lots of shade. Carmen Teresa learned the trick of covering the head and neck of the nightmares with blankets, which allowed them to go in some sunlight.

Bernardo and Thomas lay along a pathway, both contorted, both covered with burst buboes, and both lying in still-wet pools of body fluids. Raphael nearly fell off his horse, but Carmen Theresa steadied him.

"Rancid," was all he could mutter.

On reaching the manor house, they dismounted and found Miguel's body inside, his face half-up. His eyes and mouth were open.

"Just like the others," observed Raphael. "And their jaws."

The lips were curled back to expose well below the gum-line.

Raphael grabbed a cloth and reached down, but Carmen Teresa sternly warned, "Don't touch them. They fed on someone with the plague."

Turning to Raphael, she ordered, "Take the horses into the stable. I am going to search the house."

Raphael hesitated, but Carmen Teresa said, "Don't worry, Cesare is long gone."

Raphael did as he was told. Carmen Teresa strode through the house, looking for any signs of where Cesare might have gone.

Raphael called for her in a frightened voice. Was Cesare still here?

She ran outside.

Out in the back, Federigo was tied down to four stakes in the ground, face up, in a gavel-strewn clearing. Though it was less than two hours after sunrise, he had been facing the morning sun all that time. His pale body was burned in in several places, but he was alive. Raphael and Carmen Teresa untied him and brought him in to the manor house, lying him on the down feathered bed of the master bedroom. There was some wine left in the pantry that Carmen Teresa sniffed. It seemed all right. She poured some in a cup, held it up to Federigo's lips, and said, "Drink this slowly, old friend."

Federigo breathed heavily and drank.

"He told me he was going to look for someone," Federigo said hoarsely. "Two children."

"Two children?" Raphael repeated.

"The ones," Federigo said. "The ones the woman is looking for."

Federigo drank some more.

"The woman?" Raphael again repeated.

"You rest now," Carmen Teresa said, giving Federigo the cup and pushing him back onto the bed. She gestured for Raphael to leave, and they both started to exit. As they did, Federigo said, "I suspect he thought I would not survive."

Carmen Teresa turned to him, "He underestimated you, old friend." She walked away, saying under her breath, "As I underestimated him."

Outside the room, Raphael asked, "Who is this woman?"

"The flesher," Carmen Theresa said. "The red haired

one who leads the others. Elizabeth. She wants two children. The coven knows what she wants, but not why. Right now, we need to find the children. When we do, we'll find Cesare."

"How does he know all this?" Raphael asked.

"I think Dom Abbot Felice frequently spoke to him. I think the guards spoke to him. Sort of a torture, letting him know what was happening. Also, when your sight is turned useless, your other senses develop. I am sure Cesare heard many things as a prisoner in the Abbey."

"How do we find these children?" Raphael asked.

"I don't know," Carmen Teresa answered. "But we will be alert and keep our ears open. When people are being hunted like that, word gets around – especially in times like these."

## A Night in the Shining Armoire
By Riley Kilmore

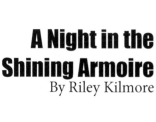

I was here, as usual, in this card shop the other day, looking over the shoulder of a woman reading a selection she'd plucked from the *Encouragement* rack. The card read:

> *Dreams take time, patience, sustained effort,*
> *and a willingness to fail*
> *if they are ever to become more than dreams.*

Boy did that take me back! Right back to the night my own dream came true.

My dream? To escape.

Escape from what, you ask? Why, my nightmare, of course. Not that there's anything too odd about that. We all have nightmares. Mine was just a little harder to escape than some since it was so real. It was so real, in fact, it had a name. I called it Mother.

I suppose I remember that night as vividly as I do because I've had to relive it a thousand times. No. No, that's wrong.

A thousand days isn't even three years. I've actually relived that night…let me see…six thousand, five hundred, and seventy times. Yeah. It replays in my brain in what feels like an endless loop, every detail a separate, shining jewel against the dark and desperate backdrop of memory. Reliving it is my punishment, because you know what they say, right? No good deed goes unpunished.

Oh, never mind me. I'm obsessed. Attaining a long-sought-after dream can do that to you. You almost *become* that moment. You've had similar moments, no? Ones that reach deep into the core of who you are. Like roots, they anchor you to the soil you sprang from, pinning you there.

Think of it. All of us are like that. Our roots take sustenance from whatever lies beneath, even if it's a tarry mire, a place of decay. Meanwhile, that part of ourselves we willingly show to the world, our broad canopy of outstretched branches, is really just a mask. My mother was particularly good at that, holding up a mask to the world. But I got to see the rot the roots of her soul were anchored to.

Let me tell you about the night my dream came true, and maybe you'll see what I mean.

It was early evening, but already dark that time of year, so I'd gone up to bed. For me, going to bed was a sort of half-way point between imminent danger and far-enough-away to be safe. For me, there really wasn't a far-enough-away, but sometimes there was Joe, my stepdad. Only, that night, he was working late. Joe working late was always bad news.

The big brick house we lived in was like something out of a Shirley Jackson novel and was painfully quiet that night as if it cowered in the eye of a hurricane. One storm front had already passed, and a second was approaching. There was a palpable anticipation in the air, a hideous humidity of hatred and hiding. The barometric gauge of my mind was falling sharply as

I lay in bed bracing for the gale. I closed my eyes, feigning sleep.

I'd been raised to believe another eye was always open, one that watched over me and was omniscient, but experience had taught me long ago that eye was blind. Either that or it was always looking the other way.

Cars passed outside. I heard their tires draw long, soggy lines of sound as they sped by, their passengers oblivious to my mute terror as I strained to hear the doorknob's squeal. If only Joe would've come walking in. My stepdad never openly confronted my mother, but his mere presence had the power to break the spells of fear she cast on me, some incomprehensible magic even he didn't understand. Whatever it was, it sufficed; his presence alone quelled my mother's demons, the ones that pointed her in my direction whenever Joe wasn't around.

But that night the doorknob remained mute, like me. The one squeal I did hear was my mother's laugh. It erupted downstairs, reminding me of that empty, ringing tone that came back to me once when I tried playing superhero using a stainless-steel bucket for a helmet. The sound of her laughter and the memory it evoked carved a hollow place in my heart because I knew no superhero was coming for me.

All the worst nights started with that laugh. Like Joe's absence, it was a bad sign.

I knew she was down there, propped against the kitchen table's smooth Formica surface, concocting clever tortures that would leave no obvious marks. Of course, that assumed she'd be sober enough to remember that twisted wisdom when she needed it.

Her laughter erupted again in a long sentence of joyless sound punctuated by glass clinking on glass, a sentence she'd carry out on me whether I pretended to be asleep or not, so I opened my eyes.

Low moonlight seeped in through the four-paned window at the foot of my bed. The light cast a shadow cross on the wall. My swim team trophy on the windowsill added to the effect, fashioning a bizarre crucifix: Shadow Jesus come to save me in a swimsuit, hands pulled free of shadow nails, and raised toward shadow heaven, pointing in the direction of freedom.

Except I didn't quite get there.

The back stairs, dressed in their worn linoleum runners, moaned beneath my mother's footsteps. It was a litany of woe I knew by heart, the creek of each step another knife against my throat. If I lay there any longer I'd wet my bed. Not good. That would only add unnecessary fuel to the volatile fire already kindled in my mother's mind.

I told myself that night would be different. That night I'd hide well and skirt the ever-present threat of hell to linger one more day in the perpetual purgatory of the living. But where? Where to hide that I hadn't, before? I looked at my window, its glass alive with slithering snakes of rain. No. I tried that once and slipped. I wound up bruising the boxelder bush below and breaking my arm in the bargain. My mother was mad about the bush.

I tried to think. Bathtub? Linen closet. Under the bed? I'd tried everything in the past, every place imaginable, but I had to decide. Once the closing note of stairsong played beneath my mother's unsteady foot, I'd be out of time. I imagined her whiskey breath wafting down the darkened hall. Then would come the silence, the worst sign of all. When my mother stopped laughing it was an irrefutable warning, like an upside-down flag on the mast of a doomed ship.

So I ran.

Moments later I heard her in my room. Her heavy breaths revved like a rusty steam shovel working the soft earth as she tore at my covers. I looked around the room I'd run to: her room. It was as disheveled as she was on mornings after a late-night date with a bottle, when she would stand at the kitchen sink in her rumpled housedress, chain smoking and staring at the tire swing. Her bedroom gave me the same ominous feeling I got when I looked in her eyes, which wasn't often. The wallpaper was old like the rest of the house and smoke-stained. In places, it hung loose, like the skin on my mother's face.

I'd never come into this room before. It was the one place I'd never tried hiding. Maybe here I'd be safe, like Daniel in his den of lions. My child's mind convinced me the devil wouldn't hunt me at the very gate of hell. I told myself she'd hunt for me every other place until Joe got home, then I'd be in the clear and could sneak back to bed.

The boxes under the bed were being shoved about. I heard my meager collection of toys spilling as she searched for me. I pictured her on her knees, her anger mounting, the red tip of her lit cigarette drawing hot slashes in the night like the menacing marks she once drew on my skin, connecting my freckles in a constellation of pain.

If you're wondering why she didn't just turn on the lights, I knew she wouldn't. She hated them. They gave her headaches. Besides, had the lights been on and she happened past a mirror, she'd have come face-to-face with the ugly truth of who she was. Most of all, lights would hurry along the hunt and ruin the fun. And any stubbed toes or banged elbows she got bumping around in the dark fed her fury. She loved her fury. She loved it like some folks love their daughters.

I guess she courted stubbed toes and banged elbows because pain lent justice to her outrage, a twisted justice to match a twisted mind—not that I thought about it that way at the time. I didn't know I was making things worse by delaying the inevitable. I just thought I was getting out of the way.

Soon, she began calling my name.

At first, it was just my nickname, spoken with a sweet

sigh as if she'd only come to tuck me in. Then, it was my given name, a name no one else ever heard who hadn't been standing at the baptismal font the day I was doused. Next, my middle name was added, and she was out of my room, teetering down the hall like a train about to jump its track. My middle name trailed like a coal tender feeding heat to the engine of her anger. Behind that came the caboose—my last name—always spoken in a tone meant to remind me it wasn't really mine, that it was Joe's. And above it all sounded the wailing whistle of interjected curses as she neared.

The safe haven I thought I'd found faltered; I'd been drawn to the site of my own undoing like a moth to flame. She knew where I was! Had I breathed too loudly? Maybe she'd heard the rolling thunder of my heartbeats like I could.

A psychosis of desperation gripped me, and a hulking ghost appeared across the unlit room. It was a broad behemoth with open arms, backed against the far wall: Grandma's vintage armoire, painted in swirls of faux white antiquing like an old actor in stage make-up trying to look even older. Shafts of moonlight stabbed through cracks in the brittle, dark green blinds, all drawn, lighting the armoire as if showcasing it in footlights for my consideration. I dove in, closing the doors behind me.

The scent of cedar was strong. It filtered through the polyester pantsuits the beastly thing had swallowed, and I curled beneath them in a pile of dirty clothes like a little bird nested beneath a camouflage of feathers.

That's where they found me, where my mother put my body back when she was through. I told you, remember? I made my escape? My dream-come-true.

So, this card shop is where I hang out now. My shadow heaven. My purgatory.

At least I got to choose.

See, I had a special reason for running that night, even

more of a reason than most of the nights my mother came for me. I'd poisoned her alcohol

I don't know if she's in hell. All I know is she isn't here. And that's heaven enough for me.

Anyway, here, I like watching people's faces. I like seeing their expressions as they discover evidence that someone, some-where understands them—even if it's only someone who writes greeting cards for a living. When customers wander in, I read over their shoulders, looking for sentiments to sum up the life I led, hoping for words that can give my nine short years on Earth some meaning. The thoughts in cards are brief, after all.

Ah. Here's a good one. This lady over here, holding up another selection from the *Encouragement* rack. See? The card she's reading says:

*Live your life like no one's watching.*

Hah! That was easy for me.

No one was.

# The Manananggal
By Arlene Schwartz

The river rocks were smooth under Cristina Sumayan's feet. She watched the water curve around her ankles, diverted but not deterred. Flowing water was like that, always purposeful and on its way. It was still early, and the women of the village were not yet out to do their wash along the river. The children not yet skipping stones, pretending to be vampires, or cocking two fingers to shoot at one another. Cristina's eyes followed the crows flying about the trees ensnared by the strangler figs, those air plants that created ropelike nooses throughout the jungle, light and harmless to view, yet slowly caging and killing their host trees.

Cristina liked coming out like this, before the business of the day, the moment before the start of things. She liked the bookends of each day best, the start and especially the finish. The middle always seemed like the space between breaths, the time controlled but not yet released.

Cristina's laundry, washed and ready to hang out in the sun, sat in the tin basin at her feet.

When the women and children came, Cristina returned to the riverbank. She was blessed by the elders, hand to forehead. The mothers with unmarried sons paid her particular attention, wishing her good morning and complimenting her long dark hair which skimmed the water when she bent at the waist.

"Cristina, how do you keep your skin so light?" Ate Edna asked.

Cristina lowered her head to blush. Aside from light skin, humility was a determiner of beauty among them, and she played her role as the shy virgin.

Ate Loling, pregnant as a ripe guava ready to drop from the branch, teetered as she bent down for her wash. Cristina rushed to help steady her.

"Salamat." Ate Loling gave thanks while cradling her round belly in both hands.

"I think the baby is almost ready," Cristina said.

"Maybe a week more at most," one of the elders said.

"My son Mario plans to come back home after university." Ate Edna smiled broadly, showing both rows of teeth, the gold crown Mario paid for glimmering in the sunlight. "He will be looking for a wife, Cristina."

"Ay! She's only seventeen. Give her time," Ate Loling said.

Edna wrung out a sheet tightly. "Well, her grandmother is getting older. She needs to think about the future."

Cristina smiled, making a point of not showing teeth, and dropped her gaze.

"Such a sweet girl," several of the women said when Cristina took her leave.

Back home, as her wash billowed on the line like sails on the fishing boats, Cristina boiled a pot of rice porridge for her grandmother.

Ate Edna was correct, her lola was getting older. An age

they stopped numbering after she turned eighty. Though, she was still quite spry, being the one who wrung the neck of the chicken that went into the rice porridge. Still spry enough to bleed and drain the carcass. Cristina used some of the chicken blood in the porridge. It turned the milky quality of the rice brown.

"I'm not really hungry. I could just wait until tonight," Lola said when Cristina offered her a bowl of porridge.

"Just a snack to keep your strength up," Christina said. "Lots of iron so you stay strong."

The day passed slowly and methodically, as though any normal day. Tending the farm animals. Planting and harvesting. Sweeping and cleaning. A walk into the center of the village to purchase flour, candles, and candied tamarind to share with the barefoot boys and girls who liked to smile at her and offer to carry her basket.

Most of the men worked their own farms, in the rice fields, or as fishermen. They toiled daily to afford things like antibiotics and clothes for their children. Things always seemed to spin on the axis of antibiotics for the villagers, deciding things like who would survive wet lungs or who could prevent gangrene from setting in. But Ate Edna's husband, Ronato, was always in the village square. He ran the only indoor market that had delicacies like powdered milk in tins and Ivory soap. His shop boasted two refrigerators with Coca-Cola and frozen meat.

Ronato's store was empty of patrons when Cristina stepped inside. The children who buzzed around her knew not to come in. Ronato had a habit of shooing them away with a broom. "Paying customers only!" he would yell.

Cristina tried to be quick about gathering what she needed. She wanted a new comb and a bottle of conditioner for her hair. Ronato had a habit of leering at her, his fat tongue darting out to lick his thick lips until they were shiny.

But the conditioner was on a high shelf in the back corner, and he came over, pretending to help. He made a point to brush against her breasts as he reached for the bottle.

"Salamat." Thanking him felt hollow in her throat. She swallowed so many other words.

"I carry this conditioner especially for your long hair because it smells like sweet coconut milk." He sniffed aggressively at the air as he put her things into a thin plastic bag.

With lowered gaze, she reached for her groceries. "Salamat."

He caressed her hand before relinquishing the bag. She could hear the wet slither of his tongue against his lips even as she aimed her eyes at the counter.

"Oh, to be young again," he said wistfully. "My Mario is young. He will want to court you when he comes home."

Cristina kept her head down even as she walked out of the store.

"Shy, Cristina. So beautiful and shy," Ronato said as she exited.

The day closed the way it always did, with God pulling a heavy blanket over the sky. The stars winked between the seams, but the darkness was absolute.

Cristina took her laundry basin and filled it with water from the well. She washed her hair at the side of their nipa hut. The water was cold, jolting her with an electric energy. The smell of promise and coconut conditioner hung in the air. She washed her body with her clothes on and toweled off outside. Propriety ruled everything.

Inside the hut, her grandmother sat at the kitchen table by one of the square cut-outs that served as a window. A soft breeze wafted through, and soon the owls sent their coded messages across the dark.

"The village should be asleep now," Lola said to Cristina,

the moonlight reflecting in her eyes like the sickles used for reaping.

"Shall we take our walk then?"

Lola gave a nod.

They walked in darkness toward the edge of their property. The jungle, barely pushed back by civilization, revealed an untamable tangle of trees and wildlife. They walked to the coconut tree marked with a circle of red thread, not that they could see the thread in the inky darkness. Still, it was the tree they chose each year. And only once a year. Too much more would betray a dangerous confidence.

There, against the tree, Cristina and her grandmother took off their clothes, so the sound of the croaking frogs and the shuffle of leaves in the breeze was the only thing that cloaked their bodies.

Cristina's lola went through the change first. Her fingers and fingernails stretched to form sharpened talons, her jaw unhinged to reveal jagged teeth, her tongue lengthening, her watering mouth dripped acidic saliva that scorched the ground beneath her. The sounds of altered bones, snapping cartilage, and ripping flesh quieted the frogs eager to mate. Wings sprouted from her lola's shoulder blades, big and black, like maniacal versions of the beautiful fans used by the wives of the wealthy plantation owners, ousted colonizers they once feasted upon. Last, splitting of the torso at the waist, her lola flew up to the top of the coconut tree leaving her human legs behind. Later she would fly back onto her lower half and reconstitute herself into her human form.

There was a legend in the provinces of a terrible monster. A woman that could split her body in half. The monster was said to fly atop the nipa huts of pregnant women, using her acid tongue to burrow a hole through the roof and eat the child from inside the mother's womb as she slept.

Cristina watched her lola fly away in the direction of Ate Loling's hut, hungering for the low-hanging fruit.

The one thing the legend never got right, thought Cristina, was that it didn't have to be just pregnant women. Ronato's greasy little mouth and fast hands flashed through her mind as her jaw cracked itself open into a gaping maw. She held her head high and soared through the air. Brains were just as nutritious as fetuses.

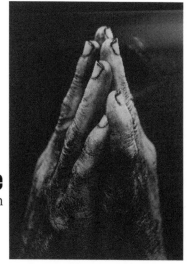

# You Had to Be There
By Thomas Elson

I will not judge.
Except for One
Who was not there.

Crammed into wagons. Doors closed. Left in darkness until arriving at this place – not unlike the other places, except this one had unpainted wood instead of concrete. Rows of us stacked upon rows, barricaded inside stockades with more rows cobbled onto more rows.

Outside and away from the bare wood and bare floors, our bare feet, and barren lives tread through rubbish – vegetable, animal, mineral – human, non-human, inhuman.

Scattered corpses. Emaciated people. Rotting smells smoldered from uncovered pits and fetid bunkers. Electric fences surrounded barking dogs, loaded guns, and filth. We waited - herded, experimented upon, raped - startled by gunfire - frozen in place each time a body thudded like a garbage bag into an open trench.

They probed me daily. I received no benefit – other than staying alive, which, under the circumstances, was not much of a benefit. Food and water: rationed. Never allowed to wash. No showers. Not even a toothbrush. Bathroom facilities? Outside – in the back. Lice and assorted insects settled on beds, clothing, skin, and inside bodies.

I survived for eighty-eight days.

After a smiling face turned his thumbs-up into a thumbs-down, the prussic acid caused my chest to sting. I convulsed as if from epileptic seizures. Blood coagulated in my lungs. Breaths turned to gasps. People yelled. I yelled. *I yelled for Him.*

Then all was quiet.

Then all were dead.

Fused to one another from the heat.

Men in masks entered, hacking with axes to separate us. Then an order came, "Burn them."

Breezes mixed the air with odors from various gasses – cadaverine, putrescence, fecal - into a hole where dust never settled.

They dumped my – our - ashes into a ditch.

Then I met Him.

I had nothing to lose.

I told Him a joke.

He did not laugh.

His voice boomed, "Human degradation is not funny."

My reply, "I guess You had to be there."

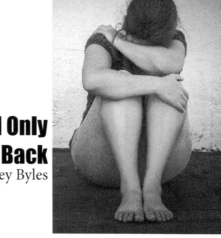

## She Could Only Go Back
By Courtney Byles

Angry tears filled Jodie's eyes as her father pushed her mother into the pool. Her heart beat so hard it felt like it might explode. The pressure in her throat was suffocating as she'd finally reached her limit. Tonight, she'd called her father out. She couldn't hold onto the hate within her heart any longer. "You're a coward. You're a piece of shit! You think you're so powerful, but you are nothing!" Her words released that tension in her throat, one by one, like a slow leak from a tire.

He turned on his heel and faced her, a venomous snake sensing new prey. The drumming of her heart consumed her as he moved closer. Her father's hand hit her face like a brick. The impact forced her onto her butt. He bent down, grabbed her by the arm, and pulled her back toward him. She could feel his warm breath on her face as he leaned in. "Don't you ever." His hand moved to her chin. The pressure from her fingers constricted her jawbone. "Ever. Talk to me like that again." He pulled his hand back to strike her again.

After years of begging, she realized her mother would

never leave, so Jodie had prepared. She'd done just like she'd practiced. She hooked her left leg behind his and pushed her hand down against his left shoulder. Using his weight against him, like a three-legged chair, she slammed him down on the concrete. The force of the blow knocked him out. A puddle of red emerged from behind his head like a sadistic crown fit for her family's tormentor.

Her mother pulled herself from the pool and screamed as she fell to her knees. "What have you done?"

Jodie knew better than to stick around. Her mother may have claimed to love her and her sisters, but the truth was she only cared about self-preservation. The body lying on the ground might have been her father, but he was a man with no boundaries. He saw women as property. All the Lancaster women belonged to him. They were to follow commands, and present perfectly to the public.

Her dad, a local radio DJ, was a small-town celebrity. His death may not make national headlines, but his popularity would have the locals calling for justice. The beloved Lucky Lancaster would be painted as a saint.

As soon as she saw the blood on the cement, Jodie ran toward her mom's blue 2018 Ford Explorer and drove as far away as she could. She didn't know where she was going, only that she needed to escape.

When Jodie took her last turn, she realized she was stuck. There were no more rights or lefts to take. She could only go back. Before she knew it the intercoastal canal was in front of her. Metal railings and yellow caution signs declared the end of the road. The end of town. The headlights from her car reflected in the moving water.

Jodie gripped the handle under her seat and pushed it as far back as she could. She needed space. She needed to breathe. She needed a plan. Her dad's voice echoed again in her head. His warning. The memory of his breath on her face. The power she felt as she landed him on the solid ground below.

She took a deep breath, like she could inhale all the air from the vehicle's cabin and pushed out a scream. The tears followed. She knew, deep down, this would only provide her a short reprieve. She'd have to eventually go home and face the consequences.

She pulled down the visor and opened the mirror. The light reflected an image that didn't look like her. Her lip was busted. Blood was dried beneath her nose. Her fingers ran up and down to figure out if it was broken.

Her watch vibrated, causing her to jump. She looked down and saw her mom's name on the screen. She'd left her cell phone home to ensure no one found her but forgot about her smartwatch. She'd officially run out of time. Her mom could use their family account to find her location. Jodie looked at herself again in the mirror. Rage boiled back up again. She did what she needed to do. She did what her mother never could. She made sure her dad wouldn't hurt anyone else. Everyone else could call her a monster and she would wear that title with honor.

Jodie put the car in reverse, realizing she could do something else her mother never could. She could go back home. Her injured face was on display in its full glory. She would appear at the crime scene showing proof of the demons her father hid so well. The proof her mother perfected hiding over the past two decades. She would blow up his integrity with just one picture.

# More Than an Eye for an Eye

By Patricia Carullo

Let's cast this world
Into unyielding darkness
Suck all the life out of it
Show them how we live

Let's decorate the streets with shards of glass
Make them all bleed while they walked
Suffer, as we have
Let them wear a path
Down the bloodstained glassy road

Let's shower the world
With our tears of agony
Let them burn like acid
Down sweat-coated, bloody-footed ungrateful folk

Let's break this world
The way it shattered us

We need more than an eye for an eye
And we will let them all feel that

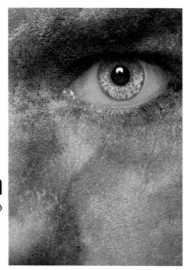

# Villain
By Patricia Carullo

Will you be quick to call me a villain
If I deign to do the things you would not choose
Once I start ripping out hearts
And watch them bleed on cold stone floors

Will it be easy for you to call me wicked
If I told you I did not bat an eye while I did it
What is a liar worth
But another blade through its deceitful spine?

Do not dare to call me a herald of darkness
For my claws only scratch skin-deep;
I have never sunk my fangs on the necks of the undeserving —
If I have bitten you, then darling you were the first one to hit
me

My soul may have been rotten
From years of flaying would-be thieves

You may have been slain by my hand
But please remember who wielded me

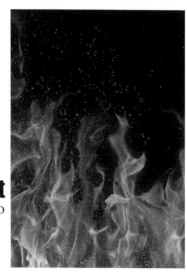

## Arsonist
By Patricia Carullo

Watching cities burn
Is my favorite pastime
The roaring fire swallowing up a tall building
Is always a sight to behold
How unkindly,
one must've thought
But I have already listened
To too many voices
Too many lies I've been told

So, I lit all their cities up
Just the way they like it
How quickly can years of building
turn into ashes
under a few hours of hellish flames?
Of course,
To this I know the answer
For this isn't my first time at all

But I want you to tell me
How would it feel
To burn the one who burnt you?

## Mark Gade

Mark Gade is from Guilderland, New York where he works with his brothers on a multi-generational family farm. It's here his love for gardening and storytelling began to grow. He has degrees from SUNY Cobleskill and SUNY Oneonta, where he majored in English literature. It was here where he began writing more seriously, having poems published in the writing journal published by the college. With a love of road traveling, he's also ventured across the continental United States several times, using these experiences and encounters in his writings.

## Tom Elmquist

Tom has always been a bit of a word nerd. He used his scribblings to express his adventures, fears, and loves throughout his life. Collecting special copies of his favorite tomes and displaying them proudly as he stared longingly, hoping to one day have a copy of his own book in the mix. While Tom has been writing for twenty-five years, this is the first time he's felt the urge to finally put his work out to the world. Watch for more stories from him as he forges forward with his first novel.

## S.E. Reed

S.E. has spent the last 20 years of her life moving around all five-regions of the United States which gives her a unique American perspective. Many of her pieces have a strong Southern theme, but she also dabbles in the strange, bizarre and fantastical.

Her work has been featured by Wild Ink Publishing, Parhelion Lit, The Writer's Workout, Tempered Rune's Press and Survival Guide for the 21st Century. She has won several YA writing contests and actively participates as a delegate for YA Hub on Twitter @writingwithreed.

S.E. Reed's upcoming YA contemporary novel, *My Heart is Hurting*, will be published through Wild Ink Publishing in July 2023.

www.writingwithreed.com

## Johnny Francis Wolf

Johnny Francis Wolf is an Autist — an autistic Artist. Designer, Model, Actor, Writer, and Hustler. Yes. That.

Worth a mention — his Acting obelisk — starring in the ill–famed and fated, 2006 indie film, TWO FRONT TEETH. The fact that it is free to watch on YouTube might say an awful lot about its standing with the Academy.

Homeless for the better part of these past 8 years, he surfs friends' couches, shares the offered bed, relies on the kindness of strangers — paying when can, doing what will, performing odd jobs. (Of late... Ranch Hand his favorite.)

From New York to LA, Taos and Santa Fe, Mojave Desert, Coast of North Carolina, points South and Southeast — considers himself blessed.

Johnny's love of animals, boundless. Current position working on a hacienda in Florida as laborer and horse whisperer has recently come to its seasonal conclusion.

— Greyhound and the Jersey Shore are drawing him North.

Some of all this Bio is true — most of Wolf's tales as well. Those illusory are hung on stories told him by dear friends or his own brush with similar, if not exactly the same.

Johnny's book, *Men Unlike Others*, will be published through Wild Ink in January 2023.

## C.L. Galan

His name is C.L. and he uses the pronouns he/they. He lives in Berkshire County, Massachusetts and has lived there his whole life. He's been in the local news, on local TV, and even on a small runway as a child. He's always wanted to be known and seen. Whether that was through instruments, singing, writing, or general interacting. His life hasn't been all sunshine and rainbows, but who's is? He loves his work and can't wait for the world to see it all. It'll take time, but you'll see his writing on many different shelves.

## James Hanna

James Hanna spent twenty years as a counselor in the Indiana Department of Correction. He spent another fourteen years as an officer in the San Francisco Probation Department where he was assigned to the domestic violence and stalking unit. Because of his background, the criminal element provides grist for much of his writing. James' work has appeared in over thirty journals, including Sixfold, Crack the Spine, and the Literary Review. His books, five of which have won awards, are available on Amazon.

## Alice de Crowley

Alice De Crowley is an author who loves exploring dark fantasy, thrilling action, and magical adventures. When she's not flying around Stonehenge on her broomstick, she is likely pursuing the lost threads of a mystery in a dusty stack of books. See her latest work at www.alicedecrowley.com or www.facebook.com/alicedecrowleyslair.

## Victoria Holland

Victoria Holland is an up-and-coming author, though she has been writing since she was seven years old. During the day, she does advocacy work, but any free time she has she moonlights as a creative, a student of magic and psychology, and a traveler. She loves beauty in all its forms. She lives in Massachusetts with her family, her friends close by, and hopefully one day with a cat she can name after one of her favorite characters.

Victoria can be found on social media @toriofthetrees.

## Maureen O'Leary

Maureen O'Leary lives in California. Her work appears recently and upcoming in Train Poetry Journal, Live Nude Poems, Hush Lit, Coffin Bell Journal, Penumbric Speculative Magazine, Black Spot Books' Under Her Skin, The Esopus Reader, Passengers Journal, Punk Noir Magazine, Tiny Frights Magazine, Reckon Review, Patchwork Folklore Journal,Bourbon Penn, and Sycamore Review. She is a graduate of Ashland MFA.

## Desiree DiFabio

Mom of four. Lover of books. Coordinator of Chaos. Believer in magic. Writer of Contemporary Adult Fiction—exploring strong females in the midst of change, often on a coming-of-middle-age journey. Grappling, always, with family dynamics and how to make peace with the past to live a better future. Desiree is completing her Master of Fine Arts in Creative Writing and has just finished her first novel.

## Wolf S. Helms

Wolf S. Helms is a cynical, scientific, irreverent person, taking pleasure in questioning set principles on scientific, moral, political and other grounds with a higher tendency towards those of science. He is from a rural section of the East Tennessee Valley.

Wolf can be found on Twitter at @ Wolf_S_Helms

## Devora Gray

Devora Gray is a yogi, Amazon boss lady, and strange mix of Sin City genteel. She's the author of Human Furniture and the Quest for the Perfect Woman and Tell the Wolves I'm Home. She writes creative nonfiction under the pen name D.A. Langley.

## Glenna Hartwell

Glenna Hartwell is a writer, designer, illustrator, and sculptor. She is an MFA candidate in the Writing Popular Fiction program at Seton Hill University. Glenna's illustrations have appeared on many book covers and in art calendars. Illustrating books re- quires an artist to visualize worlds that don't exist. That has given her the practice to create worlds with words instead of brushes. Glenna writes fantasy and horror and can read tarot cards with uncanny accuracy. She lives in Eastern Pennsylvania.

## Dexter Amoroso

Dex Amoroso is a published Filipino author who mostly does academic writings and poems when struck by a lightning of inspiration which are varied in themes, from silly to serious, in the English language. He is a registered writer/author at National Book Development Board and the VP for Research and Innovation of McKinley Publishing Hub, and the author of *"I DRINK; THEREFORE I AM LASHENG: For Bottle or Verse."*

## Melissa R. Mendelson

Melissa R. Mendelson is a Poet and Horror, Science-Fiction and Dystopian Short Story Author. Her stories have been published by Sirens Call Publications, Dark Helix Press, Altered Reality Magazine, Transmundane Press, Owl Canyon Press and Wild Ink Publishing. She also won second place in the WritersWeekly.com 24 Hour Short Story Contest. Melissa's upcoming book, *This Will Remain With Us,* will be published through Wild Ink in December 2022.

## Sehra Dylan Nikol

Sehra has always wanted to be a published author. She use to dream of holding her own published book in her hands. Following this dream, Sehra is working toward her BFA in creative writing with plans to enter an MFA program in the future. Her goal? The best seller moniker.

## William J. Connell

William J. Connell is currently a practicing attorney in the great states of Rhode Island and Massachusetts. He has also worked as a public-school teacher in the areas of Special Education and History in the same states. He enjoys writing on a wide variety of topics. Most of his non-fiction material is in the legal field, and his work has been published in many law journals. His fiction tends to run to historical adventure, which reflects his love of teaching history, mixed with elements of sci-fi, classic literature, and horror thrown in for good measure! Be Careful

What You Wish For is a short story set in Europe during the plague which today we call "The Black Death." He hopes you'll agree that his villain is not so bad, just misunderstood!

## Riley Kilmore

Riley Kilmore has been a cop, firefighter, and homeschool mom. Her award-winning short stories and poems appear in multiple anthologies, literary magazines, and online venues. When not writing, she regales her persnickety mare with tales of past glory: parachuting, sailing the world on a shoestring budget, and winning enviable recognition as runner-up to the Lititz, PA Chicken Corn Soup Queen. Kilmore has an MFA in Writing Popular Fiction from Seton Hill University and an infatuation for Daniel Boone. She lives in a cabin with one amazing husband, a dancing goat, one beer-guzzling hound who knows sign language, and four affectionate cats.

## Arlene Schwartz

Arlene Schwartz is a Filipino-American contemporary author and writing doula living in Nevada. Her fiction champions diversity while dealing with difficult themes surrounding the human experience. She helps writers tell/edit their stories using a collaborative approach. She has an English degree from the University of Nevada, Las Vegas and is an MFA candidate with Southern New Hampshire University.

## Thomas Elson

Thomas Elson's stories appear, or are forthcoming, in numerous venues, including Ellipsis, Better Than Starbucks, Bull, Cabinet of Heed, Flash Frontier, Ginosko, Short Édition, Litro, Journal of Expressive Writing, Dead Mule School, Selkie, New Ulster, Lampeter, and Adelaide. He divides his time between Northern California and Western Kansas.

## Courtney Byles

Courtney Byles grew up in the bayous of Southeastern Louisiana. She loves reading a wide variety of fiction but has always found herself drawn to young adult fantasy. It may have something to do with her obsession with all spooky things. She loves spending time with her two daughters and watching British murder mysteries with her college sweetheart. Her husband states that her goal in life is to adopt all the homeless fur babies that cross her social media feed. While her oldest daughter reports that her mother can be found spontaneously singing and dancing around their home, especially in the kitchen.

Courtney started her Bachelor's degree at Louisiana Tech University before completing her degree at Nicholls State University. She has a Master of Arts in Humanities from American Military University and will complete her Master of Fine Arts in Creative Writing from Southern New Hampshire in June 2023. She is an educator and loves to help others reach their goals.

## Patricia Carullo

Patricia Carullo is an upstart writer from the Philippines. Currently, she has fourteen cats and writes poems with so much fur floating around.

# Wild Ink Publishing LLC
## Current Titles

Into the Mirror

A Literary Collection

Calliope's Collection of Mystical Mayhem

Maria James-Thiaw

Count Each Breath

If you are interested in publishing with
Wild Ink Publishing, please go to:
wild-ink-publishing.com/submissions.

We have anthology and traditional publishing
opportunities.

# About Wild Ink Publishing LLC

Wild Ink is just starting our publishing journey. But that doesn't mean we don't have amazing authors to share with you. In fact, we would say it means we are able to bring you some of the brightest wordsmiths by unleashing the shackles that usually stop people from publishing traditionally. We are not afraid of breaking a mold or two.

You can learn more about our current, upcoming authors and projects on the Wild Ink website.

wild-ink-publishing.com

Made in the USA
Monee, IL
15 October 2022

15949710R00203